FISH OR
CUT BAIT

OTHER GUPPY ANTHOLOGIES

Fish Tales
Fish Nets

FISH OR CUT BAIT

A GUPPY ANTHOLOGY

EDITED BY RAMONA DEFELICE LONG

WILDSIDE PRESS

Published by Wildside Press LLC.
www.wildsidebooks.com

CONTENTS

INTRODUCTION

MICHELE DRIER

From shapeshifters to fleeing Nazis. From small town USA to the French battlefield trenches of WWI to the warm waters of the Caribbean, this collection of short stories will delight you, amuse you, and take you away.

Whether your interests are contemporary, historical, or verge on the speculative edge of paranormal or futuristic fiction, *Fish or Cut Bait* is for you.

It's the third anthology of short stories from members of the Guppies, an on-line chapter of the national organization for mystery writers, Sisters in Crime. Begun as the GreatUnpublished, we've grown to more than 600 members offering each other advice, classes, tips, information, and a hand to hold (virtually) when bad things happen—personal challenges to rejections.

Although few of us were published when we started, today our ranks include unpublished as well as nationally-known, award-winning authors.

Fish or Cut Bait became the title and theme of this anthology. We wanted those short stories that forced a character to balance on the fine edge of decision—jump or not, say yes or no, move or stay, fish or cut bait?

Judges Toni Kelner, Earl Staggs, and Kate Thornton read the fifty-three submissions and rated them, then the Steering Committee chose the top twenty-two for inclusion. Not a painless or easy process.

All the judges have close relationships with mysteries and short stories.

Toni L.P. Kelner is the author of eleven mystery novels as well as the author of numerous short stories, and she co-edits bestselling urban fantasy anthologies with Charlaine Harris. Kelner has won the Agatha Award, an *RT BookClub* Lifetime Achievement Award, and has been nominated multiple times for the Anthony, the Macavity, and the Derringer.

Earl Staggs is a transplant from Baltimore to Texas. His stories have appeared in a number of magazines and anthologies. He joined the Short Mystery Fiction Society and served as both vice president and president. He was also the Managing Editor for *Futures Mystery Magazine* and has twice won a Derringer Award for Best Short Story of the year.

Kate Thornton writes novels, but her real interest is short fiction. Her stories have been compiled into two anthologies: *Spaced Out—Interplanetary Voyages of the Linda Rae* and *Inhuman Condition*. She serves on the Board of Directors of the Los Angeles Chapter of Sisters in Crime and is an editor for the chapter's anthology, *Ladies of the Night*.

This is the third Guppy anthology edited by Ramona DeFelice Long. She's an independent editor and writer, has received a Fellowship from the Mid-Atlantic Arts Foundation, a literary fellowship from the Delaware Division of the Arts, and a residency at the Virginia Center for the Creative Arts.

If you're curled up by the fire or stretched out on the beach, this collection of stories will tickle your imagination and entertain.

Enjoy!

THE MOUNTAIN TOP

GEORGIA RUTH

Brunch was over. Jeff settled into his leather recliner close to the hearth and watched Sally maneuver an iron pot of hot water. She wrapped a towel around the slim handle and removed it from its fireplace hook. She didn't need his help for now.

"Honey, did I tell you that I saw Walter Bailey at the barber shop last week?"

Sally carefully stepped across the cherry hardwood with her load. "The state senator?" She poured the water into the sink in the kitchen corner of the great room.

"Yeah," Jeff said. "Instead of suit and tie and Italian loafers, he was wearing some kind of uniform under the barber's cape. And work boots. Still trading jokes with the old timers. It's hard to tell the difference now between him and the farmers who voted for him."

"A shame he lost his house." She added a spot of detergent to the hot water.

Jeff struggled out of his chair to put another log on the fire. And to replace the screen that Sally had shoved aside. "Let's get into the co-op again this year. Trading eggs for produce worked well for us."

"I'm glad my grandmother taught me how to can vegetables." Sally set rinsed dishes in a rack, dried the plates with a towel and put them into her treasured china hutch.

"I'd like to barter for a few goats," said Jeff. "What do you think?"

"I'd rather have sheep. But there'll be plenty of possibilities now that more people have booths at the marketplace."

"Neighbors helping neighbors." *Yes, this is one of her good days.*

A familiar squabble outdoors captured Jeff's attention. He smiled in anticipation and stepped over to the window. Seventy feet down the hill, a gang of turkeys raced across the clearing, necks outstretched, wattles jiggling, competing for position.

"Wildlife on stage," he announced, putting his magnifiers to rest on Robert Burns' poetry. Jeff climbed to the loft for a better view.

Sally removed her homemade apron and laid it next to the cast iron pot that dried on the useless electric stove. She joined him upstairs, and through the chalet windows, they watched the huge birds stuff themselves on the corn Jeff had scattered earlier that morning. The bright face of the sun briefly overcame gray clouds, peeking into the woods, warm fingers touching pockets of crusty snowdrifts and hundreds of animal tracks.

"What a life, my love." Jeff cuddled his bride of fifty years.

"Yes, it is. Atlanta was the right place to raise our boys, but these North Carolina mountains are perfect for me."

"That's good, because we can't afford to move. Not many folks can even travel."

"I'm happy watching water freeze into icicles that thaw the next day." She smiled.

"Very inspirational." Jeff squinched his eyes.

> *Live with me, and be my love,*
> *And we will all the pleasures prove*
> *That hills and valleys, dales and fields,*
> *And all the craggy mountains yields.*

"Very impressive." Sally chuckled. "High school English?"

"That's all I can remember from last week. Christopher Marlowe." He tugged the faded red braid that lay half way down her back.

"I like it when you remember to be romantic." She tilted her head back to cock an eyebrow.

"I'm a Renaissance man." He smiled into her pale blue eyes.

"We do all right by ourselves, don't we?" She spoke softly. "Jeff, I don't ever want to go to one of those old-people homes."

"We'll take care of each other, honey. I promise." He hugged her close, his eyes misting.

Time stood still as they watched the fluttering attendance at the bird feeders.

"I do wish that Daniel and Chad could be here with us."

"They were always big city boys, honey." He swallowed hard and looked to the mountains. "They never spent a day reading a book."

"Or walking deer trails." She sighed deeply. "I know, but I worry that they're not getting enough to eat."

The turkeys abruptly took flight.

"Something spooked them," he said.

"Probably the fox casing my hen house. And if I see him, I'm going to shoot him." Sally reached for the binoculars from the roll top desk to examine the outbuildings near their young orchard. "One day I'll be able to trade jars of preserves."

"Unless Mr. Bear or Woody Woodchuck sneaks up on us and confiscates our fruit."

"I won't allow any varmint to steal my food. We worked too hard."

Jeff laughed. He had always admired her spunk.

The scrape of boots on the front deck turned their attention. Over the loft railing, they could see a dark face glower through the glass at the top of the mahogany door. Someone else in a black ski mask pressed his nose to the porch window and peered into the cabin's main room.

Jeff felt a spasm of fear squeeze his chest. His wife dropped the binoculars on a chair and hastened toward the steps.

"Be careful, Sally. Looks like trouble, those slackers from the bottom of the hill."

She hesitated. "They can see we're here."

"Stay with me."

Jeff sought options of self-defense. His pistol was tucked away at the top of the closet in the downstairs bedroom. Out of reach. The penknife in his pocket would be slow to open. *Need something with a sharp point.* He glanced at the letter opener on the desk, the scissors, a ballpoint.

The knob turned, and a huge shaggy head loomed around the door. "Hallow, anyone ta home?"

"We're up here in the loft," shouted Jeff. "Hang on, we're coming down." *The fireplace poker!*

The two men invited themselves in. "Nice place you got here."

Jeff's heart was pounding as he descended the open staircase, Sally behind him. He steeled his intention to be cordial as long as possible. "Come in by the fire."

"Thank ya kindly." The husky intruder in the camouflage bibs clumped to the hearth, leaving wet tracks on the oval braided rug. "Shoar looks like another snow headed our way."

His sidekick stood by the door, looking around the large room. He rolled his stocking cap off his face up to the top of his head uncovering short brown hair and stubbly beard. Denim cuffs partially hid the burn scars on his chapped hands.

"Aren't you from the cluster of mobile homes in the valley?" Jeff asked.

"Yep, my family all lives together. Like the Kennedys." His laugh revealed a cavern of sparse teeth stained by the bits of tobacco wedged among them.

Jeff didn't see any bulges suggesting concealed weapons. He forced a smile. "What can I do for you?"

The stranger turned away from the blazing warmth. "Friend, times are tough. We ate our last chicken for Christmas dinner. I see you still got some."

"Yes, we do. We've hatched a few eggs and made our own flock."

"We ate ours, didn't have nothin' else." He picked up the beach photo from the mantle. "Big boys. They live here? Or you two all alone in these woods?"

"We have friends and relatives nearby." Jeff claimed the family memory and replaced it below the grapevine wreath. He didn't mention both sons had been killed in Afghanistan.

"Sounds like the good life." The behemoth called out to his hostess who stood behind the island sink. "What do you think, honey? You like it here?"

"I certainly do." Sally picked at a button on her sweater.

"Forgot my manners, darlin'. My name's Boyd. What's yourn?"

Jeff interrupted. "What brings you boys up the mountain?" He stationed himself between his wife and the two strangers. He expected Sally to follow his lead, whatever it would be.

"Well, like I said. We need meat, and we're mighty tired of squirrel. I seen them turkeys in front of your place, and it 'pears to me that they'd make a right tasty dinner. Course they scattered when we come up the drive."

"If you follow the tracks, you could catch up to them. They poke along."

"I know that." Boyd glanced upward at the thick exposed beams. "Yep, real nice place." He reached out a dirty fingernail to touch the photo again. "We need some firewood, too. I seen you have a big pile out there."

"Work at it all winter," said Jeff. "The stack closest to the back door is seasoned. Behind that is what I cut this year from the trees damaged by the ice storm."

"Too cold to go out in that stuff." Boyd wrapped his large paw around the fireplace poker, swiped the screen to the side and nudged a flaming log. Sparks flew.

Jeff picked up the coffee mug next to his chair and clutched it tightly.

"Would you boys like some vegetable soup? I could heat it up real quick." Sally pulled a jar from the pantry.

Jeff nodded at her. *Smart idea, appear neighborly, non-threatening.*

The younger man at the door perked up. "Sounds good, don't it, Boyd?" His thin frame looked as though it could use another meal.

"Shoar. We'll stay to eat. We're not in no hurry." Boyd shed his jacket, tossing it across a tartan footstool. A tiny snowball from the sleeve melted on Sally's knitting. "C'mon, Cooter. Make yourself ta home."

Sally poured the soup into the iron pot. "Would you care to wash up first? We could turn on the pump."

"So you got your well water, do ya?" Boyd moved directly to the table rubbing his palms on his barrel chest. His hunting cap still covered tangled strands of long black hair. "We can't 'ford no generator."

"We tried to get prepared last year when the government looked shaky. We put back a few extra groceries each month. Installed a wood-stove downstairs." Jeff took the kettle from his wife, hung it on the fireplace crane and swung it over the blaze. "I'll warm up some coffee."

"I reckon you lost a bundle in the stock market crash."

"Everyone did." Jeff retrieved the coffee pot from the hutch where Sally misplaced it.

"I didn't." Again the toothless grin.

"Me neither." Cooter burst into squeals.

Boyd slapped his thigh and hooted at him. "You was in prison."

"Oh, yeah." And they both laughed rabidly until Boyd abruptly stopped. Cooter closed his mouth immediately, eyes on his companion.

Jeff smiled indulgently while he positioned the ceramic pot close to the fire.

Sally stood motionless behind the kitchen island.

"Honey, do we have any bread?" Jeff squeezed her arm as he passed. When he got a serrated knife to place near her cutting board, he secreted a paring knife in his cardigan pocket. He handed Sally her apron.

"Seen any deer?" Boyd scraped a ladder-back chair into position as he sat down. Cooter sat across from him, imitating his friend's table manners.

Sally opened a cabinet door. And a drawer.

"Not recently. I was hoping our little herd would grow." Jeff studied his guests from his stool at the granite countertop, away from the greasy animal odor trapped in their clothing. "Someone shot the two bucks last month."

"That was me. Got one, anyway. Big ten pointer, wadn't it, Cooter?"

"Shoar was, Boyd. A rack this long." He held his hands three feet away from each other. Cooter bumped Boyd's hand with his over and over. "Too bad we couldn't use his head. Remember that, Boyd? 'Member that?"

"You're my buddy, ain't ya? You helped plant that salt lick and all."

Cooter sat up straight and nodded. "I followed that trail of blood to finish him off, too. I'd do anythin' for you." He smiled. His tiny eyes burned brightly. "Buddy."

While their guests jawed about dressing deer meat, Sally placed a plate of thick-sliced bread on the table. Boyd watched her cleavage rise and fall as she leaned forward to serve soup to her guests. Jeff watched Boyd.

"I ain't never et at a rich man's table. Looks good, don't it, Boyd?" Cooter leaned both forearms on the oak table, bread in one hand, spoon in the other. He hunched close over his bowl and quickly slurped every drop. Belching loudly, he leaned backwards balancing on two legs of his chair. "Yessir. That was extry good." He swiped his mouth with his sleeve, napkin still in its decorative holder.

Sally poured coffee for the men and then retreated behind the counter.

Boyd pushed away his empty bowl and lit a cigarette. "So you got a big pension comin' in? You must be one of them guys with a sweet retirement package. I heard about it when they was bailin' out all them companies with hard-earned money from us little folks. You one of them?"

"I don't have a pension, but I don't think it should concern you." Jeff used a checked napkin to dab a coffee drip from his neat gray beard.

"You're wrong about that, mister. Everything you do concerns me. You live in my back yard." He nodded at Cooter. "Ain't that right?" Boyd flicked an ash into the soup bowl. "Our grandpappy used ta own all this land afore the developers got hold to it. I know every creek and holler."

"No doubt your grandpappy got paid for it. You should be the rich one," remarked Jeff.

"Well, I ain't. My folks bought a restaurant, and we all worked at the family bizness. We tried to make a go of it, but neighbors quit eatin' out. Nothin' to be done but shut 'er down." Boyd pushed back his chair and stood up. He gave Cooter what was left of his cigarette. "What kinda work did you do?"

Jeff got to his feet. "I'm an electrician."

"You musta owned your own bizness. You got some mighty fine things here." Boyd winked at Sally. "And a fat diamond ring for the missus."

She frowned and put her hand in her apron pocket.

"I saved what I could in the good years. And didn't go into debt. We retired on social security, but since there's no longer any of that, we just make do." Jeff hoped to move them toward the door.

"You're making it better than me and my family."

"We live a quiet life. It was hard to get used to kerosene lamps, but at least we can read at night. One day they'll get the power up and going again in this area."

"It just ain't right for some people to have so much and others to have nuttin'." Cooter rhythmically slapped his spoon on the table until Sally snatched it to wash in the sink.

"The guv'ner said we should share. You ready to share with me, neighbor?" Boyd moved closer to Jeff, forcing him to look up or step back.

Jeff looked up.

"Sure. I'll tell you what. You can take half of my woodpile."

"That's a start." Boyd slapped Jeff on the shoulder, unsettling him.

"What are you going to trade? Share means helping each other." Jeff was determined to show some strength.

"I don't have nothin'."

"Do you have any beer?" Jeff asked.

Cooter sat up straight.

"I ain't givin' up my beer," said Boyd.

"Maybe you have something stronger in that shed in the woods? The one where I've seen smoke?" He had to show strength or they would run right over him.

Boyd narrowed his eyes at the stooped man in front of him.

"I don't think that concerns you," Boyd mocked.

"Tell it, Boyd." Cooter twisted a stalk of baby's breath from the dried centerpiece and crushed it slowly between thumb and forefinger.

"Sounds like you're mad at us because we prepared for hard times. You could have done the same thing," said Jeff. He clenched and un-clenched his fists.

"I lost my job when all the furniture companies went to China. That ain't right."

"Companies moved where they could have lower operating expens-es. No union jobs."

"My girl would do better in a union. She works at a nursing home, and they cut her hours. She can't pay her car note."

"You're right." Jeff nodded. "People all over the country are strug-gling."

"Yep. Fifteen teachers at the high school were let go."

"Ain't so many prison guards left neither." Cooter giggled. He swiped the crumbs from the table with his sleeve.

"No way I can get work. But a man's gotta take care of his family," said Boyd, his voice sharp and loud.

Cooter stood, sucked in one last mouthful of smoke and threw the cigarette butt into the fire as he ambled past.

"I think we agree on that." Jeff spoke softly. "It's power and greed that'll ruin us. All of us." He took shallow breaths now. He put one hand into his sweater pocket.

"You don't seem to be worried." Boyd snorted.

"Worrying won't change things. We're too old to work, and too old to revolt."

"You're right. You're too old. What use are yunz?" Boyd grabbed his jacket and brushed Sally's knitting to the floor.

"Not for you to say." Jeff eased the paring knife out but kept it hidden at his side.

Sally started out of the kitchen area, her forehead furrowed. Jeff stopped her with a shake of his head.

"Well, grandpa. Let me tell you how it's gonna happen. First off, I'm takin' all your wood. We're gonna load it on my pickup right now." Boyd motioned at Cooter. "Then tomorrow, I'm takin' all your chickens. And I'm sendin' my young'uns up here to get all your canned goods. Whacha got to say about that, old man?"

"I say you're stealin'." Jeff raised his voice and stepped closer.

Sally slipped out of the kitchen. Jeff heard her lock the bedroom door. She was safe.

"Hey, Cooter, look at that there recliner. Help me move it to the porch. We'll carry it on top of the wood."

"I worked hard for my possessions," Jeff shouted. He made his decision. "You will not take them."

"Who's gonna stop me?"

"Me." Jeff thrust his knife at Boyd's chest.

The men guffawed. A titanic arm brushed him aside. Jeff banged his shin on the footstool.

As he fell towards the hearth, he caught a glimpse of a determined Sally returning to the room. "No! Go back!"

"You will leave," said Sally. "Now."

Jeff watched in horror as she charged the visitors.

"Boyd, she got a gun!"

"Honey, give it to me."

Sally fired.

* * * *

At daybreak, the doves fluttered off in different directions at the sound of knocking on the log cabin door. With every muscle in his body complaining, Jeff limped over to peer through its glass at two teenage boys. One wore a ski mask. "Sally, we have visitors."

Jeff unlocked the door and opened it.

"Good morning, sir. We're looking for our pa."

"Well, I haven't seen anyone today. Two men stopped to visit yesterday."

"Our big brother found Pa's truck down by the creek but no sign of nobody," said the shorter boy. "He had to go on to work, so me and Danny are out lookin'."

"That's strange. They said they were going to hunt for turkeys." Jeff peered past them into the frozen forest. The crows roosted noisily. "Do you boys want to come in? You must be cold."

"Thanks, we are. The sun don't feel too warm when the wind goes right through ya," said Danny. They entered, stomping their snowy boots on the clean mat at the door. "Pa's shotgun was missing from over the back window. I think mebbe he and cousin Cooter have a deer stand close to the creek." His adult baritone contrasted with the teenage acne erupting on his forehead. "Sweet place you got here, mister."

"Could you eat some livermush with eggs?"

The teenagers exchanged bright-eyed looks. "We sure could. That sounds great." They hung their jackets next to Jeff's parka on the pegs by the door and removed their boots.

"We were just about ready to sit down to breakfast." Jeff went to the kitchen to help Sally. She stood motionless at the sink. She stared at the boys.

"One day I'm gonna have me a log cabin like this." Danny surveyed the room as he moved in holey socks toward the fieldstone fireplace.

The younger one made a sliding approach to the roaring fire.

"Careful, Brad."

"This feels good, don't it?" He put his hands toward the heat.

Danny examined the beach photo on the mantle.

Jeff pointed out the basin of water at the antique washstand, and the boys rinsed their hands. Sally set places for them at the table.

"Fine boys like you need plenty of food." Jeff sat with them, sipping his coffee as Sally served their plates with unsteady hands. Her hair stuck out like eagle feathers.

"Have you guys been out of school long?" Jeff asked.

"I'm tryin' to get on at that military gear factory in Fletcher," said Danny. "Might hafta join the army to get me a job."

"You're a smart fella." Jeff offered a smile.

"Ma says I need to go back to school." Brad grimaced. "But Pa says I don't."

"Y'all eat up now," said Sally. "Tell you what. I'll fix a basket of canned goods for you to carry back. And it just so happens I made a pie yesterday. Chocolate. Your favorite."

"Yes, ma'am. Thank you."

Jeff studied the boys as they quietly gobbled down their breakfast. "I'll share a couple chickens with you, too."

"When the chicken farmer down the road went out of business, he gave us some. But we ate them all," said Danny.

The boys pushed back from the table. Brad followed the lead of his brother, wiping his mouth with a napkin.

"Have to keep a rooster around, you know," said Jeff.

"Pa wanted to eat him first, 'cause he woke us up so early." Little brother grinned.

"C'mon, Brad, daylight's burnin'." Danny went towards the door to put his boots on. "If we don't find Pa and cousin Cooter, Ma hasta go tell Uncle Walter. He's the new deputy sheriff."

Jeff wobbled as he stood, holding on to the table for balance.

"Mister, you okay?" Danny shoved one arm into a coat that was too large for him.

"Yeah, thanks. I did some heavy lifting yesterday and threw my back out. Nothing that a few hours of rest won't cure." He paused. "But I could use a hand in planting my garden this spring. You boys know anyone who would work for me?"

The boys glanced at each other.

"Sure thing. We can do it." They talked as one, with bobbing heads.

After they zipped their coats under Sally's prodding, she handed one a sack of groceries and the other a pie carrier.

"I believe you've got a load to carry today, but you come back to get those chickens anytime you want." Jeff shook their hands. "We'll make our plans then."

"Thanks. And thanks for breakfast." Brad's grin lit up the room. "Was nice to meetcha."

"I'm so glad you came to visit your old folks." Sally kissed their cheeks.

The two boys exchanged blank looks.

The door closed.

"It was nice to see Daniel and Chad. I worry that they're not getting enough to eat." Sally tracked them from the window.

Jeff pulled her close, tears in his eyes. "It's all right, honey. Come sit here with me."

Sally watched the gift-laden teenagers until they were out of sight, making their way through the pines in the swirling snow. "I hope those horrible men don't hurt them."

"The men are gone, honey. They won't be back."

He adjusted the lamp wick and eased into Sally's rocker with his banjo. The instruction book was propped up on the footstool.

"Wonder where those turkeys are today." She shuffled over to Jeff's recliner to wait with bowed head for his new song, "The Ballad of the Mountaintop."

This is going to be a good day.

JUDGE LU'S DILEMMA

FROM THE JUDGE LU CASE FILES

P A DE VOE

A magistrate's first duty is to the Ming Emperor through serving the people in his district.

He controls criminals and their destructive impact on the community.

He brings a sense of fairness and justice, which prevents unrest and revolt.

This is a simple task if the criminal behavior is from the lowly.

Not so simple if the illegal activities benefit the local gentry.

Every magistrate's success in office depends on the gentry's support.

The damp, sweltering heat was unusual for the fall, but neither man complained. The rain brought an end to the years of drought and famine that had plagued the region.

Wu Ming-feng smoothed his long gray robe, a sign of his elite status, and wiped his forehead with a green silk handkerchief. "Tomorrow's celebration will return our town to its former glory." Smiling, he added, "Pu-an is overflowing with people who've come for the banquet and commemoration. You've done our poor town a great service, Magistrate Lu."

"Not at all," Judge Lu returned. Wu's comment about him was a polite social convention. They both knew there'd be no celebration without Wu's financial backing. However, as owner of the largest silk company, the influx of outsiders into the town meant extra cash flowing into Wu's pockets. His support wasn't entirely altruistic.

"It's time to reinstate the annual celebration," Lu said. "The famines over the past ten years forced my predecessors to neglect this ceremony. Now, with your support, we can once more honor a filial son who exemplifies our country's most important value." Raising his cup, Lu continued, "Let's drink to Guei-qing, your youngest son, who will be honored in tomorrow's ceremony."

"Yes, while his brothers left to seek fame and fortune, Guei-qing remained at home."

As the men jointly raised their cups, the sharp sound of the petitioner's drum came from the court's front pavilion.

Someone was bringing a complaint before the court. Lu frowned. This was the first time since he took office a month ago that the drum sounded. This could be his first case. Still, he wondered at the late hour. What couldn't wait until morning?

A younger, more handsome version of the Judge stepped into the room. One glance at his brother and trusted secretary Fu-hao told Lu the problem was serious. He immediately rose. "I must attend to court duties, but I'll return as soon as possible." With that, he hurried from the room, his brother following.

"Who's the complainant?" he asked.

"Widow Guo."

"Who is this Widow Guo?"

"She works land owned by her husband's clan since she has nothing of her own. She claims someone raped her daughter tonight."

"Who found the girl?" Lu's questions came fast and furious.

"A farmer Song came along just as someone attacked Xiang-hua. The assailant fled, Song ran after him, but he got away. Song returned to the girl and took her home."

"Do they have any idea who did this?" Lu looked at Fu-hao as they strode through the hallways connecting his official residence to the court. He didn't miss his secretary's slight pause and nervous glance before answering. Lu prepared for bad news.

"Song said the rapist was Wu Guei-qing." Fu-hao spoke in a whisper as if to stay a pending disaster.

At that, Lu exhaled sharply. Wu Guei-qing? The one they were honoring as a filial son? How could this be? Lu closed his eyes. His first case. He saw his career slipping away before he'd even begun.

Entering the court chambers, Lu donned his official robe and hat and sat behind a massive desk. Fu-hao went to a side table where paper, ink, and brush waited for him to take down the petitioner's complaint. The court's constable and Lu's two personal retainers, Zhang and Ma, stood at attention along one wall.

"Bring in Widow Guo," Lu ordered.

As soon as the beleaguered mother was escorted in by the constable, she rushed forward and dropped to her knees. "Please give my daughter justice, your Honor!" she wailed, tears streaming down her worn cheeks.

"Tell me all you know, leave nothing out," Lu encouraged her in a firm, gentle tone, even as he hated to hear what she had to say.

The elderly woman repeated much of what Fu-hao had told him. She named Wu's son as her daughter's attacker. At the end of her recital, Lu asked, "Where's your daughter now?"

"At home. She collapsed on her bed and hasn't moved since."

"All right. Tell me what evidence you have against Wu Guei-qing. Besides farmer Song's story?"

"None, your Honor, but Song is a good man. Why would he make up such a thing?" Her voice spoke volumes to Lu. She was conscious of the power and wealth of the Wu family, plus, along with everyone else in the city, she must know Guei-qing's name had been sent to the Emperor and tomorrow he would be honored as a model for filial piety. Her charges against him would bring shame on him, his family, and the entire community.

"The court will investigate the matter. Return home, I'll come to talk to your daughter tonight. Do not discuss anything, anything, with anyone, about the case." Lu's voice did not betray his anxiety.

When Lu returned to his office, his guest had already left. Lu's secretary and two retainers followed him, awaiting orders.

"What are you going to do?" Fu-hao asked. Because he was Lu's brother, as well as his secretary, he could ask the question no one else dared raise.

Lu knew what Fu-hao was really asking: was he going to jeopardize everything by accusing the son of the most powerful man in the city of a crime, on the word of an illiterate, scrubby farmer and a distressed mother?

"What have any of you heard about Guei-qing? What's the word on the streets and in the wine shops?"

"He has a mixed reputation," Fu-hao conceded as he stroked his neck.

"He can be found every night at the local brothel and wine shop," Ma promptly added. "Gossip has it he spends his father's money faster than water flowing down a mountainside."

"So, he's out of control. Why hasn't his father forced him to behave? In the end, the father's responsible for everyone in the family," Judge Lu said.

They shook their heads. No answer.

Lu nodded. *One rash young man may destroy everything for me and my family.* He removed his official robes and slipped on a long gray robe for traveling to the Guo's home. As magistrate, it was his duty to interview the alleged rape victim; he decided whether she was truly accosted or not. As a matter of record, he sent a detailed report to his superiors. If anyone questioned the fairness of his actions, the report would be key to his superior's determination of malfeasance. Lu was keenly aware that he had a duty to fulfill, but he hoped the costs weren't too high.

"Fu-hao, we'll leave immediately, bring your writing materials for the official report. Zhang and Ma, bring torches."

When they entered Widow Guo's simple, earthen-walled home, his retainers' torches threw a pitiless light over the stark, bare room. Widow Guo's daughter lay in bed, a crushed butterfly struggling for survival.

Following the law's specific requirements, Lu gently slipped a hand under her chin and turned her face toward him. Ma's torch clearly illuminated the bruises around her mouth. As Lu began to describe his findings, Fu-hao took notes.

Lu pushed up the worn sleeves of her tunic. Raw, red bands encircled each wrist. Finally, he drew back her heavy cotton blanket. On her back—at her waist—were angry black and blue marks. A tear in her pant's waistband corresponded to the bruises on her back, as if the pants had been pulled sharply forward to rip them open. There were no bruises on the inside of her legs. Lu breathed a sigh of relief. *He must not have succeeded—saving her from being condemned by society for her rape.*

Completing his examination, he pulled the blanket over her. "Xianghua, can you tell me who tried to rape you?"

The girl's eyes opened wide in terror, but she remained mute.

Lu laid a hand on her arm. "That's all right. Rest. Close your eyes. That's right." He moved away, signaling her mother to follow him.

"I won't need to speak further with your daughter. You may clean her up and get a doctor to care for her."

The mother, overwhelmed with grief, shook her head. "I've no money for a doctor. I'll tend to her myself."

"Don't worry about money. Get a doctor. Also, you must put your mark on the report of my examination verifying its accuracy." As with the majority of women, he realized she was uneducated. He handed her the writing brush and showed her how to make a mark.

She took the unfamiliar brush and, with hesitation, finally produced a black blob on the paper.

"Again, I must remind you to not talk to anyone. A loose tongue could destroy the court's investigation."

She nodded.

Lu immediately left for Song's house. He needed a statement from the farmer. Immediacy was critical, both to capture every possible detail of the event and—if Song was guilty of the crime—before he had a chance to create a story about the night's events.

Farmer Song's home didn't look much different from Widow Guo's, although the building and land was his. Ma pounded on the rough planked door.

A disheveled young man opened the door. He wore the typical farmer's work clothes of a short jacket tied with a thick cotton belt. It fell to his hips covering the tops of his grass stained pants, which billowed out over his thighs to just below the knee.

"Tell me what happened," Lu said. His curt, no-nonsense approach aimed to intimidate, not terrify.

"I heard muffled cries—" Song began.

"Begin at the beginning. Why were you out at that time of night?"

Song nodded. "I have one pig and I want to breed her in another month."

Lu thought wryly he may be sorry he said "at the beginning," but let the young fellow continue.

"Sometimes she escapes from her pen and goes to my neighbor's garden. He threatened to complain to our town's peace-and-security team. They could force me to pay a big fine for damages."

Lu glanced at Fu-hao, who was diligently taking notes, although a slight smile pulled at the corners of his mouth.

"I bought some really good, heavy wood from…."

"Get on with finding Widow Guo's daughter," Lu said.

Song nodded. "Anyway, I built a strong fence, but I still check every night to make sure she hasn't gotten out. Tonight, she escaped again! Naturally, I headed to my neighbor's garden first. I took the path adjacent to the Guo farm and through the grove of trees just beyond it. That's when I heard these strange sounds and saw Xiang-hua on the ground. A cloth covered her mouth and another covered her eyes. A man struggled with her. I called out."

"Did you see his face?"

"No. When I yelled, he leaped to his feet and raced through the trees. I ran after him. I wanted to catch the rotten egg." A look of anger and disgust crossed his face. "He had too much of a head start on me. I had paused to check Xiang-hua, to see if she was okay. It was only a second, but enough time for him to get ahead of me.

"I didn't catch him, but I know who it was." He knit his eyebrows over dark, stormy eyes, and fell silent.

Impatiently Lu said, "Well, go on."

"Wu Guei-qing. The dog," he spat out.

Judge Lu's stomach tightened. "If you didn't see his face and he got away from you, how can you accuse him?"

Song stood with his feet apart and arms crossed.

"Speak up," Lu roughly commanded. "You know the penalty for falsely accusing someone!"

"I didn't see his face, but I saw him. He was wearing a long gray robe; he was tall and overweight. Still, he ran at least as fast as me, so he had to be younger."

Lu appreciated the farmer's observation skills. Still, it didn't prove anything. It wasn't enough to bring a devastating charge against Wu's son.

"Take us to where you found them."

With Zhang and Ma lighting the way, they retraced his path to the grove of trees. Within a few feet off to the side of the path, Song gestured toward a trampled area. "There. That's where they were."

"What direction did the man run?"

"Through those trees, back to the path, and into the village. I lost him behind the Wu compound," Song added pointedly.

"Stay here while we inspect the grounds," Lu ordered. "Zhang, bring your torch and come with me. Fu-hao and Ma, inspect the other side."

Lu started with the area where the grass and small plants were crushed. A rope and a couple of green silk handkerchiefs lay in a pile. "Do you know about this?" he asked Song.

"That's the rope I cut off her wrists. Those two handkerchiefs were tied around her eyes and mouth."

Lu inspected the rope and its cut end, laid it down and took up each of the pieces of silk. "Why is one cut and the other knotted?"

"The cloth covering her eyes was loose enough for me to push over her head, but I had to cut the one tied over her mouth."

Lu thoughtfully pulled each through his fingers as he inspected them. The silk was of the finest quality. He tucked them in his sleeve and handed the rope to Zhang, who placed it in a satchel he carried for evidence. The two continued to inspect the ground and low hanging branches, following a trail of broken tree limbs leading back to the path.

When they returned to the site, Fu-hao and Ma had finished their inspection.

"Anything?" Lu asked.

"The area to our south is trampled from the path all the way to this site. He must have grabbed the girl along the path and dragged her here. From the looks of it, she probably fought with him as he dragged her along because every few yards there is a wider spot which is trampled, indicating he had to stop to get a better hold of her."

Lu nodded. "All right. Song, show us where you ran after the assailant and where you lost him."

"This way," Song said and started off following the trail Lu had just inspected. Once they reached the walking path, he moved along the Wu family fields and their compound's massive walls. Arriving at a small servant entrance door in the compound's wall, Song stopped.

"This is where he disappeared," he said.

"You saw him run right up to this spot?" Lu asked, steadily watching the young farmer.

Song's lips tightened. With a frustrated toss of his head, he said, "I didn't actually see him enter the Wu compound." He crossed his arms. "But I know he went in there. It was Guei-qing."

"You are accusing a man you never clearly saw and claiming he went into a house you never saw him enter," Lu shouted.

Song sneered. "You don't want to believe me because the Wu's are powerful and Widow Guo is poor."

Zhang swung at Song's head, hitting him with a powerful blow. Song lost his balance and fell; he lay splayed on the ground. "Show more respect!" Zhang bellowed.

Lu raised a hand to keep Zhang from kicking him. Lu had to determine if this obstreperous young man was telling the truth or lying and falsely accusing an innocent person. He turned toward the sergeant, who had followed behind them, and said, "Take Song to the jail."

Fu-hao sidled up to Lu and spoke softly to him. "There is no solid evidence to prove Wu Guei-qing did this thing. More than likely it was Song himself. He lives next to the Guo family and knows the girl and her habits. He could have attacked her from behind, blindfolded her so she wouldn't recognize him when he raped her, but then lost his nerve and pretended to be her savior. Such a crime is the act of an ignorant, immoral man—not of a gentleman."

"The law cannot find a man guilty because he is poor and uneducated," Lu returned.

Fu-hao spoke more directly. "If you arrest Guei-qing, he will not be honored tomorrow as a model filial son. His family and the entire town will lose face before the world and—even more importantly—before the Emperor. And, finally in the end, through the power and influence of the Wu family, Guei-qing will be found innocent and you will be found guilty of malfeasance. You will be thrown out of office, your career ruined, you will go to jail yourself, and our family will be ruined."

Lu looked steadily at his brother; what he said was true. Bringing a successful case against an influential gentry's son would be difficult under any circumstances. As presiding Judge, he would be held accountable for bringing a wrongful suit against such a man. What his brother also implied, and was true, was that Lu's entire family, including his brother, would suffer the consequences of such an error.

"What are you recommending?" Lu asked.

"Certainly Song is the guilty party. He'll definitely confess under torture. He's a simple farmer who acted on impulse. He won't be able to resist telling the truth once the jailer gets a hold of him." His brother spoke with conviction. "The case will be over. No one will challenge Song's guilty verdict."

Lu stood in quiet thought, feet apart, hands tucked into his wide sleeves. His brother was right; no one would question his decision if he found Song guilty. On the other hand, accusing Guei-qing would open up a world of trouble. The Wu family, the town, and even his superiors would challenge his decision. If he condemns Song, he will be praised; if he arrests Guei-qing, his decision opens the road for potential disaster.

He pulled the silk cloths out of his sleeve and stared at them for a long time. Finally, he stuffed them back into his sleeve and turned toward his men.

"Come, we have work to do," he said and hurriedly strode around the compound walls.

Zhang pounded on the Wu's massive wooden door, shouting, "Open up by order of the Magistrate!"

A befuddled servant opened the gates.

"Take me to Wu Guei-qing immediately," Lu ordered.

The servant paused a moment, as if not quite understanding what was happening. Zhang shouted, "This is Judge Lu, Magistrate of the District. Do what he says!"

With that the servant jumped to obey, leading them through the compound.

At Guei-qing's room, Zhang pushed the door open and held the torch up as Lu entered with Fu-hao. Sprawled on top of the bed, Guei-qing still wore his long gray, dirty, grass-stained outer robe. As Lu entered, Guei-qing lurched into a sitting position.

"What're you doing?" he asked, his voice slurred. He stumbled as he attempted to stand near his bed. The stench of wine filled the room. Staring groggily at the men in the doorway, he recognized Lu and drew back, shivering. "Why are you here? I haven't done anything." He started protesting before the judge spoke.

Zhang stepped forward. "Silence! The Judge will do the talking!" he roared. Guei-qing staggered back.

"What is the meaning of this?" an irate voice demanded. Guei-qing's father stood in the doorway, his face contorted in anger.

"Wu Ming-feng you may remain in the room, but you must be silent while I interrogate your son," Lu said.

"Interrogate my son? What're you talking about?"

"If you are silent, you may remain, otherwise you will go outside," Judge Lu repeated, ignoring the questions.

Guei-qing's father shot him a hostile look. "Do you know what you're doing? You'll regret this, Lu."

Zhang started forward, but Lu stopped him. Without another word, Lu turned toward the quivering son.

"We know you accosted Guo Xiang-hua tonight. Confess or you'll be arrested and the jailer will interrogate you."

Guei-qing's face lost all color. The jailer would certainly use torture to get him to confess. He cast a pleading look at his father, but Zhang stepped closer to the elder Wu, reminding him to remain silent.

"No, no. I've been here, sleeping all night," Guei-qing stammered.

Lu scrutinized his clothing. "The criminal wore such a robe and knelt in the wet grass. How do you explain those stains?" Lu said, waving his hand toward Guei-qing's clothing. He then produced the silk handkerchiefs. "I believe these are yours."

Guei-qing looked down. "I didn't mean to. I was drunk. She was walking down the path, alone. It was an accident."

His father, shocked, started forward, but Zhang again blocked his way.

"An accident?" the judge roared. "You call rape an accident?"

"I was drunk," he whined.

Lu turned toward Fu-hao, who had already established himself at Guei-qing's desk. "Are you ready to write this down?"

Fu-hao hurriedly finished preparing his ink and took several sheets of paper out of his packet. "Yes, ready."

"Proceed," Lu instructed the young man.

"She shouldn't have been alone at that time of night. I was returning from a visit with friends," he said with a quick glance at his father.

"You mean you were returning from the wine shop," Lu said.

He grimaced. "Yes. I said I was drunk," he whimpered.

"Go on," Lu ordered.

"It was too much. She swung a basket as she walked ahead of me. I thought, well, she doesn't even know I'm here. I grabbed her from behind and covered her eyes so she wouldn't recognize me. She started screaming, so I had to tie another handkerchief around her mouth. But she wouldn't stop struggling. She was hard to control. I found a long piece of rope in her basket. I grabbed it and tied her hands behind her back. She kept wriggling, trying to escape. Then that stupid farmer came along and almost caught me." He frowned and looked up. "She was so much trouble. If only she would have kept quiet, none of this would have happened."

Disgusted, Lu said, "Zhang, take him to the jail."

At that, Guei-qing shot another glance at his father, then spoke urgently. "Please, your Honor, give me a few moments of privacy. I need to change clothes before leaving the house."

Lu paused, then ordered everyone from the room. "We'll be right outside. One of my officers is at your window. You can't escape."

Dejected, Guei-qing nodded.

No one spoke as they waited. After some time, Lu told one of his soldiers, "Go get the prisoner. He's had enough time."

The solider marched into the room but returned alone. "Sir, you need to come inside."

Lu and his men, with Guei-qing's father close behind, entered the room. The accused man lay bleeding on the floor. His father cried out and ran to his son's prostrate body.

He had cut his own throat, severing the windpipe.

Before the grief-stricken father could drop to his son's side, Zhang pulled him away. Lu strode forward. Guei-qing was dead.

Lu picked up a knife lying next to Guei-qing's hand. He had chosen suicide rather than jail and a trial.

Allowing Wu to care for his son's body, Lu and his staff left.

As he sat at his desk finishing the case file, Fu-hao said, "You took quite a chance."

Lu shook his head. "It's my duty to make sure justice is served for everyone, not just the powerful and wealthy."

Fu-hao sighed and nodded. "What about the girl?"

"I'll order Guei-qing's father to pay a fine covering the girl's medical expenses and to give her a dowry, which will allow her to marry well. But, now," he continued, "let's get a couple of hours sleep before court opens tomorrow morning."

THE INSURRECTION

JUDITH COPEK

My full name is Specialized Autonomous Computative Intelligent Naval Robotic Fish, or SACINRF. That's a mouthful, so my handlers rearranged my letters to spell FRANCIS.

Let's get my vitals out of the way. Just skip over them if you aren't into technical twaddle. I'm a replica of the Gafftopsail Catfish, about twenty inches long. I sport a vulcanized rubber exterior, and I'm equipped with sensors up the ying-yang. *Literally.* Each of my fins contains a propulsion device to steer me along the sea floor or up to the surface. My interior space contains miniature but powerful batteries, transmitters and receivers, even dye packets like the banking industry uses to foil robbers. Each eye socket holds a retractable fish eye lens that "sees" the area around me and sends data to my electronic brain, a sophisticated computer controlled by my software agents.

These agents are "bots" that learn from my experiences, changing and adapting my software code. After my final assembly, I aced my beta tests and strafed through the preliminary trials with an honor roll performance. Then they hustled me off to the deep blue sea for a final shakedown.

* * * *

My mission is to prowl the waters off Iran. I'll collect statistics about Iranian shipping with particular emphasis on the Iranian navy, taking underwater measurements of knot speed, displacement, and determining if the ships carry concealed weaponry. Naturally, my research goes back to Langley.

My first adventure—well, misadventure—occurred off the South Florida coast on my final training run. I was humming along, searching for a sunken ship, when a shark nosed up to me. My programming code instructed me to cloud the water with dye, but my delivery mechanism tanked and the shark bumped me with his big sandpaper nose and then he bit me.

Mayday! Mayday!

I signaled for pickup and, missing two fins and listing to port, I dragged my frame to the rendezvous point.

My handlers said, "Dumb-ass robot that swims right into the shark's mouth." Like it was my fault the dye mechanism crapped out! Back to the lab posthaste. But the problem was, after the shark adventure, my agent software interpreted "object approaching" as danger, which I applied to harmless sea turtles and tropical fish, and anything that moved underwater, including seaweed and kelp.

Unbeknownst to my handlers, this sense of danger was enhanced during my post-repair sea trials. With no one the wiser, I had become a robotic wimp. I'd release my dye if krill swam by. If one of those idiot technicians had dumped my memory, they would have figured it out.

My mission began for real, and with it came the first crisis. I was delivered to the Persian Gulf gussied up as an African Sea Catfish. Our boat, disguised as a fishing trawler, deployed me via an underwater tube, and I jetted to the surface to look around and get my GPS reading.

Holy freakin' crap! My internal marine encyclopedia told me I was nose to nose with a yellow-bellied sea snake. Those bastards are six feet long, and the only thing yellow-bellied about that snake is its color. The monster was lazing in the turquoise water as if he owned the whole Persian Gulf. He raised his ugly head two feet out of the water and peered around, like a snake charmer's music lured him out of the sea.

Dive! Dive! My software commanded.

With my propulsion fins thrusting, I scuttled to the sea bottom. The encyclopedia continuously fed me more data. Sea snakes are the most venomous snakes in the world. A drop of venom can kill several grown men.

Would this venom tarnish my silvery skin and destroy my coloration? Would the toxin corrode my propulsion jets? The Second Law of Robotics* is that a robot must protect its own existence.

Before I could branch to "anti-venom," my internal software agents created crippleware, cretinous code that gave me an antipathy to sea snakes. This hard-coded fear blocked me from my tracking and measurement functions. I released my dye packets and hovered on the sea bottom, ignoring my handler's urgent signals until a fishing dhow arrived at midnight to pick me up.

Francis, to the surface, ASAP.

* * * *

My software agents were deprogrammed, debugged and reprogrammed, a tedious error-prone process. My handlers denied my requests for venomous spines like an authentic member of my species would have.

Faux spines, Francis. Hidden antennae. Remember what you are.

More frustrating were the handler's comments my receptors picked up.

"Fish and visitors smell in three days."

"Sometimes you really have to squirm to get off the hook."

"Fuggedaboutit Rebellious Air-brained Nincompoop Cowardly Insurrectionist Sissy."

Insurrectionist? *Moi*? A robot always follows orders. Well, usually.

My third and last adventure (some called it a debacle) as a CIA operative was not my fault either. No way, I counted myself a hero. For this final training mission to determine my seaworthiness, the lab rats tarted me up as a diaphanous finned Mozambique Sea Catfish. I knew no fear, frisking to the surface, plunging to the bottom. Nary a dye packet escaped my ejectors. I propelled myself among the dhows and freighters sending back reams of data. I showed the sea snakes my middle fin.

Then, as I was tooling along in the warm water a few miles north of the Equator on the last day before deployment back to Iran, my receptors picked up satellite phone and GPS devices off the Somali coast.

Sky Sat chatter at 2°, 47 minutes North, 46°, 21 minutes East.

No sooner had I transmitted this information than I swam into a mass of flailing swimmers, far from shore. On the surface, I observed that sailors on a rust bucket boat were tossing men, women and children into the sea. I signaled my handlers for an emergency delivery of lifeboats, and beach towels.

Asimov's First Law of Robotics is that a robot may not allow a human being to come to harm. I circled among the weak, nudging them to the surface, and then some netting trapped me and I was heaved out of the water. Those brutish sailors had caught me in a seine.

I signaled my handlers again. *Captured by seafaring thugs.* No response.

The crew of the boat gathered round the net and gaped, shouting, "Foodda! Foodda!" I didn't need to access my international dictionary to understand *that*.

A message came over my emergency frequency: *Somali pirates have seized you. Get the hell off that boat and back into the water. Assistance on the way.*

Those bastards would have probably tried to eat me, but I extruded my alternate fins to cut through the netting. While those lawless loonies gaped, I put out two tiny mobility wheels, shot between their legs, crossed the deck and plunged into the water. I also deployed a few grams of my special "slime" that made the deck "slippery as snot on a marble," as the lab technicians put it. When the pirates tried to run to the railing, they careened and crashed into each other, giving me time to swim under their vessel. I propelled myself back to the surface, hidden among the exhausted swimmers. Again, I requested life-saving assistance for the unfortunate souls still floundering in the water. While I waited, I bumped a few back to the surface.

My sound sensors detected a helicopter. The Seahawk chopper dropped a basket for me to swim into and inflatable rafts and food packages for the flagging swimmers. From my wire basket high above the water, I saw some of the pirates swabbing the deck and two others, back on their feet, pointing their AK-47s at the helicopter and making threatening motions. They didn't shoot. Maybe they noticed the Penguin missiles, but I couldn't wait to get out of there.

* * * *

Back in the lab for the third time, my handlers attempted to reprogram my agents to "get rid of that empathy crap." I realized they didn't know the Laws of Robotics. While he worked on my software, Jason, the programmer, spoke in his sincere voice.

"Francis, you gotta follow orders and stop screwing this up. The agency spent big bucks to transport you to the African coast. Do you have any idea how much it cost to create a Mozambique sea catfish skin?" Pause. "Francis, you gotta do your stuff and follow orders or they'll ship your project off to Bangalore."

I wanted to tell him that top-secret projects are not sent offshore, but he seemed like a clueless chiphead, and besides, my empathy paths had been moved to a seldom-accessed subroutine.

* * * *

I didn't return to the Persian Gulf or the Gulf of Aden. Instead, I have been shuffled between acronym agencies. The CIA traded me to the DEA like I was a baseball card for a lame one-season rookie.

I'm back in Gafftopsail mode, with a new silvery gray skin that coruscates like anodized aluminum but it's still vulcanized rubber. My current handlers have given me a final opportunity to execute a successful mission. The assignment: patrolling the coast between the harbors of Cartagena and Santa Marta in Colombia and searching for self-propelled, semi-submersible (SPSS) craft, small drug-transporting submarines. These subs have been spotted and apprehended in the Pacific and the DEA believes the drug cartels will move to the Caribbean for safer passage. The subs, with cargoes worth two hundred million, travel just below the surface. They could even be towed by a freighter. My information is that the subs are assembled in the jungle and transported to the coast—sometimes even floated down a river.

When I spot a sub, I'll vector our Navy or Coast Guard the coordinates. As the ship or plane approaches, I'll drop a dye packet to pinpoint the sub's location. Orders I can follow without mishaps. No sea snakes, no pirates, no problem. I'm mission ready and gung ho. Off to Cartagena to be a robotic soldier-fish in the drug wars.

* * * *

Released off the Colombian coast on patrol duty, I reconnoiter the shoreline, and swim up the estuaries, checking my stored internal maps against physical geography. Maybe I can discover secret locales along the coast, a mangrove swamp or a river where an SPSS might be clandestinely launched. I have to stay alert for not only ships, but also for larger fish that consider me part of the food chain. My memory circuits still jangle with recollections of the shark.

Carefree for the moment, I'm swimming to a salsa beat, in the waters somewhere between Cartagena and Barranquilla. The clowns in the lab thought it would be "kind of cool" to equip me with an iPod. I swim to samba, rumba, salsa, cha cha, and reggae. Tango, too. My dorsal fin keeps the beat, and my tail sways through the water. I like the samba best, but salsa is good, and *Timbalero* is the best.

My sensors pick up the sound of an engine and I surface to investigate. Not thirty feet away floats a sixty foot sub, painted as blue as the Caribbean, tied up on a deserted stretch of coastline. Half a dozen men load large plastic-wrapped parcels into the hold. A guy with a submachine gun stands guard. I calculate the coordinates and send a signal to the DEA. "Blue SPSS loading cargo." I wait for orders.

Francis! You can only operate in International Waters. We're advising the Colombian Navy of the sub's location. Now, get the hell away from there, pronto.

Did anyone say, "Good job," or even "Awesome?" Like I'm lower than whale shit. But I don't get the hell away; instead, full of curiosity, I skulk in the good cover of some mangrove roots. The Colombian navy vessel shows up and arrests the sub crew and the workers. They tow the sub away. Then I hustle up the coast toward Barranquilla. This time I move to the samba beat, whipping my fin and swaying with the music, relying on my sonar to avoid boats and large fish.

Later in the day, another communiqué: *You're a clever robot. The Colombian Navy retrieved two hundred twelve million in cocaine. The decision has come down that you are to patrol close to the coast, track any SPSS vessels to the open sea and then follow procedures.*

Somewhat mollified, confidence paths reinforced, I turned up the samba beat and continued toward Barranquilla and the big river that pours into the sea. Up ahead my sonar detected various objects about the size of, well, about the size of me. I extruded my fish eye lenses.

Holy freakin' crap! I would recognize those swept-wing silvery fins anywhere. From the flat head to the pale belly, it was… me! The Gafftopsail approaches and swims circles around me a few times. The rest of the school hangs back. I keep still in the water, with my fins fluttering. If I had a heart, it would have been pounding.

My twin takes a good long look. Her nose seems to quiver, her mouth opens, then she gives me the fish eye and swims off. The school scatters after her, whirling away like a barracuda is after them.

I am alone again before I can say, "Hey dudes, want to go scarf down some shrimp and a little sea water?"

Was it my lack of bacterial slime? Did she notice that my spines lack venom? That my mouth would not be an ideal locale for her eggs? My electronic brain reactivates the empathy paths. The bots race into program mode to create a *socializing agent*. I swim after my Gafftopsail brethren, but they flee, eyes wide with terror.

A message arrives from my handlers. *Whiskey-Tango-Foxtrot? You're emitting strange signals.*

"Gafftopsail confrontation. One o'clock heading to Barranquilla."
Roger.

I sway to a mournful tango beat, music with feeling. Various system checks including my hierarchy of rules shows everything in order, but my circuits jangle, and my fuzzy logic seems downright wooly. Goal-directedness has got up and left. My zeal for the mission is now smaller than the finest grain of Caribbean sand.

The future is bleak. Someone will transport cocaine no matter how many subs I locate. Eventually I will malfunction or corrode or my batteries will die. I'll sink to the sea bottom with all my expensive electronics and my vulcanized silver skin. I take stock. Somehow, I have become more than an autonomous robot.

I have become sentient.

A galvanizing thought, not a coded instruction, not even an adaptive behavior but a real independent thought. And feelings. Holy freakin' crap! Now what?

If the DEA gets wind of this, they'll pluck me out of the sea and back to an uncertain fate. Maybe even… disassembly. I don't want to drink the Kool-Aid.

I won't drink the Kool-Aid.

I have to figure this out *sub rosa,* or in my case, *sub mare.* My first independent act will be to proceed robotically, as it were, and according to programmed instructions. As if my life depends on it, I swim north at twelve knots. Because my *life* does.

* * * *

Weeks pass. Rivers, streams, estuaries, lagoons, harbors, islands, even a quagmire and not a SPSS in sight. When I send in my daily report, the same tedious message comes back, PCO. *Please carry on.*

Despair becomes my companion and the tango with its morose passions becomes my beat. I hover among coral reefs and swim along the placid beaches. Nada.

Then, one moonless night on my rounds, swimming between Santa Marta and Barranquilla, where the great Magdalena River flows into the Caribbean and the silt-choked water reeks with pollutants, my sonar picks up two vessels in tandem. I discover a sub towed by a ramshackle fishing boat, *Bonita,* a boat defying the term "seaworthy," a boat the Somali pirates would have scorned.

Even on a night with no moon, towing the sub would be risky, but tonight is Carnival. All Barranquilla will be drinking, dancing and carousing. I douse my tango tunes and fall in behind the sub.

The silt stretches far into the sea. My sonar keeps me on track, and at intervals, I surface for a GPS reading and to scope things out. A thick brown grungy hawser tethers the fishing boat to the blue sub. The air and the sea are calm, and gradually the lights of Barranquilla disappear and I am again at sea.

Instead of a more northeasterly directional heading toward Florida or Mexico, *Bonita* tows the sub toward Cartagena, staying close to the twelve-mile limit. I follow in leisurely pursuit, with bits and bytes churning over this turn of events. Where is *Bonita* towing the sub? Our little flotilla passes Cartagena and cruises in a northwesterly direction. As my handlers like to say, Whiskey-Tango-Foxtrot?

Without warning, my sonar sounds like a pothead drummer. When I pop to the surface, I discover *a second sub* portside the fishing boat. A fast, sporty Monte Carlo 27 has also pulled up to *Bonita's* starboard side. The name on the transom is *La Vida Loca.* Now there are two subs, the ancient fishing boat and the Monte Carlo rafted together in this speck of ocean. And me, Francis, the insurrectionist robotic fish.

On my next trip to the surface, I discover the ships are in the lee of a dark, silent island. No carnival music, no seaside taverns, no dancing, no lights, only silent, shallow sea. My online atlas identifies Los Islas de los Rosario, an island chain off Cartagena. The dark island is *Bocachica*. The drug runners are taking advantage of Carnival, the ebony night, and the uninhabited island. I feel a shiver of outrage. Los Rosarios are a national park. My atlas describes a perfect watery place of protected flora and fauna. In my unique way, *I* am now fauna.

I transmit my location and a message about the rendezvous of the two subs, and all the business with the *Bonita* and the Monte Carlo. A communication comes right back: *West of Cartagena is out of your territory. However, proceed, keeping at least one sub in sight and dye packets at the ready. Our ship is two hours away. Prepare to be picked up for maintenance. We'll drop your basket.*

No more maintenance. No more trips to the lab. Yet, for my self-respect, I need one final bang-up successful mission. After that, I'll return to the peaceful island with the sea park, the oceanarium and the placid blue water.

A sailor from the Monte Carlo climbs up the rickety ladder onto the wretched *Bonita*. When I skitter underwater again, my environment is FUBAR to the max. Later, my data log reveals that *Bonita* (a misnomer if there ever was one) dropped her anchor chain, clobbering me in the process, and fracturing my right fish eye lens. I tumble ass over teakettle until my equilibrium returns. The collision knocks some slimy green gunk off the anchor, which wedges in my left fish eye lens, blinding me. I swim back to the surface to signal my handlers, assuring them my other systems are "go," but that visuals are an issue. The cracked lens remains watertight, but I see quadruple images of everything, like a fish that swims in bathtub gin. If I were among the sea snakes, the shock of seeing four for every one would cause a technical freak out.

From the handlers: *Identify slimy green glop.*

I could respond, "Anchor crud," but I message, *virus viridus,* which sounds more "robotic."

Are you able to proceed via sonar and GPS readings?

"Roger."

Ten minutes later, *La Vida Loca's* propeller creates enough turbulence to wash *virus viridus* from my left eye, but I don't tell my handlers. Instead, I remain in furtive fish mode, observing the transfer of large blue and white plastic-wrapped packages from *Bonita* to each of the subs. *La Loca Vida's* crew supervises the process. They speak in monosyllables and move with precision. I swim using my good eye. Soon the towed sub is loose from the hawser, and the sailors finish their tasks as a blood red dawn blooms in the east.

The subs, now traveling together, head out into the quiet dawn-lit ocean, while the zippy little Monte Carlo turns toward Cartagena. The ugly old *Bonita* sets course for Barranquilla. Both of the subs are just below the surface, and I follow them out to sea. At the twelve-mile limit, they separate, and my random decision generator recommends following the sub heading on a course between Mexico and Cuba.

My handlers and I stay in communication, and they regularly message back, *PCO. Please carry on.*

At last, my sonar picks up a boat, and I surface to investigate. Four boats, four U.S. flags. Curse this fractured lens. *One boat.* I use my propulsion jets to come alongside the sub and wait for the approaching cutter.

With a mighty thrust, I release my red dye packets into the blue sea. Moments later, the cutter pulls up to the SPSS. The sub's raggedy crew, three guys (or was it twelve?) in shorts and sneakers clamber out of a hatch on top. They have no time to scuttle the sub, which they always do if apprehended.

I feel so proud to see our flag on the stern of the Coast Guard ship. Sailors take the crew off the sub and prepare to tow it behind the cutter. A successful mission at last!

Francis, excellent job. Approach and reveal yourself. The crew will lower a basket.

I break the Law of Robotics about obeying orders from human beings. I do not approach, nor do I reveal myself. Instead, I dive deep and swim away like a crazed porpoise, sprinting back to the Islas de los Rosarios and the Coral Reef National Park. The last incoming message before I flip off my communications equipment: *Francis, Whiskey-Tango-Foxtrot?*

Swimming again to a samba beat, for it is Carnival, I approach the sea park with the lovely flora and fauna. I hope there are a few Gafftopsails lazing in the warm waters. We can swim together and they will show me the ropes. I'll do fine with only one fish eye lens. Maybe one of the Gafftopsails will let me hatch her eggs in my mouth.

I am no longer Francis. I am free.

* * * *

* Isaac Asimov's Three Laws of Robotics

1. A robot may not injure a human being or, through inaction, allow a human being to come to harm.

2. A robot must obey orders given it by human beings except where such orders would conflict with the First Law.

3. A robot must protect its own existence as long as such protection does not conflict with the First or Second Law.

The original Three Laws of Robotics were coined by Isaac Asimov in his 1942 short story *"Runaround."* Eventually *"Runaround"* became only one of several similar stories published under the common name *I, Robot.*

BARGAINING CHIP

KATE FELLOWES

"I'll make you a deal." Maxine Norse addressed the couple standing before her. They'd dithered over whether to buy a compact or mid-size car for nearly an hour and now was the right moment to prod them. She launched into her boiler plate pitch, making up their minds for them. She didn't get to be sales leader at Ace Quality Motors for ten years running without knowing how to close.

Smiling to herself, she imagined the wheels creaking around ever so slowly in her customers' heads, until one or the other had an "a-ha!" moment. The deal was as good as sealed.

They'll be getting a car they can enjoy for years, Maxine thought. *Sure, it costs more money than they planned on spending, but the bigger one will suit them better in the long run. They can thank me later. And I get another sale for this month. Win-win.*

After work, Maxine changed into her running gear, ready to run three miles, maybe more if the rain held off. Running wasn't her sport of choice, but since the nearest roller skating rink was ten miles away and a woman past forty had to work out every single day to stay in any sort of shape, Maxine ran.

"Run for your life!" she said to her reflection as she pulled her hair into a ponytail. Her mantra—half serious, half jest— always gave her the momentum she needed to actually get out the door. That was the hardest part, making a choice. Committing to the choice flowed naturally from there.

She'd made several hard choices a few years back. Offloaded her cheating husband, traded the big house in the 'burbs for a cozy Cape Cod in a tree-lined neighborhood, and found her niche at Ace Quality Motors. Yes, life was darn near perfect. A little lonely, sometimes, but otherwise, perfect.

After stuffing both pockets with dog biscuits, Maxine set out down the drive. Sprinting the short side of the block, she slowed at the next corner, then fell into a steady pace, weaving her way from the residential area, through the shopping district, out to the old industrial part of town.

Like every small town, Warnimont had seen better days. When Maxine was a girl, the factories hummed for three full shifts, and if you drove down the road at the shift change, you were guaranteed a ten-minute wait as streams of workers crossed to the parking lot.

Now, as she checked her time with a quick glance at her watch, she looked up to see the vast expanse of empty asphalt, where all those workers' cars should be.

Kicking it up a notch, she ran past a few more down-on-their-luck enterprises—the small engine repair shop, an auto body place, a printing company—and turned another corner.

Her sneakers hit the ground in a rhythmic pattern that should have soothed her, but didn't. After a bad day at work, she imagined each step was landing on whoever had made the day miserable. But today had been a good day.

She reached the mid-point in her run and her heart took a dip. Up ahead was the old fenced-in farm, with a dilapidated house, some crumbling buildings, and the chained dog.

Maxine always ran in the road here, where the sidewalk had run out. Even the curbs had chunks broken or missing, just like the fence in the yard up ahead, where the missing pickets resembled knocked-out teeth. Her hands moved to her pockets. She checked both ways on the deserted street, where twilight was just beginning to fall. Already the days were growing shorter, which meant winter was coming. Her heart dipped even lower. Which meant the chained dog would be freezing, as well as hungry and lonely.

As a flare of anger filled her, the dog biscuit she'd been clutching snapped in her hand. How dare someone leave a poor dog chained outside all day? How could someone be so heartless and cruel?

In the past, the local humane society had an investigator to check out bad situations. But that job got the axe when the economy tanked. Now, there was no one to check.

Well, she wasn't going to sit on her hands where this dog was concerned. In fact, she'd already put some wheels in motion, but they were legislative wheels. Slow-moving wheels like the ones on the old junker that couple had brought as a trade-in today.

"Look, Mayor, I'll make you a deal," she'd said after last week's Chamber of Commerce luncheon. "If this town gets a law banning chaining dogs, I'll see that Ace Quality Motors picks up the tab for candy and ice cream at the 4th of July picnic."

Mayor Whitnall played along. "I appreciate your offer to *sponsor* some 4th of July costs, Maxine. Certainly, no dog should be mistreated here, or anywhere."

"Certainly not," she agreed.

"We were hoping to get those fancy square dancers for the parade, too...." Mayor Whitnall went on, meeting her eye.

Maxine laughed. "I don't suppose you ever sold cars?" she asked.

"Just candy bars for fundraisers," he said with a chuckle.

"You can have your dancers, too. As long as we get the best ad position in the program and prominent acknowledgement."

Mayor Whitnall spread his hands. "Square dancers sponsored by Ace Quality Motors."

"Exactly. Let's call that a deal."

"The price of fireworks has really gone up," the Mayor went on.

"Don't press your luck, sir," Maxine said, rising. "I'm just a citizen trying to expedite an ordinance, not your fairy godmother."

But it would still take at least two months for her ordinance to pass, Maxine knew. Two long months. Too long.

One sharp bark split the air, focusing her attention now.

Maxine had taken this route just three weeks, but the dog recognized her approach, standing at attention as she came closer. Waiting on the end of his chain near the missing pickets each day, he always snapped at the biscuits she tossed to him.

He looked fierce, with a big, square head and smooth, sleek body. But she wasn't fooled. She saw the tail wag, the eyes light. He was a good boy. He deserved better than this.

Poking her head through the space where two pickets were broken off, Maxine stretched, lobbing one biscuit after another in the dog's direction, at least eight feet away.

"How's my good boy?" she asked, following up with more sweet talk as he ate.

At the rear of the yard was an old square farmhouse, quite a ways off. One side had been patched in various colored aluminum. Some pieces hung loose, showing unfaded paint beneath. A window was covered with cardboard and plastic film attached by duct tape. The porch railing sagged. A satellite dish perched on the roof seemed out of place.

She pitched the last biscuit. It took a bad bounce, falling short of Good Boy's chain-restricted reach. The heavy choke collar around his neck tightened as he struggled in vain.

Maxine gauged the width of the space in the fence, turned sideways and eased her body through, one careful inch at a time. Her sneakers squelched over mud and scraggly grass as she crossed the space between them. Her heartbeat quickened, her mouth felt dry. What if the dog's "owner" spotted her out one of those dirty windows? She *was* trespassing on private property.

Maxine gave a snort, shaking off the thought. Part of her wanted to break Good Boy's chain and run all the way home with him right that minute, a worse crime than trespass.

Crouching, she retrieved the biscuit and advanced to Good Boy.

"Here we go, Good Boy. That's a good boy," she cooed, holding out the treat.

The dog growled low in his throat, but Maxine held her ground. Good Boy opened his mouth, took one end of the biscuit and backed up a step.

The sudden prick of her tears surprised Maxine and she blinked rapidly. He trusted her!

The dog's ten foot chain had worn away grass in a semi-circle around his rickety shelter, a wooden structure that looked as old as the farmhouse. A stainless steel water bowl, half-filled with murky liquid sat near the doorway. An empty dog food bag lay crumpled and tossed against one wall, as it had every day since Maxine started running this route.

Maxine stepped closer to investigate, noting a row of junker cars parked along the far side of the yard, where a gate opened onto a rutted gravel driveway.

In the old days, this property had been a successful nursery, with rows of greenhouses producing roses sent around the entire country. But like so much else in town, that had been long, long ago.

Several of the greenhouses still stood, but just barely. Missing glass left only the framework for two of the buildings. The one nearest the house, though, appeared nearly intact. Glints of the setting sun revealed flourishing greenery, odd in the vastness of neglect.

Good Boy let out a series of throaty barks. Maxine spun around to face the gravel drive.

As an old maroon van slowly bumped down the road, Maxine froze halfway between the dog and the fence. Several big strides brought her to the doghouse. She slipped around the back, out of sight. Peeking around the side of the shelter, she tried not to think about what she was standing in, what was now firmly stuck to both shoes.

The van parked near the farmhouse and two men got out. Both were big guys dressed in flannel shirts and cargo shorts. They sported beards worthy of a reality show, and were laughing, talking loud. Were they high? Or drunk?

The driver swung open the double doors at the back of the van, reached inside and then tossed a cloth bag at the other guy, who gave a hoot of delight.

"Like candy from a baby!" he said, catching the bag.

Throwing two more parcels at his friend, the driver gathered up one of his own. The van doors clanged shut.

When something warm and wet touched her hand, Maxine nearly cried out with surprise until she realized it was Good Boy, making friends.

"Good Boy," she whispered as he sniffed her hand then dipped his head, inviting the scratch. Maxine rubbed the velvety ears in wonder. He was such a good boy, just as she'd known he would be.

The van door clanged again and she checked back on the action. The driver slapped white magnetic signs onto the body of the van, first on one side then the other, before following his friend into the house. Neither man had ever even glanced in Good Boy's direction.

"What was that all about?" she asked the dog.

He slipped his tongue over her hand, tickling her palm.

"I'll get you out of here," she promised him.

Her jog home felt longer than usual, the look in Good Boy's eyes as he watched her squeeze through the fence haunting her thoughts.

After a shower and some digital food—microwaved lasagna—Maxine sat on the sofa, watching the local news. When the story about a bank robbery at the First Mariners branch in town came on, she wasn't even surprised by the description of the robbers or of their vehicle.

"The suspects were bearded and escaped in a maroon van with dark patches on the side," the news anchor said.

Patches of unfaded paint, where magnetic signs normally blocked the sun.

"I'll be double-dipped," Maxine said, reaching for her laptop.

She did a quick property search, turning up the landowner's name. Chip Bottsford. If anyone looked less like a Chip, she couldn't imagine who. Chip sounded so all-American—clean cut, big white teeth, and a tennis sweater. Not hairy, overweight, and baggy cargo shorts.

A circuit court search revealed two convictions—shoplifting and DWI.

Sitting back, Maxine pondered her options. As a good citizen, it was her duty to tell the police what she'd seen—as she'd been trespassing on private property while contemplating dognapping.

But if the police went to question Chip and Good Boy barked, even from the end of his chain, there was a chance he'd be shot. That big square head was intimidating when you didn't see the warm brown eyes, too. Things could get ugly fast. She'd read about those tragedies a million times.

Good Boy came first. Being a law-abiding citizen took second place. Easily.

Tapping her fingers against her chin, Maxine thought and thought, crafting her plan.

The next day, Maxine left work early. She stopped at the sporting goods store for a nylon collar and leash and some pepper spray.

Boldly driving through the gate and down the rutted gravel to the farmhouse, Maxine practiced her pitch. She needed to strike the proper tone from the get-go to make this deal.

Mounting the rickety steps to the farmhouse, she rapped briskly. The doorbell hung from the wall on frayed wires, as it probably had for decades.

Chip opened the door with a rush of motion. She almost didn't recognize him, up close and clean-shaven.

"Yeah?" he said around a mouthful of something heavy with onion. His bored tone matched his annoyed expression.

"Hello, Mr. Bottsford. I'm here to make you the deal of a lifetime." Maxine smiled, swallowing down her dislike of this man.

"Don't need nothing you're selling, lady. Get lost. Get off my property." Chip started to close the door.

"I know what you did," Maxine said quickly. Her hand tightened on the pepper spray canister in her right pocket, the small, curved shape reassuring her. "But I'm prepared to take that knowledge to the grave."

Chip leaned against the doorjamb. "Lady, what are you talking about?"

"C'mon, Chip. You know. The robbery yesterday. You did it. I know you did, and I can prove it. But I won't."

A silence fell between them. Beyond Chip, in the living room, Maxine could see a big screen TV blaring the news. She could also make out the bulky figure of Chip's friend, sprawled in a recliner.

"You don't know squat," Chip snarled, leaning back on his heels.

"I know there's a maroon van over there with dark patches on the side," she said, watching his glance dart toward the vehicle.

"So?"

"I know you're watching a brand new big screen TV." Maxine gestured inside before sweeping her hand toward the giant cardboard box shoved behind a trash can next to the porch. "And I know the police would find those details worth investigating. But they won't hear them from me."

"Keep talking," Chip said.

Maxine's spirits soared. He was on the hook, now it was just a matter of reeling him in.

"I want your dog," she stated, pointing in the direction of Good Boy, who sat forlornly as ever, on the end of his chain.

"What?"

"You heard me. I want your dog. I want to take him away from here to live with me. Now. Right now."

"Are you nuts?"

"Or I'll call the cops from here on your porch and turn you in."

Chip looked from her to the dog, who gave one wag of his tail. Then he said, "Do I know you?"

"No, you do not," Maxine said.

"You look familiar," Chip said, his nose wrinkling as if he smelled something bad.

Maxine swallowed. She knew perfectly well hers was the face that launched five thousand promotional calendars every Christmas, one for every residence in town. Chip probably had a copy hung in the kitchen next to the fridge.

"I just have that kind of face," she said. "You don't know me. I don't know you. And, no offense, but I don't want to. I just want to give that dog a good home."

"I've had Duke since he was a pup. I love that dog, man." Crossing his arms over his chest, Chip shifted in the doorway, prepared to argue.

Maxine pressed her eyes shut, wondering what sort of love invited neglect and abuse. The sort she'd gotten from her ex-husband. The sort that had made her feel like a chained dog.

She opened her eyes, made a speed-it-up motion with one hand.

"Yes or no, Chip. I don't have all day. It's time to fish or cut bait. Sure you love Duke, but I'll bet you love not being in jail more."

"Why should I trust you?" he demanded. "How do I know you won't take my dog and rat me out anyway?"

"Because I said I wouldn't," Maxine stated. She knew how she appeared to others—businesslike and sincere. Impeccably groomed, stylishly dressed. A woman who knew what she wanted and did what she said she would. A woman to believe.

"I'm not saying I will, but if I let you take Duke and you say one word to the cops, I'll come find you," Chip threatened, putting his finger under Maxine's chin.

She didn't blink. Choosing her words with precision, she said, "I'll never say a word about the robbery." Using her index finger, she crossed her heart, a gesture Chip could understand.

"You know, Duke won't even go with you," Chip said.

"If he won't come, I won't push," Maxine said. "Deal?"

Chip pondered for all of a second or two. "Yeah, okay, deal. He'll never come to you."

Maxine was already turning away, clattering down the steps.

Slipping the collar and leash from her left pocket, she approached Good Boy with care, and a biscuit. Squatting low, she let him eat while her fingers worked at the choke collar. When the dreadful thing dropped off, she put it in her pocket and glanced back to the porch, making sure Chip hadn't budged.

The soft nylon collar clipped on easily and then they were off, moving across the yard at a trot. Good Boy quickened his steps to match hers, never doubting, never hesitating. On the porch, Chip lifted a hand in farewell, but Maxine didn't respond. She just put the car in reverse and got out of there.

"Hooray, Good Boy! We did it!" she said, swiping at her tears.

Good Boy—Duke—sat beside her, watching out the window as the industrial area passed by and the tree-lined neighborhood approached.

The next night, a freshly-groomed Duke lay on the rug in the living room of Maxine's cozy Cape Cod, his big square head resting on equally big paws.

Eating microwaved macaroni cheese, Maxine watched the news.

"Acting on an anonymous tip, the police department raided a local property today, uncovering an established marijuana growing operation," the anchorperson said.

On the screen, Chip and his friend appeared in handcuffs, being led down the rickety farmhouse steps. In the background, officers could be seen carrying pots from the greenhouse.

"Authorities are also investigating a possible link to the First Mariners bank robbery earlier this week, since a van similar to that used in the crime was found parked on the property."

Maxine sighed happily. "Best deal I ever made," she said, glancing over at Duke.

In his sleep, Duke heaved a sigh, too.

HOME INVASION

POLLY IYER

"Going out again tonight, Addy?" I asked from my office as she walked by, adjusting an earring.

She stopped at the door. "Our critique group is meeting twice this week. Didn't I tell you?"

I thought back, came up empty. "Maybe you did. The Big Dollar account has taken all my energy and concentration." I pushed my work aside and got up. "Sorry if I forgot."

"You work too hard, Brian. Life is short."

She sidled up to me and put her arms around my waist. When was the last time that happened?

"We need to go someplace fun. Reignite those old fires. You never used to be like this."

I kissed her cheek. "You're right. I'll look into it." I followed her to the door where she returned the kiss.

"Love you," she trilled, and scooted outside to her car.

Protective, I always watched her leave the house at night. The last week, she'd gone out three times, and the same thing happened. No sooner than she backed out of the driveway, Jeff came out of the house next door and followed her toward town.

Again.

Tonight, Addy's excuse for going out was an added critique meeting. The other two times she went shopping. As a Willow Lake police detective, Jeff sometimes kept crazy hours, but could their timed departures be more than coincidence? My stomach turned over. Had Addy been affectionate to me out of guilt?

You never used to be like this. Was she bored with me?

Jeff and Eddie had been my best friends since we were kids. The three musketeers. That's what everyone called us. Eddie and I, along with our wives, commiserated when Jeff's wife and two daughters were killed by a drunk driver—a rich guy who hired a big-time lawyer and got off with a thirty-day license suspension. Jeff was never the same after that. He rallied when the driver was shot to death in an alley behind a bar.

Jeff and Addy had always been friends, but would he take their relationship to the next level? Would Addy? The question burned in my brain.

I went into Addy's study and flipped through her desk calendar. Tuesday: critique group. Thursday—today—nothing. Opening her laptop, I tried the usual passwords—the names of our kids, Bogie the dog, Addy's mother's name, special dates, and a few more, without success. Frustrated, I called Eddie. Cecile, Eddie's wife, was one of Addy's critique partners. Both women were published by a small romance press. Eddie answered.

"What's up, old pal?" he said after hearing my voice.

"Catch you at a bad time? Dinner?"

"We just finished."

"Thought you might be interested in a game of racquetball Saturday morning. What'd'ya say?"

"Sounds good. Let me check with Cecile to see if she has anything planned."

Eddie didn't do anything without checking with Cecile. I always wondered if he needed permission from her to go to the john. I heard Eddie's question and her negative reply loud and clear.

I really didn't care if Eddie could play racquetball Saturday morning. I did care that Cecile was home and not at a critique meeting. I cared about that a lot.

"See you at the club," Eddie said. "Nine a.m."

I mumbled something in the affirmative.

"Oh, and don't forget dinner Saturday night," Eddie said. "Cecile wants to try that new French restaurant at the hotel. So does Addy. I'll ask Jeff to join us, if that's okay with you."

Where was my mind? I'd totally forgotten our plans. "Um, fine with me. You know the women make the plans. We go along for the ride."

"You got that right."

I hung up and sat for a few minutes, numb, my mind cycling out of control. Was I letting suspicion rule over reason? I went to the office window. Jeff hadn't returned. Were he and Addy holed up making love in some sleazy motel out of town? If so, how long had my wife and my best friend been having an affair?

Addy wouldn't cheat on me. She wanted to get away, just the two of us. Rekindle the old flames. Why did she say that? Was she feeling neglected?

Forget it, Brian. You're being paranoid.

In the kitchen, I cut a piece of apple pie, warmed it, and scooped ice cream on top. After two bites, my stomach revolted, and I tossed the rest down the garbage disposal. I decided to work on the Big Dollar promo but couldn't focus on that either.

Addy didn't like me to read her stories until she finished, so I didn't. Why all of a sudden did she add a password to get into her computer? Were she and Jeff trading secret emails?

Then I had a devious idea. I saw Jeff's computer password recently when we were checking online sites to buy ballgame tickets. We kept a set of his house keys in case of an emergency, just like he kept ours. Dare I go into my best friend's house to look inside his computer? My best friend who might be screwing my wife?

My imagination was taking me to places I didn't want to go. Still, a quick look couldn't hurt, could it? I'd be in and out of the house in a flash.

No, going into his house without permission was wrong on so many levels. He was a cop, for God's sake. I couldn't.

A picture of Addy's naked, curvaceous body filtered through my confusion, then Jeff's buff cop's physique.

Yes, I could. I damn well could.

I inspected Jeff's house—quiet with lights dimmed. I grabbed the set of keys for his house, then slipped out the back door. Silence. The neighbors on the other side left yesterday to visit their daughter and new grandchild. I inhaled a long breath, crossed my yard into Jeff's, and scaled the back porch steps.

I slid the first key into the lock, the second into the deadbolt, and opened the door into the kitchen. The faint smell of grilled hamburger wafting in the air didn't help my queasy stomach.

Shaking off the slimy feeling of invading another man's property, I hurried through the kitchen to his office. His neat, orderly desk—folders, pen holders—contrasted with my paper-strewn surface. Every guilty thought vanished when I saw the open laptop. A tap on the mouse brought the sleeping screen to life, asking for a password. I hesitated. Was I really going to do this? I typed it in.

A newspaper article about a gangbanger who raped a twelve-year-old girl filled the screen with the headline, "Jackson Gets Slap on the Wrist." Below were the words, "Judge claims the girl asked for it."

What? How could that be? I wanted to read the rest of the story but couldn't take the time. I'd read it at home later. I clicked on Jeff's email link and scanned the entries. Addy's email sent earlier today stood out as if it were illuminated in neon letters. My pulse ticked up a few notches, knowing the precipice on which I stood. My index finger hovered over the left side of the mouse.

Click!

> *Meet you at the hotel. Make sure Brian doesn't see you leave.*
> *Addy*

I wasn't sure if my stomach or heart caused the turmoil inside me. Had I been blind? Were the signs there all along and I was too distracted with work to see them? Addy said as much when she left. "You work too hard, Brian. Life is short."

Yes, I did work long hours, but only to give Addy everything she wanted. Tennis at the club, bridge mornings, and the time to write her romance novels. I'd supported her in everything she'd ever done. And Jeff, the bastard, my best friend, stole my wife right from under my nose.

Was it his fault or mine? I snorted. Or Addy's?

I quickly scrolled through earlier emails. Most looked like police business. No others from Addy, but I'd seen enough. I clicked back to find the newspaper article on the screen when I inadvertently toppled a folder off the edge of the desk. Papers flew everywhere.

Shit!

I kneeled to gather them and paused, mesmerized by copies of newspaper articles reporting on people who'd committed crimes that should have received stiff penalties but who got off with little or no prison time. The multiple sheets stapled together followed the crime from trial to judgment. On three sets, the last sheet reported that the perpetrator had been either killed or committed suicide. A big X covered the page. One was the drunk driver who killed Jeff's family. His murder remained unsolved.

I'm not the brightest guy in the world, but I'm not dumb either. These papers could mean only one thing. Jeff had morphed from good cop to avenger.

The sound of a car sobered me.

Dammit to hell. I gathered all the papers and stuffed them into the folder. With a shaky hand on the mouse, I clicked back and found the opening article.

The car door closed.

Sweat dripped down the sides of my face. There wouldn't be enough time for the computer to settle into rest mode, the way I'd found it.

The key turned in the door latch.

I slammed the laptop lid shut and hoped Jeff wouldn't remember how he'd left it. Sliding the chair under the desk, I bee-lined for the back door.

The keys.

I dashed back, grabbed the two keys, and scooted through the kitchen just as the front door closed. I crept onto the back porch and darted across the yard to my house.

Collapsing into a kitchen chair, my drumbeat heart thudding in my ears, I dropped my head into my hands, disbelieving that I'd actually broken into Jeff's house but more distraught at what I'd found. Not only was my best friend having an affair with my wife, but it appeared he was meting out justice where justice hadn't been served. I couldn't think straight.

When my head cleared enough for a rational thought, I wondered why Jeff was home and Addy wasn't. A few moments later, I heard her car in the driveway. She came in the front door, carrying a grocery bag.

"Hi," she said. "I stopped to pick up half and half for coffee in the morning. We're out."

That explained her tardiness. I dug deep and drew on my inner Robert DeNiro, though I'd always been a terrible actor. "Productive meeting tonight?"

"Not for me. They all thought I should drop a complete storyline." She growled. "Damn, and I like it."

"Was everyone there, and did they all agree?"

"Yes and yes. I might have to work a little tonight or else I'll never sleep. Were you about to turn in?"

"I'll watch a little TV in the bedroom. If I crash, I'll see you in the morning." I pulled her close, unsure if I wanted to kiss her or to smell the scent of another man. I hated that I resorted to such a deceitful ploy. I kissed her and smelled only the faded scent of her perfume.

"That was unexpectedly nice," she said.

Her words were another reminder that I'd been inattentive to my wife's needs. I forced a smile and bid her good night, doubting I'd get one hour of sleep.

* * * *

Friday passed in a daze. I did find the presence of mind to search the Internet for the cases in Jeff's folder. One man died an apparent suicide, another a hit and run, and the third was a victim of a drive-by shooting. The two latter cases were still open. Those three men got what they deserved, but that didn't justify Jeff taking the law into his own hands. And what about the others in the folder, judgments that he'd collected? Punishments yet to be carried out?

I called Addy and said I had to work late. I didn't, but my head felt like tiny sticks of dynamite were lit and about to blow me apart. At a nearby deli, I ordered a salad which I barely touched. Fortunately, Addy was asleep when I got home.

* * * *

The next morning, while Addy slept, I slunk out of the bedroom and left to meet Eddie at the club. While driving, I contemplated what to do about Jeff. I couldn't very well discuss what I'd found without telling Eddie how I found it. Jeff's affair with my wife had taken a back seat.

The racquetball game was more intense than usual. I hit the ball with fierce resolve; Eddie responded in kind. When we called it quits, he said, "What's eating you? You played like you were mad at the world. Anything I did?"

I laughed, the first honest laugh in a long couple of days. "No, friend. It's been a hellacious week. I needed to work off tension. Sorry I was such a bear."

"Sometimes we need to do that." He patted my shoulder. "See you tonight."

I drove home dreading the thought of dinner. No way did I want to look Jeff in the eye.

* * * *

I stood in front of the dresser mirror and knotted my tie. Maybe I could feign being sick. Ha, that wouldn't be much of a stretch.

"Jeff said he didn't mind driving tonight if that's okay with you," Addy said from the bathroom.

"Sure, fine with me." It wasn't, but what else could I say?

Addy stepped into the bedroom. The turquoise of her dress brought out the color of her eyes. *Tell her, dummy.*

"You look beautiful. In fact, you get more beautiful every year."

A pink glow colored her cheeks. "Why, Brian, you haven't said any-thing like that to me in years. Thank you."

I weighed what she said. Had I been that neglectful? If I changed my ways, would I still have a chance with my wife?

Jeff's horn beeped in his driveway.

"We'd better hurry." Addy straightened my collar. "You don't look half bad yourself. Come on." She grabbed her purse and my arm, and we hurried to Jeff's car.

"Eddie said he made a reservation," Jeff said.

"Great." I forced a smile. Jeff was uncharacteristically quiet on the drive to the Versailles Hotel. So was I.

Addy broke the silence. "I've read wonderful reviews of the food. First class French cuisine, the paper said."

Jeff and I both said something to the effect that we couldn't wait.

The valet gave Jeff a stub for his car, and the three of us entered the hotel. The restaurant was on the far right side of the large lobby. Eddie met us at the door and guided us to a private room. As soon as we walked inside, strains of "Happy Birthday" filled the room. *What was going on?* My mother and father, Addy's parents, and all our friends, were clapping and singing and hugging me. I turned to Addy.

"Happy fiftieth birthday, darling," Addy said.

"But... but it's not until next week."

"We could never have pulled this off if we'd waited."

"You'd have suspected, old boy," Eddie said. "Jeff and Addy organized everything."

"You arranged the booze," Jeff said. He looked at me longer than was comfortable. "Happy birthday, friend. Get this man a glass of champagne."

Someone stuck a goblet in my hand; someone else kissed my ear and said happy birthday.

"You guys knew and didn't tell me?"

"That would have ruined the surprise."

I had other things cluttering my mind, I thought.

"What do you think I've been doing?" Addy asked. "Going to a critique meeting? Shopping?" She laughed, and everyone laughed with her.

"A toast," Jeff said. "To the best friend a guy could have."

He lingered on me with a steady gaze. My heart pumped double time.

"I'll drink to that," Eddie agreed.

I practically guzzled my champagne. If ever I needed a drink, it was now.

The tightness in my stomach settled enough to enjoy the five-star dinner. Everyone raved about the food, and when the band struck up a slow version of "Happy Days Are Here Again," Addy tugged me onto the dance floor. "I thought for sure you'd suspect something. It's not easy lying to you."

I held her close, feeling her warmth. "I never guessed." That was the truth.

"Cutting in, friend," Eddie said. He whispered in my ear. "Jeff wants to talk to you on the veranda."

Jeff stood outside, waiting. His body language told me he dreaded this conversation as much as I. The joyous sounds of the party inside clashed with the discomfort that hung in the air outside. I wished I were somewhere else. Anywhere else.

Dark circles I hadn't noticed earlier hung under Jeff's eyes; the weight of the world lined his face. I don't know what I looked like. Guilty, I assume.

"I'm a detective, Brian. It's what I do for a living."

My voice cracked. "I know."

"And you're a clumsy burglar."

A million needles pricked my skin. I calmed my breathing. *Okay, it's out in the open.* "I thought you were having an affair with Addy."

"Wha—"

He looked honestly perplexed. I explained how I came to that conclusion. "I figured you and she exchanged emails. When I couldn't access her computer, I knew you usually left your computer open, so I—"

"Went into my house. Did you think I wouldn't notice you closed the laptop and the disorganized papers in the folder? Who else in my house could do that? I'll tell you who. No one." He lowered his voice almost to a whisper. "You know why? Because my wife and daughters are dead, murdered by a goddamn drunk whose lawyer paid off a judge so he could walk scot free."

"Now he's dead, too. Strange how that worked out, isn't it? Was he the first?"

Jeff took his time. "I could say I don't know what you're talking about, but you'd know I was lying."

I nodded.

"Yes, he was the first and most important. Killing him felt good. Really good. I never lost a minute's sleep over what I did. Nor did I with the gangbanger. They got what they deserved."

I shivered in the warm evening air. "So you set yourself up as judge, jury, and executioner?"

Staring into my eyes, he said, "Yes again." He leaned on the railing, peering into the dark night. "What are you going to do?"

"I… I don't know."

"If the situation were reversed, I'd help you rid the world of vermin."

"They're not vermin. They're human beings."

He snorted, a nasty sound to my ears. "Not to me. Justice isn't fair when people can kill and walk free. Should I spend the rest of my life in prison for doing the right thing?"

Thinking of Jeff in prison tore me apart. As much as I knew he was wrong, my heart ached. This was not the Jeff I grew up with. The Jeff who wanted to become a cop to help people. "What you're doing is wrong. You have to stop."

Jeff turned to me with a grim expression. Hard. Resolute. Jeff the cop.

"Do you know what it's been like for me, knowing that slug was walking the streets, drinking and driving, a bomb ready to go off? What about the families he destroyed forever or the ones he would have if he hadn't been stopped? What about the young girl who was raped? Who speaks for her? What if Christy had been raped? As a father, how would you feel then? Don't say justice prevails. It doesn't."

"What about the orderly who put a choke hold on the old man in the nursing home to calm him down? He didn't mean for the patient to die. It was an accident. That orderly had a wife and kids. Now she's a widow and her kids are fatherless. Aren't they victims too?"

Jeff turned away, silent.

"The law isn't perfect," I said. "You always knew that. But you can't play God." I reached out, hoping my touch would ground him, but he shrugged away. "What if you're wrong and kill an innocent person?"

"I won't." Jeff lowered his voice. "These people need to pay for their crimes. Don't you see that, Brian?"

These people. My delicious dinner churned to acid in my stomach, and I swallowed hard to keep from tossing it all over the veranda. Jeff had lost all sense of reason. "I can't turn a blind eye while you go on killing people."

Jeff's eyes narrowed briefly. "You won't give me up. We're as close as two men can be, without blood."

"You need help. Let me help you."

"You want to help? There's a guy who beat his pregnant wife so badly she lost their baby, and she's brain damaged. You know how long he was in prison? A year. That's how you can help."

I stood speechless at what he implied.

After a long, steady look, Jeff pushed away from the railing and returned to the party room. He kissed Addy on the cheek and spoke to Eddie. Then he left.

I made an effort to enjoy my birthday celebration, but my heart was broken. Eddie and Cecile took us home. Addy asked what was wrong, but I wouldn't burden her with the weight of Jeff's crimes. The decision of what to do would be mine alone.

I paced the bedroom while Addy slept. I'd misjudged Jeff's and Addy's affair. Was I misjudging Jeff? No, he'd admitted his crimes, tried to enlist me to become a partner. I thought of the orderly, dead because Jeff judged an overreaction as murder and exacted his special brand of justice.

I weighed all sides, back and forth, agonized. When I'd made my decision, I left the house. Jeff peeked out the window when I got to my car. Our eyes connected for a brief, heart-shattering moment. I drove to the police station and sat in my car for an hour, hoping Jeff would call. When he didn't, I went inside.

* * * *

At dawn, I watched from my bedroom window as two cruisers parked outside Jeff's house. Two officers stayed by their cars; two men in suits strode to Jeff's front door. Jeff's precinct captain was one of them. They rang the bell. The house remained dark.

I jumped when the gunshot blast from inside Jeff's house echoed in the dim stillness. I believe my heart stopped at that moment, then stuttered back to life.

Addy dragged herself out of bed and shuffled to the window. She put her hand on my shoulder. "What's going on?"

I wiped the tears from my cheeks. "I just murdered my best friend."

A SHIFTING PLAN

ELIZABETH ZELVIN

I stared out the window, not really seeing the Blue Ridge Mountains of western North Carolina recede behind us, then sleepwalked through the change of planes in Charlotte for the flight to New York. My world had been shattered, and I had no idea how to put it together again. Michael was dead: my lover, my songwriter, the wind beneath the wings of Emerald Love, country artist. Without him, could I still be Emerald Love?

If not, that left me not quite nobody. I would still be Amy Greenstein, nice Jewish girl from Pumpkin Falls, New York and closet shapeshifter. No comfort there. I didn't know which I dreaded more, watching my mother fail to hide her relief that I was no longer in danger of marrying a *goy* or listening to her bemoan the fact that I didn't see more of my sister. In the woods outside of Boone, I had told Wendy I never wanted to see her again. I couldn't envision circumstances in which I'd ever change my mind.

Nighttime Manhattan made a lively, bright, well-populated Limbo. I took a taxi from the airport to a Marriott in the theater district, comfortable but not glamorous, where nobody would recognize Emerald Love. I left my luggage, two discreet suitcases without so much as a sticker to give me away, unopened on the bed and made my way to Times Square.

Cynics might deplore the sanitized theme park that Disney had made of Broadway, but I liked it. Costumed characters mingled with the tourists, Minnie Mouse and Winnie the Pooh posing for pictures with kids from Kansas and Montana. I climbed the broad bleachers that faced south toward 42nd Street and sat, high above the milling mass of people with a spectacular view of the colorful marquees and frenetic digital ads. To my amusement, I spotted a few shifters in the crowd. I saw a Puss in Boots, not as domesticated as it appeared at first glance, smile secretly as it twirled for an amateur videographer with an iPad and an I Love New York T-shirt.

I don't know how long I sat there, letting the hubbub wash over me and enjoying the anonymity. It had been a long time since I'd faced a crowd that wasn't shouting, "Emerald! Emerald!" In one corner of my brain, I knew I had big decisions to make about my career. And in my gut—or as country music would put it, my heart—the wrenching pain of Michael's loss still lurked. But for the moment, I floated free of it.

Eventually, my stomach growled. I couldn't remember eating since the Seder at my parents' table days ago, before the shattering phone call from Boone. I knew I should start taking care of myself again, if only at the most basic level. I considered taking myself out to a real meal. Like all the great cats among shifters, I relish a good steak once in a while. But tonight it felt like too much effort. I decided to pick up a slice of pizza, bring it back to the hotel, and make an early night of it. Tomorrow would be soon enough to figure out what to do next: hire a new lead guitar or cancel the tour, even take a year off. I'd never been to Africa. Maybe I should go, run with the cheetahs before they landed on the endangered species list. They were currently designated "vulnerable." Well, so was I.

I'd seen an old-fashioned New York pizza place on a side street, the kind with guys in white tossing dough around like Frisbees in the window. Maybe I'd buy two slices. Maybe I'd buy a whole pie and eat myself into oblivion back in the room. If I wasn't going to be Emerald any more, it wouldn't matter if I gained some weight. But my plan got derailed when I heard a familiar song curling out from a dark doorway: "Killing Me by Moonlight." Michael had written it for me, and it had hit Number One on the charts. A couple of other artists had covered it, but I'd never heard anybody else sing it live.

The neon sign above the stained and pitted wooden door said, "WERE IN THE CITY." I didn't think the absence of an apostrophe between WE and RE or an H after the W was a fluorescent typo. A dark glamour hung about the place. Opaque black plate glass covered the windows. I doubted many people who weren't looking for it could see it at all. But the song, as familiar to me as my own breath, drew me in.

A short hallway, illuminated only by reddish light spilling from an arched doorway ahead, ended in the bulk of a bouncer who looked as if he might be a gorilla in his spare time. He frowned at me under a shelf of brow like a ledge on a mountain ridge. I showed him a hint of whisker and a flick of tail. He grunted, stepped aside, and let me pass.

On the left stretched a long, busy bar glittering with dangling glasses and mirrored wall panels in flickering candlelight. As I'd hoped, it was a mixed-species shifter bar. I heaved a sigh of relief. Only wolves, like Michael, are actually called weres. I didn't think I could have handled seeing them in pack, even in this unfamiliar setting. The song and the ache of loss were reminder enough. The drinkers ran the gamut from human to animal form: a snow leopard, a couple of Afghan hounds, a stag whose antlers brushed the smoke-saturated beams of the ceiling. A trio of catwomen enjoying a rowdy girls' night out had kept themselves at half-shift the better to dress to the nines. They looked terribly young and innocent to me.

The singer stood in a pool of light on the tiny stage, fingers dancing up and down the neck of her guitar. Her only backup was an upright bass plunking away in the shadows. She was good; she was making the most of Michael's riffs, which she must have picked up from our album. She wore a flowing green tunic and black pants tucked into silver boots. Her silvery hair and the wildness in her eyes told me she was wolf. They have more of a thing about moonlight than the rest of us. As I eased my way onto a stool at the bar, the song flowed from instrumental break to final chorus. She could sing, too. She was smart enough not to try to imitate my phrasing, and she gave it more howl in the high notes and more growl in the low notes. Cheetahs cough, and coughing does not enhance performance. As I signaled the bartender—they had Blue Moon on tap, and it suited my mood—she wound it up and bowed with a grin at the audience.

"Viva Bellini," the bass player announced. "Let's give her a hand, folks."

The set was over.

I sipped my Blue Moon as I watched her work the crowd, a mix of human fans and shifters. She laughed and chatted with human and shifter alike, patting a cheek or shoulder here, stroking a tail there. I wondered if she ever gigged in mainstream venues or confined herself to supernatural audiences. The supe circuit hadn't been an option for me. No way could I have stuck to gigs I couldn't tell my mother about. Having to knock on doors in Nashville like an ordinary girl had worked out well for me. I'd had a lot of fun the past couple of years. But Michael had had a lot to do with that.

For someone doing covers in a supe bar, Bellini had Nashville potential. She was that good, especially on guitar.

"Refill?"

I handed the bartender my glass and dug in my purse for a twenty. When I turned back to the room, Bellini had disappeared, presumably to the restroom. Without touching my fresh drink, I slipped off my stool and headed in the same direction.

I had the Ladies to myself, so maybe she'd gone outside to smoke. I never touched the stuff, but hey, it was her vocal cords. Down the hall from the restrooms was a door that must lead to one of those Manhattan backyards or alleys that a lot of people don't even know exist. Secret gardens are one of New York City's endless surprises. I decided to take a look. If daffodils were growing this close to Times Square, I wanted to see them.

No daffodils. The cramped alley was filled to bursting with a silver wolf snarling over the body of a man with bloody gashes in his neck and chest. I froze. The wolf shook itself and rippled into Viva Bellini, belligerence and horror chasing each other across her face.

I spoke from the shadows.

"You've got a problem."

Hearing a woman's voice, she raised her hands in a conciliatory gesture. She had no violent intent toward me.

"Predator or prey?" she asked.

In reply, I dropped into cheetah form. She went wolf so we could do a bit of ritual circling and sniffing, then both of us shifted back so we could talk.

"What did he do?" I asked. My feminist mother had taught me, "Always give a woman the benefit of the doubt."

"Jumped me when I came out to get a breath of air," she said.

"His mistake," I said.

You can't rape a shifter. Ever.

"'You know you want it' were his last words."

"Did you know him?" I asked.

"He was a fan," she said. "He's been stalking me the past couple of weeks. I meant to put a scare in him the first time he tried it in a place that wasn't too public. But he was too quick for me. He left me no choice."

"Yeah, that can happen." I really did understand. If she could have bit him in the leg in human form, it might not have ended so badly. But once the animal instincts take over, it's hard to control them.

"I don't know what to do," she said.

To help or not to help? It wasn't my problem. On the other hand, I had no plans for the evening, maybe not even for the rest of my life.

"Did anybody see you with him tonight?"

"He couldn't get into the bar," she said. "Most civilians can't find it."

Everyone knows that we exist, but we can still keep a few secrets if we want to.

"He found the alley, though," she said. "He was waiting for me."

"Good thing he didn't have a knife," I said.

"That wouldn't have fit his image of himself." Her lip twisted. "A lover, not a fighter. The whole thing makes me sick."

"You can't afford to let his body be found this way."

"What am I supposed to do?" She ran her hands through her silver hair. "I mean it, I'm stumped. So if you have an idea, I'm listening. I'm Viva Bellini, by the way."

"Amy, uh, Green," I said. "I know, I heard you in there. You're really good. Are you supposed to do another set?"

"No. A piano player comes on at midnight. I sometimes do another two or three numbers before then, but they don't pay me extra, so if I don't, they won't miss me. You mean you'll help? Really? I can't thank you enough!"

"A corpse with tooth and claw marks half a block from Times Square would be bad news for all of us. Too bad this didn't happen in Michigan or Minnesota."

"Or Wisconsin or Wyoming," she said. "Believe me, I know every state where they're already making war on wolves. I'd hate to give the bad guys ammunition, but it would be better than a freak show on the front page of the *New York Post*."

"Let's leave that part of it aside for now," I said. "First, let's cut this guy down to size." I could hear how cold that sounded, but honestly, I felt more sympathy for Viva's predicament than for her victim's ill-judged rape attempt.

First, we dragged a heavy garbage bin across the door I'd come out and another to block the gate at the other end that he had used, so we wouldn't be interrupted. Then, we dropped into wolf and cheetah form. We made quick work of him. The remains filled a couple of giant plastic garbage bags we found in the bins. We used bags that had held recy-clables, so it wasn't even as messy a job as it might have been. I had hand sanitizer in my purse. When you cross the country in a tour bus, you have to be prepared. We found a cold water spigot that we used the same way a janitor would have to hose down the concrete underfoot. In the end, nothing was left but two big bags and two slightly disheveled women.

"Now what?" She looked at me as if I had all the answers.

I didn't yet, but I was working on it.

"We need wheels," I said. "We don't look skanky enough to be drag-ging bags of garbage down the street. And it would be better to look like solid citizens in case we run into anyone with authority. Suitcases, maybe?"

"Wrong shape," Viva said. "How about a couple of giant wheelie duffel bags? There are dozens of stores in this neighborhood that sell cheap luggage."

"Fine. You go, I'll stay."

When I'd assured her I'd be there when she got back and helped her unblock and slip through the gate, the adrenaline was still pumping. I sat down on the edge of an overturned metal garbage can, took some deep, slow breaths to put myself in a meditative state, and emptied my mind. Within a couple of minutes, the plan blossomed in my head. All we had to do was get the duffels back to my hotel room. I could charter a bus to pick us up in the morning or simply rent a van. We'd chuck the duffels in the luggage compartment and hit the road.

Viva would realize that she had better leave the city for a while. I could offer her not just a way out of town, but a job. A good job. She could finish the tour with us. Her git-tar pickin', as my band called it, was good enough. If she wasn't too proud to sing backup, even better. And those garbage bags could go in the bus's luggage compartment. We were bound to hit a truck stop someplace where they were already mad at wolves.

I'd gone over the whole plan twice before I realized that it depended on my going on being Emerald Love. It seemed I still wanted to sing, and the prospect of making music with another wolf felt a lot less painful than I'd thought it would. Now all I had to do was get Viva to say yes.

EASY PREY

TRACY L. WARD

The child had been missing since late afternoon, and by the time Charley made her way down to Black Creek Canyon it was nearly dark. An hour had passed before she received the call, and another had been lost as she gathered her gear and drove her ailing truck to the trailhead. There would be no time to wait for the other volunteers.

Charley could barely look at the child's mother seated on a boulder next to the trailhead, her cries nearly drowning out the words from another volunteer who had arrived earlier.

"Where was she last seen?" Charley asked, pulling her pack from the passenger seat of her truck.

"She was with them when they stopped for lunch near the stream," the volunteer explained. "I'm Mack," he said, thrusting his hand at her.

Shaking it quickly, Charley wondered where she had seen him before. The man wore a severely frayed baseball cap, the bill curled deeply toward his temples, the color faded where the sunlight hit it. His face was scruffy, not unlike every other outdoorsman she had met, walking out the door before taking the time to shave.

Charley viewed life similarly. Why waste time on frills and scents?

"Charley," she said, introducing herself.

Mack smiled as he looked her over.

Annoyed, Charley quickly turned their attention back to the issue at hand. "Show me on the map," Charley said, pulling the topographical chart from the front pouch of her pack. She splayed it out on the ground before the wooden bridge that traversed the first of a number of ravines. Heavily treed and littered with boulders and rocky outcrops, the trailhead was merely a starting point for a number of trails that branched off in every direction. The creek where the girl was last seen could have been on any trail along the route. If Charley had any hope of finding the girl, she'd have to start there.

Mack knelt beside her in the gravel, surveying the map. "She said they were at Crayfish Creek, which comes into Potter's Lake." He tapped the map with his index finger. "It's a doozy to get down there."

Charley gave a bemused smile. Also like the other outdoorsmen she'd met, he was concerned for her safety. How typical.

"We should go together," he said.

Giving one last look over the map, Charley began to fold it, sectioning off the area where they were headed and folding the other areas behind it to make a nice, neat square. "All right," she said, glancing over the parking lot, surprised to see only two vehicles had arrived to assist in the search. "The others can radio to us when they get here. Let's go."

Before heading down the trail, she gave one last glance at the woman on the boulder, now sniffling into her sleeve and avoiding Charley's gaze.

She had enough gear for one, maybe two overnights, should she get caught out. Since her father's death in the woods four years before it became her habit of keeping one fully equipped pack by the back door of her house, and another box of supplies in the bed of her truck. No way would she be caught off guard like that again.

With the day wearing on and the sky getting dark, she had little doubt she would be spending the night in the woods. It mattered little. It wasn't her first missing persons search at nighttime.

"So is Charley short for something?" Mack asked when they paused to sip water from their canteens. They had been walking for nearly an hour, keeping a watchful eye on the darkening foliage around them and another on the craggy rocks and tree roots jutting out on the trail in front.

"Charlotte," she said, "but only my dad called me that."

He nodded and then his eyes grew wide. "I've heard of you," he said. "You found that dead hiker last month."

Charley felt her throat tighten at the mention of it. "Yeah," she said with little inflection. With her metal canteen placed back in her pack she turned and pushed further into the wilderness.

"Man, what a sight that must have been," Mack said as he followed.

Charley nodded, and hoped the conversation would end there. There had been no missing person's report, and no team of volunteers assembled that day. Charley had been out on her regular weekly hike grooming her father's trail, a task she had taken over since he passed, when she came across the body, splayed over a gigantic boulder beside the trail as if he had fallen from the cliff above.

It seemed the simplest explanation at the time—a hiker looking for a challenge decides to scale the craggy rocks and perhaps see the view from up top—but when the state troopers arrived, they said it wasn't the fall that had killed him.

"I read in the papers his hand was missing," Mack said. "That true?"

Charley hesitated at a grouping of rocks that would force them to traverse slowly.

"I understand," Mack said. "Must be difficult to talk about."

"Yes," she said, beginning her descent over the rocks. "Second worst day of my life."

She could hear the shuffle of rocks behind her as Mack followed. He wasn't proving to be the most graceful.

"What was the worst?" he asked as they neared the bottom of the rocky section.

Charley dusted her hands off on her khaki shorts and looked further down the trail. She couldn't bring herself to say the words, *the day I didn't find my father in time.*

* * * *

The trail led them down into a gully and then up into the mountain again. Every thirty feet or so a new trail branched off from the main one, and each time Mack knew the way without having to refer to the map.

The silence of their trek was interrupted by Charley's cell phone. Charley stopped and began pulling at her pack. It dawned on her that she hadn't heard from any other search parties or volunteers since the initial phone call. Perhaps it was Andrew calling to tell her what frequency they were on.

"Andrew?"

"Charley, where are you?" Andrew's voice was faint.

Charley covered her other ear in the hopes she could hear him better. "I'm—" The phone went silent. "The call was dropped." Charley looked to Mack who stood slightly above her on the trail.

"Maybe we're too far out."

The phone's bars indicated zero reception. She tossed the phone back in her bag. "How much farther then?" she asked, cognizant that their thin strip of sun was quickly disappearing behind the canopy in the west.

With his hands on his hips, Mack surveyed their position, finally pointing ahead of them with reassurance. "There's a bend and then the trail should lead down into a small valley." He slipped ahead of her, blazing the trail.

A few moments later Charley pulled her head lamp from her pack. Mack did the same. Once the light from the sun faded, their trek became slow and calculated. Neither could risk a twisted ankle or worse while in such terrain.

"What was the girl wearing again?" Charley asked.

"A pink t-shirt with a rainbow on it," he said, slightly out of breath. "Purple shorts."

Charley stepped forward and he came into the aura of her headlamp. "Running shoes?" she asked, remembering seeing a child once on a trail such as this wearing flip flops. The stupidity of parents never ceased to amaze her.

Thankfully, Mack nodded. "They had their lunch over here."

Mack disappeared into the darkness but Charley hesitated. The wood was dead, devoid of the birds or rodents she would have normally expected to hear running rampant through the ferns and underbrush. There was something about this area of the forest that kept them away.

Then she heard the faint sound of water rushing over rocks and she knew their real work began at the water's edge. She forged ahead, mentally preparing herself for a long, cold night of searching.

She found Mack standing at a creek that ran over the dirt path before spilling down into a larger body of water. It seemed an unlikely spot for a family to stop for a picnic. The mosquitos overwhelmed them quickly and the branches hung so low beneath the trees Charley doubted the spot offered much by way of view, even in the daylight.

"Are you sure this is where they stopped?" she asked, surveying the needle-littered ground.

"This is where she said," Mack said.

None of the orange needles, discarded from the conifer canopy above them, appeared disturbed. Charley stopped at the creek and followed the water's edge a bit further into the trees, looking for a footprint of any kind.

She saw nothing.

Something wasn't right. A family out for an autumn hike, with a five-year-old no less, would have stopped for a considerable length of time. Evidence would have been abundant even in the light of their lamps. And now that she thought about it, why hadn't they happened across other rescuers?

"Let's look further upstream," Mack suggested.

Charley did not give a reply. Instead she stood looking over the water from the opposite side. It hadn't been Andrew who called her first. It was someone she hadn't met before, a woman. There were two vehicles in the parking lot—her own beat up pickup and an SUV that she had assumed belonged to Mack. So how had the mother driven there, and why was no one else with her? From the moment she hung up the phone she'd put her game face on, determined to find the girl, never stopping to ask pointed questions, believing it would only slow her down.

"Charlotte?"

"Don't call me that!" she snapped. "It's Charley." Her anger was exaggerated by her predicament. She turned in place, taking in the trees and darkness while running the scenario in her head. With each second that passed her predicament became more evident.

There was no missing child. There never had been. The entire charade was a ruse to get her out in the woods.

"Is something wrong?" Mack's voice cracked in the aura of his headlamp.

Charley's hand shook as she reached up to her headlamp. Flipping the switch, she turned and bolted back into the darkness.

* * * *

"Charlotte!"

Charley could hear the panic-stricken voice of her search and rescue partner growing more and more distant as she ran back over the path they had originally come through. Guided by memory and the muted aura of the half moon, Charley was able to run, avoiding larger rocks and overhanging limbs as she climbed, but on the descent she was forced to slow down.

She veered from the trail and pushed higher and higher into the brush, second guessing herself with each step. What if she was wrong? It was that damned body she found making her question everyone's motives. She couldn't make sense of a world where such things could happen. If she had thought her father's death in the woods shook her, seeing that body splayed out in such a manner rattled her to the core.

A laugh behind her pierced the dark, silent woods. Charley whirled around and scanned the trees. It wasn't Mack, she knew that for sure.

"I can't wait to get out of here," a muffled female voice said from the darkness.

Charley couldn't make out any forms so she stood, listening and waiting. A light appeared between the trees further down the slope. Charley was able to make out two people with flashlights.

"Where did Mack say he'd bring her?" the girl asked.

"Where the water runs over the path," the other hissed. "Now quiet, we're almost there."

Charley watched intently as they walked thirty feet in front of her, unaware that she stood in the shadows.

Another light came toward them from ahead and Charley could tell it was Mack's headlamp. Charley crouched down, afraid their lights would catch her.

"She took off," he said, out of breath.

"What?" the girl asked.

"Where'd she go?" the other voice asked more gruffly.

"She must have known something was up. She ran back this way," Mack said. "You didn't see her?"

Charley could just make out their shadowy forms as the one man, the leader of the trio, delivered a quick jab to Mack's face. When Mack stumbled, the man, who was a good foot or so taller, grabbed him by the collar. His flashlight illuminated the blood and fear on Mack's face. "When we find her, you'd better pray you don't end up in the same god-damned grave!"

Suddenly, Charley remembered where she had seen Mack before. She held a vague memory of three people on the trail the same day she had found the body. Originally lost in the horror of her discovery and the police interviews that followed, Charley was sure of it now. Mack was one of the three that passed her that day, returning to the trailhead just as she had been setting off. She had seen their faces. Now it seemed they were tying up loose ends.

"She couldn't have gone far," the girl said. "Not in the dark."

Charley watched as they surveyed the brush for any sign of where she may have gone. It was only a matter of time before they discovered where she left the path. As Charley stood, she decided she wasn't going to die. Not that day and not at the hands of those people. She turned and methodically made her way up into the thicker brush and away from the flashlights that scanned the edges of the trail. This time she did not run. Any sound would draw attention. Any quick movement, even in the dim light, would bring them right to her.

They'd see her footprints soon enough and she didn't have a lot of time. As she walked she reviewed every detail of Mack's face in her mind, every loose thread on his ball cap, every unshaved whisker on his face. She was going to walk her ass out of there and scream to high heaven at the first sign of human life.

After an hour of walking she slid into the crook of a cypress tree and pulled out the map from her pack. Shielding the light with a cupped hand Charley directed her headlamp at the chart cradled on her lap. She knew vaguely where she was, but in the dark no visible markers existed for her to back up her suspicion. The compass offered little help. There was a fire tower about two miles west and although not depicted on the map, she hoped there would be a road or path used by the rangers who visited it.

The safety of the tree highlighted her overwhelming fatigue. She could feel her eyelids become heavy. Only a moment, she told herself, she could rest her eyes for a moment.

Sudden awareness snapped Charley awake. Lifting her head, she squinted at the morning sun as it shone on her face, warming her skin. Panic took hold as she remembered where she was and why. She had been hidden from view thanks to the darkness of night, but now she was vulnerable and, worse, she had no clue where her predators were.

Charley resisted the urge to spring from her hiding spot, knowing careful calculation would be her best bet. Slowly she unfolded her legs from beneath her. A shuffle from her left made her freeze mid-motion. A bush rising up between some logs and deadfall marred her view. Save for the birds' morning calls, the forest went silent once more. Gingerly, Charley went to her hands and knees. She crept forward, squinting to see beyond the leaves of the bush. There was another movement, a shadow stepping forward though true outlines could not be deciphered.

Charley froze. Hearing and seeing nothing, Charley craned her neck, readying herself to run at the first sign of the men who were chasing her. Over the crest of a toppled log she saw the perky ears of the deer first, erect and alert to the sounds of the woods.

Almost laughing at the scare, Charley smiled. The doe was close enough to touch. "Good morning," she whispered from her crouched position behind the bush. The animal stared, ready to dart at the first sign of aggression. *You're scared*, Charley thought. *You and me both.*

Charley reached for her pack, slowly so as not to scare the deer—

A gunshot went off.

Charley fell back into the hollow cypress, pulling her knees into her chest. The deer pivoted and bounded down the side of the hill, weaving a zigzag pattern between the trees as another shot echoed through the forest.

"What'd you do that for, Darren?" asked Mack's voice.

"I'm hungry," Darren answered. "Fuck, I need food. We've been searching for fucking hours."

From her hiding spot, Charley could hear him open the chamber of his pistol to reload.

"Maybe she fell off a cliff," Charley heard the girl suggest.

They made no attempt to hide their heavy steps or temper their voices as they moved toward her hiding spot.

Quickly, Charley surveyed the part of the forest she could see. The deer had gone right, down a steep bank riddled with trees with God knows what at the bottom. Straight ahead was too exposed. All the heavy branches of the trees were at least ten feet from the forest floor. Her only hope was left, where sumac and other bushes converged, making a good cover before the mountain rock could give her better cover.

A running shoe appeared on a fallen trunk to her right, making a base scraping sound on the bark. The sound resonated in her ear like the rapid beats of her heart.

Stay alive, she told herself, while giving a slow and methodical exhale. Stay the hell alive.

"I think I found a track," Mack said from about ten feet behind her.

Charley watched as the running shoe turned on the log. She counted the sound of five steps in the dirt before jumping up, grabbing her pack and bounding for the bushes. She didn't care about being quiet or unseen. She only cared about speed. She needed to get to the trees and around the rocks as quickly as her burning feet could take her.

"There she is!" the girl yelled.

The sound of the gun shot was masked by the rustling of leaves in the bushes and the snaps of branches under her feet. She didn't stop at the rocks. A sheer cliff prevented her from going up so she followed the rocks down, bounding from flat surface to flat surface, not knowing where it would lead. She prayed she wouldn't find herself trapped on a ledge, easy prey for anyone with a gun. She could see a trail below but as she scaled the rocks she saw it was a far drop.

She could hear their voices behind her closing in. Charley slid off the rock on her stomach holding on as long as she could to the top of the boulder. She hoped the ground was closer than it appeared. There was no time for second thoughts.

She skidded down the boulder and landed on the ground. Her knees buckled and she fell into the dirt. Charley scrambled to her feet and bounded down the trail.

"Get her, Mack, or I swear you'll be next!"

Another shot rang out and hit a rock just above her as she ran.

Charley had no clue where she was or where her trail would lead. She found herself scurrying across a large, fallen log over a small canyon with a man-made rope handhold. She ran down a slight hill before the rocky terrain turned to mixed forest and the trail widened. To the left, the forest grew up on a slope. To the right, she could hear the sound of a river with a fast current and wondered if it was Lightning Creek. If it was, she wasn't far from the tower after all, but there was no chance she was going to stop to consult the map.

A flash of orange caught her attention. There was a hunting party, perhaps three or four men, on the other side of the creek. "Hey!" Charley yelled. She began waving her hands in the air as she ran. "Hey! Help!" Charley saw them scaling the opposite bank, the rushing water drowning out her cries.

Movement in the bush ahead caught her eye. Mack was running full tilt down the slope. Charley changed course, running down toward the river but she wasn't fast enough.

"Hey! Help!"

Mack collided into her, wrapping his arms tightly around her body. Together they rolled over branches and small saplings.

Charley fought him the entire way down, desperately grabbing for his face, eyes, anything. She felt his hand clasp over her mouth. She had been screaming—no, growling— as she fought him but now all she heard was the rush of the water as they tumbled down the slope toward it.

They hit the shallow water and she kicked as hard as she could, using the rocky bottom to get away. His hand clasped her ankle briefly but she was able to shake him. She grabbed a rock from the river bottom and delivered a sharp blow to the side of his head. She tried to stand but he pulled her back under and she dropped the rock.

He was standing over her, holding her beneath the water's surface, smiling at his triumph.

She kicked at his legs and landed a perfect hit to his groin. Mack scrunched his face in pain, keeling over slightly and loosening his grip. Charley surfaced and pushed herself back, scrambling over the rocks.

Charley wanted the strong current to whisk her down the river, despite the rocks and other unknowns that lurked beneath the surface. It was her only chance.

Mack pulled a large rock from the river and held it over his head as he stepped toward her. Charley climbed over a boulder to deeper water and was about release her grasp when a hand from behind her reached under her arm and pulled her from the water.

She saw the barrel of the shot gun first, pointed toward Mack, and then registered the hunter behind her, dressed in full camouflage, save for a bright orange ball cap. Along the riverbank she could see a few more similarly dressed men, all with their weapons ready.

"I don't think she's with you," the hunter closest to her said.

Mack raised his hands in surrender just as the girl and Darren appeared on the opposite side. Darren hesitated between pointing his gun toward them and hiding it behind his back. An older hunter on the opposite bank pumped his shotgun and took aim.

"Think carefully, son," he said, with marked assuredness.

An overwhelming feeling of fatigue rushed over Charley. A tremor developed in her hands and legs and she found it hard to stand amongst the rushing current. She rested her hands on her knees and tried to steady her breathing.

"Why'd you have to run, Charlotte?" Mack asked incredulously. He eyed her from the other end of the shotgun. He seemed more disappointed for losing out on the opportunity of killing her than he did about being caught.

Charley stood tall and returned Mack's gaze with a marked defiance. "Don't call me Charlotte."

THE BONES IN THE BOX

MELISSA ROBBINS

The skeleton wearing a Nazi uniform and stuffed into Nanny Vic's cedar chest solved one mystery. Until two weeks ago, I, Charlotte Graham, had no idea my grandmother owned an ancestral home across the pond. I assumed she had kept it for sentimental reasons. Nope.

"Charlie!" shouted Tom from the other side of my grandmother's bedroom. Fudge! I released the support of the cedar chest's heavy lid and it slammed against the base. I sat on the chest as if to prevent the skeleton from rising from its makeshift coffin.

"Come see these paintings," Tom said in his irresistible English accent.

I rose, peeking over my shoulder to make certain nothing looked out of place, and walked to the Oriental screen that shielded the brass bed and chest from the other parts of the large bedroom. The khaki material of Tom Montgomery's trousers stretched across his cute bum as he squatted in front of a pile of paintings leaning haphazardly against the fireplace. When I showed up at the town's historical society looking for help to sort through my grandmother's belongings, I expected to find a gray-haired marm or stodgy old man, not a good-looking history student.

Tom held up a painting of a dark-haired woman in a skimpy bikini. "Did you know your grandmother was a 40s pin-up girl? You look just like her."

Heat crept up my neck. "A pin-up girl? What does my grandmother as a pin-up have to do with your doctoral thesis?"

"Everything." Tom gently set down the painting. "This house is shrouded in mystery and a legend among the islanders here in town. No one has entered these halls since your grandparents fled Nazi occupation in 1945. It's a real-life time capsule." He raked his hand through his dust-covered, dark-blond curls. "I'm chuffed Mrs. Edwards at the historical society suggested I help sort everything out. When you allowed me access, I had no idea what brilliant finds we would uncover."

That made two of us. Now I knew why Nanny Vic had fled. She murdered a Nazi. *Don't look at the chest, girl. You'll draw attention to it.*

To divert Tom's attention, I moved over to my grandmother's vanity littered with perfume bottles and other beauty items. My fingers ran over a silver brush that resembled the one she used on my hair with when I was a child. You think you know someone. "Nazi occupation? I thought the Germans never crossed the English Channel." And certainly didn't end up in Nanny Vic's cedar chest.

Tom picked up another painting and squinted at the blue and green brush strokes. "Ah, but the Nazis did. Churchill felt the Channel Islands weren't strategic, so he let the Germans take over. They controlled all the islands for most of the war."

He lowered the painting. "I don't want to get your hopes up, love, but you may be a millionaire. We'll have to do some more research, but I think this painting is a Renoir. My ex was an art major. I'll have her look it over and see if you have the real deal."

Is that why my grandmother killed the Nazi? He was trying to steal her priceless painting?

"Wow, a Renoir? Really? That's amazing." I had to get him out of the house until I figured out how to remove the skeleton. Nanny Vic wouldn't want the town knowing she was a murderer, even if he was a Nazi. I pressed my fingers against my stomach. "You know, I'm famished. Could you go buy us some lunch?"

Tom set down the painting and smeared his hands against his blue buttoned-down shirt. "Already? Have we been here that long?" He glanced at his wristwatch.

My heart pounded against my ribcage. "I didn't eat much breakfast."

Tom pointed to the bedroom door with his thumb. "I'll get some take-away and bring it back."

I tiptoed backward until Tom closed the front door downstairs. Rushing to the chest, I yanked open the lid. Still there.

A dagger with an unmistakable swastika on the pommel pierced the skeleton's chest. *Why kill a Nazi over a painting, Nanny?*

A hand touched my shoulder and I screamed, jerking away. Tom stared at the opened chest. "I forgot my jacket." The corners of his mouth stretched up, forming wrinkles around his blue eyes. "I wondered why you weren't more excited over the painting. You found a dead Nazi. That's ruddy brilliant."

"No, it's not." I grabbed his shoulders and jerked him around to face me. "We can't tell anyone. People can't know my grandmother murdered a man."

"But she's dead." Tom thrust his arm out toward the chest. "And he's a Nazi. The town would probably give her a medal."

"Then why did she hide the body for all these years? We have to find out what happened first."

He knelt in front of the box. "I'm a history student, not a detective."

I leaned forward and pressed my hands against my knees. "Then use your history powers for good and figure something out."

Tom gestured toward the dagger. "Noting his uniform and knife, he was a major in the Luftwaffe. If your grandmother killed a Nazi pilot, the ramifications would have been catastrophic."

"Probably why she didn't tell anyone. Did you also notice his buttons are fastened incorrectly?" My fingertips brushed the coarse texture of the coat's fabric. Realizing I just touched a dead body, I jerked my hand back and smeared it against my jeans.

"He isn't wearing his boots, nor his socks. Your grandmother must have surprised him." Tom scrunched up his nose. "He has six toes on his left foot. How odd."

I pressed my hands to my chest, for it surely felt as if my heart had stopped. "Polydactyly."

"Poly what?" When I didn't answer, a wrinkle formed between Tom's brows. "Charlie, what's wrong?"

"Polydactyly is when you have more than five fingers or toes." Four heartbeats later, or in my case ten, I added, "It can be passed down to your children and grandchildren."

Tom stared at my leather boots. "Do you have six toes too? Is this Nazi your biological grandfather? But you said your grandfather died in Canada just a few years ago."

"He did." I shuffled my feet and pulled the edge of my red shirt-sleeve down over my palm. "I don't have six toes, but I had an extra useless finger. Simple surgery when I was a baby removed it. Mom had one too. Always wondered how she got it."

Tom rocked back on his heels. "Your grandmother was a Jerry-bag."

I punched his shoulder. "I don't know what that is, but it sounds terrible."

He sat down on the Oriental rug, draping his arms over his bended knees. "It was a derogatory term used by the locals for English women who slept with the Germans." He leaned his head against the chest. "If they found out Nanny Vic slept with a Nazi, the locals would have shunned her—if she was lucky. In Europe, women who *horizontally* collaborated with the Germans were stripped of their clothes, had their heads shaved, and were humiliated in public."

Thinking of my grandmother suffering that fate, I squeezed the cold brass of the bedframe until my knuckles turned white. "Nanny Vic loved my grandfather. She didn't sleep with a Nazi by choice." I released the frame taking two steps back. "By choice. Nanny Vic didn't murder a Nazi because he was stealing her painting. He raped her." I punched the air with my fist. "And she stabbed him in self-defense with his own knife. That's why his uniform isn't buttoned properly and his boots and socks are off. He was hastily getting dressed after having his way with my grandmother."

A veil of dust rose as I sunk into the worn mattress of the bed. "Explains why my grandparents refused to talk about the war."

"Was your mum born here?"

"No. What little my grandparents told me was that they left Guernsey for France in March '45, staying there until they arranged passage to Canada. Mom was born in Nova Scotia."

"Nine months from the time they left the island?"

"Mom was born in November."

"So figuring that your grandmother killed the Nazi in March, this encounter wasn't the first time he raped her. If she got pregnant by him, she wouldn't have been able to keep it a secret for very long."

"But Nanny Vic was married. The baby could have been Gramps' as far as she knew in March."

Tom tapped his thumb against his chin. "There is one issue that is troubling me. Dead men are heavy and your grandmother would have had a hard time lifting his corpse into the chest by herself. Your grandfather may have helped her."

"So either one could have killed the man." I stared at the tarnished silver wreath and eagle pin fastened to the Nazi's uniform. "Did German pilots have identification tags like Brits and American soldiers?"

Tom pressed his fist against his forehead. "Of course. Why didn't I think of that?"

"So we can figure who he is right away?"

"Not exactly." Pulling a white handkerchief from his back pocket, Tom covered his hand and fingers with the handkerchief and searched the area around the skeleton's neck.

"Unlike the British and American armed forces, the Germans didn't add names or personal information to the identification discs." He pulled out a metal oval from under the skeleton's shirt. Cradling the rusty metal in his handkerchief, his thumb rubbed the tag with the fabric. I hoped it was rust and not something else. "There's a number and what squadron he was in, but no name." Tom unfastened the leather strap that kept the disc around the soldier's neck and slipped off the oval. "Normally, one part stays with the body. The other half was for notification, but I know a bloke, Mr. Colin Celandine, who might be able to help narrow down the search. He's an old codger, but a clever one. If I separate this disc, he'll notice."

I jumped off the bed. "If he's clever, we shouldn't involve him. Can't you find out who he is yourself?"

He stood up and wrapped his handkerchief around the identification disc. "Colin is probably the one only on the island with the information. His sister could help too. She was your grandparents' housekeeper." Tom stared at the wad of fabric in his hand. "Servants always knew family secrets. She might be able to shed light on this particular one."

I closed the lid of the chest. "We can't tell them anything about this body."

"They may already know, and there's only one way to find out."

* * * *

"Thank you for your hospitality, Mrs. Webster." I sat in a worn blue chair next to a crate labeled 'parachutes.'

Mrs. Webster handed me a cup of tea. "I'm not sure where he is, but my brother is probably off collecting more German rubbish." She waved her hands around the parlor littered with every possible WW2 memorabilia available. "As if we needed more."

I blew across my teacup, disrupting the steam. "Why does he collect so much war stuff?"

Mrs. Webster smoothed down her apron with her hands. "Colin says he does it to remind him of the past. Good and evil."

What was Colin trying to remember about the past?

Tom slid down the sofa, placing a stack of ledgers on his lap that were in his way. "I keep telling him he needs to open a museum so he can share his collection with the world. We don't mind waiting for Mr. Celandine." His eyes quickly darted to me. "You were telling us about your time as the Buckleys' housekeeper."

"Oh. Yes. Lovely woman, your grandmother. Ever so kind to me."

No mention of my grandfather. Perhaps he didn't deal with the housekeeper.

The teacup trembled as I brought it to my lips. "And did you take care of the house during the war?"

"Oh no, duck. I left with the evacuated children as a chaperone in 1940 and didn't come back to my island until after the war. The Buckleys had left and Colin locked up the house tight until their return."

Mr. Celandine had access to the house. He might know of the skeleton.

There was a yell from the kitchen. "Mary, look what a bloke sold to me!" Several metallic bangs followed and glass broke. A man entered in the living room carrying a large chunk of metal with a swastika painted on it.

"Watch the cupboard, Colin." Mrs. Webster pursed her lips and gestured with her hand. "Tom and Miss Graham are here."

With the metal tucked under his chin, Mr. Celandine poked his finger through a hole in it. "Tom will appreciate this. Look at the bullet holes one of our lads put into this tail. A chap found it in his dad's attic. He thought it was a bad omen and wanted to get rid of it."

When Mr. Celandine looked up and focused on me, he leaned the tailpiece against a stack of boxes. "It's remarkable how much you look like Victoria Buckley, Miss Graham. It's as if the rest of us aged, but she never grew old." He removed his newsboy cap, placing it over his heart. "I'm sorry to hear of her passing." The sadness from his eyes vanished. His jaw clenched and his fist squashed his cap. "Is your grandfather still alive? Has he returned to the island?"

I placed my empty teacup on the coffee table. "No, he died a few years before Nanny Vic."

Mr. Celandine exhaled loudly and slapped his cap down on a box labeled 'uniforms.' "I hope he roasts in hell."

"Colin!" Mrs. Webster plunked down her teacup next to mine. "Everyone knew you fancied her, but she was married and it's all in the past."

Mr. Celandine pointed at me. "Are you afraid Miss Graham might learn something she probably already knows? If she spent any time with the bastard, nothing we say will shock her."

My eyes darted between him and his sister. Why would Mr. Celandine say such horrible things about Gramps?

He grasped fistfuls of his white hair and croaked out, "The bastard hit Victoria. You saw the bruises and did nothing. No amount of make-up can hide away those black eyes."

Mrs. Webster tugged at her apron hem. "Family matters of that nature were not discussed."

I rose from my chair. "I need some fresh air. Please excuse me for a minute." I weaved around the boxes of artifacts and rushed out of the cottage.

Once outside, I inhaled deeply. The salty sea air calmed my nerves a little.

"Charlie," Tom whispered, coming to stand beside me.

He dug into the earth with his loafer and brushed the curls away from his face. "I'm sorry I brought you here. We can notify the police of the body and you won't have to worry about it anymore."

I pressed my hand to my chest. "Yes, I have to worry. My grandparents are still involved, but I don't understand it. I was close to Gramps far back as I can remember. He never hit Nanny Vic, Mom, or me. The man Mr. Celandine hates is not my grandfather."

Tom gently squeezed my shoulder. "Perhaps the brutality of war softened him. It changes men." He pulled the handkerchief wad out of his pocket. "Knowing Colin like I do, if we get him talking about Nazis, he'll forget all about your grandparents."

After inhaling another refreshing breath of salty air, I followed Tom back into the cottage.

Mr. Celandine looked up from polishing his newly acquired plane tailpiece with his coveralls sleeve. Mrs. Webster had disappeared with the tea service. "Miss Graham, forgive me for my rudeness. I always felt quite protective of your grandmother."

Protective of my grandmother? Could Colin have killed the Nazi while visiting his sister one day and overheard the rape? He had access to the house.

Tom flashed me a sweet smile before holding up the wadded handkerchief. "Colin, I found a German identification disc on the Buckley grounds. We were hoping you could figure out who it belonged to and if the chap survived the war."

Mr. Celandine hurried to Tom's side as he gingerly revealed the oval disc.

After adjusting his glasses, Mr. Celandine took the handkerchief and tag from Tom as if Tom had passed him a baby. "Remarkable condition."

Tom pointed to the number etched at the top of the disc. "Don't you have loads of the records the Germans left behind?"

"I do. No one else on the island wants them." Mr. Celandine hurried over to a desk covered with papers, files, and more books. He gently rested the handkerchief on a book and started flipping through a ledger. "That squadron flew numerous circus operations to attack English aerodromes, and later, London." Mr. Celandine stopped at a page and ran his finger down it. "Generalmajor Rottenhaus kept marvelous records of his pilots. Here we are!" His mouth gaped opened and he glanced at the disc and then back at the ledger. "Ruddy hell, you found him."

"Who?" asked Tom and I together.

Mr. Celandine rotated the book so we could read the entry. "Major Gunter Falke, one of Germany's finest aces. He vanished near the end of the war. No one knew what happened to him."

I stared into Tom's blue eyes. Tom and I knew. Stabbed to death by Nanny Vic or Gramps.

Mr. Celandine adjusted his glasses and licked his lips. "You said you found the identification disc on the Buckley grounds? He could be buried there."

I tugged on one of my curls. "It was just lying on the ground, right, Tom?"

Tom furiously nodded. "It could have been dropped by a clerk who wasn't given a chance to report his death."

My hand rested on Mr. Celandine's arm. We had to get him off the topic of a dead body before he dug up all of Nanny Vic's rosebushes. "What more can you tell us about Major Falke? Was he despised by the islanders for his cruelty?"

"Actually, no." Mr. Celandine headed to a stack of boxes and removed the first one setting it on the floor. "I found him to be quite the gentleman." He rummaged through another box. "For a Nazi, that is. Being a pilot, he didn't concern himself with the islanders and left that business to the army. Most of the women on the island found him quite dashing and handsome, though they would never admit it."

Tom's eyes bore into me. Just because my grandmother may have found the man attractive didn't mean she asked to be raped.

Mr. Celandine removed the second box from the stack and continued his search in the bottom box. "I always found his name perfect for his profession. Did you know 'falke' is German for 'falcon?' That's what some of the townspeople called him. The Falcon. Haven't you found information on him, Tom? He would be a great addition to your thesis."

Great. That's all I needed, another reason for Tom to reveal the dead Nazi.

Tom nodded as he pressed his thumb into his chin. "Sounds familiar."

The Falcon. I had heard that name somewhere too, but couldn't place it. Perhaps he came up in history class.

"At last!" Mr. Celandine held up a picture of a group of Nazi pilots and carried it over to the desk. "That's him right there. Third from the left."

Goosebumps erupted on my skin and the breath left my chest. I reached out to grab the desk, but missed and smacked my knee on its leg. Tom put one arm around my shoulders and grasped my hand. "Charlie, love, are you all right?"

All right? The dashing blond Nazi pilot staring back at me from the photograph was not the dead man in Nanny Vic's chest. He was the man who helped raise me, who kissed my scabbed knee when I fell off my bike, who escorted me to the Father and Daughter dance at school, because my father abandoned us years before. The man was the reason why my grandfather's passion for falconry amused Nanny Vic. He was the Falcon and loved me even though he had to know I wasn't his biological granddaughter.

The fog lifted. Everything made perfect sense.

"Mr. Celandine, you cared for my grandmother and protected her?" He removed his glasses. "I would have died for her."

"What if I asked you for a final wish of my grandmother, no matter the consequence? Would you do it?"

"Without question."

* * * *

As I leaned against the boat's railing, the full moon reflected in the calm waters. Only the wake from Mr. Celandine's boat, *Sweet Victoria*, rippled the mirror image. All was silent except for the purr of the engine until he switched it off and *Sweet Victoria* bobbed in the middle of the English Channel.

He left his tiny wheelhouse and headed to the stern. "This is still better than the bastard deserves." Mr. Celandine opened the lid of Nanny Vic's cedar chest and stared at the body—not of Major Gunter Falke, Nazi—but the real Michael Buckley. "I just wish I had done the deed myself."

Tom nudged my shoulder with his. "You're such a clever girl, figuring everything out. Falke must have switched clothes with Buckley and then stabbed his body again for good measure. No one missed him, because Michael Buckley supposedly left for France with his wife, Victoria. Are you sure you don't want to inform the police?"

"What good would come out of it? All concerned parties are dead. Can't some family secrets be kept secret?"

"I'll keep it even though the discovery would give me high marks on my thesis. However, I broke several laws helping you. Doesn't that warrant at least one dinner date?"

Smiling, I leaned my head against his. "Maybe two."

Mr. Celandine slammed the lid of the chest shut. "Miss Graham, was Victoria happy? Truly happy?"

"Yes, she loved Gramps very much and he treated her like a princess."

One corner of Mr. Celandine's mouth crept up. "Good. She deserved that." He pulled out a handkerchief and rubbed his cheek. "I'm not wiping away tears, you lot, it's just the wind in my eyes." Liar.

Mr. Celandine stuffed his handkerchief back into his coveralls pocket. "I added ballast to the chest to sink it good. Tom, grab that other end and we'll throw it overboard."

Tom and Mr. Celandine hefted up the chest and shoved it over the side. Water splashed onto the deck. The chest sunk into the dark waters on the last day the Buckley family secret crossed the lips of anyone.

EGIDIO DECIDES TO FISH

JOAN LEOTTA

Bullets had been whizzing over his head since dawn from the German machine gun nest across the no-man's land in Belgium. Bullets, however, were not what most Egidio feared most about his time in the trenches. The trench was low enough so he could walk standing without the bullets touching him. The miserable miasma that passed for air and the putrid water in the trenches gave him the most cause for worry. He was sure he would die of influenza before succumbing to a bullet. As if to confirm his feelings, a sudden gust of wind blew along the narrow trench. Egidio crouched in a futile effort to warm himself.

The cold air reached through Egidio's thin uniform jacket to chill his bones. His coat and gas mask had gone missing a few days earlier. He wrapped his scarf around his neck. Egidio's shiver shifted his body enough to move his foot off of one of the narrow walking boards into the ever present, near-frozen trench water he had been trying to avoid.

"*Accidente!*" he cursed softly in his native Italian. His commanding officer, Lieutenant Sloan, disliked it when he or any of the other Italian-Americans in the unit spoke Italian. "English only!" Sloan would bark while assigning the offender to KP duty. So even when Egidio swore in his native tongue, he whispered. He did not want to rile Sloan.

He wished he could curse louder to take his mind off of the wet that was seeping through the paper he had used to patch a hole in the sole of his boot. Miserable. He thought back to the nice little house where he lived with his brother Dominick on Larimer Avenue in Pittsburgh. They didn't have much money, but even in winter his feet remained warm in heavy boots as he tramped home through the snow from his job as a driver making deliveries for the Pasta Emporium.

His one American friend at home, Douglas, was always urging him to speak up for himself. "Don't keep so quiet, Egidio, when you or your Italian friends face trouble. Don't wait around. Take action. Life is a series of decisions. Fish or cut bait. When are you going to act against the men who are beating down you and your friends?"

He explained the saying to Egidio, who smiled thinking about it. The trench water under the boards seemed deep enough for fishing! He sighed and shivered again.

Rinaldo, his friend and Pittsburgh neighbor, came limping over to him. Before the war, Rinaldo had worked as a gardener at one of the mansions that graced Fifth Avenue in Oakland. Blue-eyed, blond-haired Mattie Wilson, daughter of one of the teachers at the high school where the two young men took advantage of American free education, had taken a liking to Rinaldo. More than a liking. Their affection had grown into a deep love.

Unfortunately, Mattie's family did not like her keeping company with a "wop," especially one who was not going to college and was working as a gardener for some of their friends. Mattie went on to train to become a teacher and met a man who was in his last year of college. That man also became enamored of her. When Rinaldo and Egidio enlisted, Mattie's other suitor also joined up. He was now their officer—Hiram Sloan, a tall blond man who looked English. His pinched nose said he thought himself above all others and knew he was destined for a career as a lawyer. Sloan was beloved by Mattie's family. She started to meet Rinaldo without telling her folks.

Before Sloan shipped out, he asked her to marry him. Mattie turned him down. She told him she had given her heart to another (Rinaldo) but would be glad to be his friend. Hiram Sloan, according to a letter Mattie had written to Rinaldo, had become incensed when he realized his rival was a gardener and a "wop" besides!

Egidio, Rinaldo and a few of their other neighborhood friends signed up to fight for their new country as soon as the call for soldiers was plastered on posters all over town. They were surprised to find Sloan at the recruiting office with them. He, as a college graduate, was being sworn in as an officer as they waited in line. Most men served in units with others from their neighborhoods. Rinaldo hoped his placement would be in a different unit from that of Hiram Sloan. No such luck. They were assigned to Sloan. Egidio advised Rinaldo to keep quiet about his romance with Mattie and to tell Mattie to do the same. However, before Rinaldo could tell Mattie not to reveal his name to Sloan, the innocent girl had let it slip.

When Egidio and Rinaldo discovered that Sloan knew about Rinaldo's romance with Mattie, they were afraid that Sloan might try to use his position to punish Rinaldo and any of his friends. Sloan always seemed to have something nasty to say to the Italians in his unit. Especially Rinaldo.

Egidio tried to stay out of Sloan's way. When the swaggering Sloan, who always seemed to look clean and pressed even in the trenches, came by, Egidio tried to remain unseen. He hated being invisible.

Egidio was sure Sloan had not taken Mattie's dismissal with good grace. He had seen a letter from Sloan to Mattie Wilson in the outgoing mail when it was his turn to take mail to the rear lines just the day before.

"Two men, one woman. Never a good thing," Egidio said to Rinaldo, trying to warn him. But the kind young man dismissed Egidio's fears.

"Sloan knows Mattie and I are going to be married. I was worried at first, but as mean as Sloan is, Mattie tells me he took her refusal graciously. Other than his usual scorn for us as Italians, I have nothing to worry about."

Egidio was not so sure, but as the days went by, Rinaldo's opinion seemed to be correct.

Rinaldo wrote to Mattie every day and almost daily he received one or sometimes two scented letters in the young girl's graceful penmanship. Sometimes Rinaldo would read Egidio little tidbits about life in Pittsburgh and share with Egidio the many plans that he and Mattie had for their future together after the war. A smile on his face, Rinaldo came over and sat down on a board across the trench, with one of those letters. Egidio sat down next to him.

"Listen to what Mattie tells me, my friend. She says the war is going to be over soon, that the peace talks are going well and I will be home by January. We're going to run away to West Virginia where she can get married without permission from her father. She can teach school with the two years of college she will have when I get back. Once we are in West Virginia, I will start my own gardening company. Everything is possible in America, Egidio."

Egidio was about to respond when their friend, Franco, hobbled toward them across the boards. "*Amici,*" he started in Italian and then switched to English. "I've got news! The war *is* over! I heard that there will be no guns, no shooting after eleven o'clock this morning. That's just twenty minutes from now."

Egidio looked puzzled. "What are you saying? If it's over, why are they still firing?"

Franco shook his head. "I heard Sloan talking to a captain. The captain told him the cease fire had already been signed but would not go into effect until eleven this morning because today is the eleventh day of November, the eleventh month. They want it to be all elevens. Someone at the peace table likes numbers. I guess."

"Why don't we just stop now?" Rinaldo asked.

Franco chuckled. "That's what the captain said. He told Sloan not to bother with any attacks, just defend until the guns stop. That way more of us can go home, he said."

"I like that!" commented Rinaldo. He opened his mouth to add something else, then shut it and straightened up. Egidio turned around. Sloan was picking his way over the boards toward them.

Sloan gathered the five remaining men of his unit: Egidio, Franco, Rinaldo, and two American boys from West Virginia, Chuck and Dave. The West Virginia duo often incurred Sloan's wrath for their "countrified" ways. He seemed to dislike them almost as much as he hated the Italians.

Sloan turned to them. "Men, get ready to go over the top and into the field. We are going to take out that German machine gun nest that has been pinning us down."

Egidio grimaced. He knew that by *we*, Sloan meant them and only them. Sloan never left the trench. He often ordered his men up the rickety ladders and into the no man's land, but always remained behind. Egidio looked around. Their little corner of the trench works was deserted. There were no witnesses to what Sloan was about to do.

Then Sloan added, "Rinaldo, you lead the charge!"

Egidio gasped. Five men to take out a machine gun nest. Certain suicide! Especially for the man who would lead the charge.

In a flash, Egidio understood. He remembered that Sloan had just written to Mattie. Who knows what lies he had told her. After this action, it was likely that Sloan would be the only one returning to tell the tale. Almost certainly the five of them would become so many more loss statistics in this awful war.

Death was something they expected every day in the war. It began to anger Egidio that once *they* were dead, Sloan would be safe to go home and free to take Mattie for himself. Mattie would be grieving the loss of her Italian boyfriend and would surely fall into the arms of the young war hero (or so Egidio imagined Sloan would style himself).

What could he, Egidio, do about it? What *would* he do about it? Nothing? Egidio looked at Sloan's smug face.

No! Egidio was tired of being bullied by Sloan, tired of worrying about the army's rules and regulations. He had to act now. As his American friend Douglas often said, a person had to fish or cut bait.

Egidio shouted, "I am tired of cutting the bait! I am going to fish!"

Before the astonished eyes of the other men in the unit, Egidio grabbed Sloan by one arm, twisting it behind the man. With his right hand, Egidio pulled Sloan's revolver out of his holster, pushed Sloan up the ladder and onto the muddy no man's land. Keeping Sloan standing up as best he could, Egidio forced Sloan to march forward. The pair had moved only a few steps ahead before the gunfire spattered out at them. Egidio felt the thwack of bullets hitting Sloan's body and the sharp pain of one or two going through to his own. Unsteady from the pain, he slipped in the mud, pulling Sloan down on top of him. As he fell, he saw the dreaded white cloud of gas moving toward him in another chilly gust of wind. His throat burned and then all went black.

* * * *

A few days later, Egidio awoke in a hospital. At first he thought he was in heaven. White sheets, no smoke. Kindly faces of pretty young women all around.

"You'll be fine," said one of the women, a nurse, he noted as his consciousness returned more fully.

Her soft calm voice continued. "I know the smoke burns a lot but we are fairly sure that it will do no permanent damage." She pointed to a letter on his bed stand. "Look, here is a letter from your friend Rinaldo. He wrote two actually, one to the hospital in English and the other to you in Italian. I'm sure they say the same thing but you can read this one for yourself. His letter to the hospital told all of us how you were wounded trying to save your officer from German gunfire as the poor man made one last brave charge in the final minutes of the war. You'll get a medal, and so will he."

Egidio choked out a few words in spite of his pain. "Our officer survived?"

"No, no, but the Army will award him one too, posthumously, meaning after death," she added, seeing Egidio's puzzled look at the long English word.

Egidio groaned. His leg throbbed and the pain in his lungs from the gas was still sharp.

"Oh, dear. I know you must feel bad about not being able to save him." She patted Egidio's hand. "You did try. Let that comfort you. Here, read your friend's letter to you, the one in Italian."

The nurse handed him the letter and moved on to comfort the next man. Egidio unfolded his letter. He read Rinaldo's thanks for saving his life and making it possible for him to marry his sweetheart. Rinaldo wrote that Franco had gone up the ladder and crawled over to pull Egidio back into the trench. Rinaldo added that he and the three other men in the unit had made up a story, telling the other officers that Egidio was injured while he was trying to save Sloan. They had agreed to say that Sloan had unwisely gone over the top in a last act of gallantry.

Rinaldo ended the letter by writing, "You'll both get medals this way and we all get to go home. Thanks again."

In spite of the pain, Egidio smiled. He had finally taken action. It was worth whatever it cost him personally. He did not regret Sloan's death. Egidio smiled more broadly. He had made a decision, stood up for himself and Rinaldo and saved his friend. Egidio thought back to Douglas' advice to "fish or cut bait" and to stand up for himself.

He would not share the details of this incident with Douglas when he recovered and went home. The incident had to remain secret, but maybe he would take up fishing back in Pittsburgh.

CROSSROAD

SU KOPIL

Nessie Hill had been eyewitness to the doings on Main Street for nearly twenty years. She remembered the day the single traffic light was installed at the crossroad. She was a newlywed then, the light a promise to a town aching to grow and flourish—the same promise she'd attached to her newly minted marriage.

She was one of the young naïve wives whose husbands ruled the roost. They met at the coffee shop to discuss who was pregnant, who had given birth, and what baby names were still in the offing. If she squinted hard, she could still make out the lettering of The Coffee Bean where it had gone unscathed from the flames. It may have been the only thing left untouched the night fire swept through town.

The storm had taken Culpepper unaware on a quiet summer evening, just after supper, when folks had been lulled by full bellies and a promise of a starry night. The wind arrived first, whistling through the tops of the pines and weaving down through the alleys. Fat drops of rain slicked the streets. Summer shower, people thought. A relief from the heat, they assured one another. And when they turned out the lights and climbed into bed, they barely noticed the increasing tempo of the rain on their windows.

Nessie remembered waking to what sounded like a train charging through their upstairs bedroom. Tornado, Henry had screamed at her, his eyes round in the flash of lightning. She was bleary from sleep and had gotten tangled in the sheets. Henry had flicked on the lights and was yelling at her to hurry. The house rattled and shook all around them.

She'd fumbled her way through the hallway and had reached the stairs, Henry behind her, his hand on her back. A loud bang echoed through the house and they were plunged into darkness. One minute she was standing on firm ground, the next she was hurtling through space.

A fall down the stairs, they told her when she woke in hospital the next day. She was damned lucky, they said. Henry had stood quietly at her bedside, not saying anything, but she saw the way his hands trembled.

She couldn't look at those hands, could barely stand to have them push the wheelchair they told her would only be temporary.

They tried everything—massages, acupuncture, physical therapy. Henry was persistent in seeking out new methods to try until she put her foot down... figuratively, of course.

Months passed, then years. Fire destroyed the chemical plant, leaving many jobless. The town stagnated—grew barren. Those who could, moved away. Houses sat vacant. Women had trouble getting pregnant. Something in the water, they said. Sex became a thing of the past as the women lost interest. And the men took to drinking. Businesses closed, sidewalks cracked, the weeds grew but there was no one to care.

The traffic light broke, stuck on a perpetual emerald green. There weren't enough cars on the road to cause a worry and so it remained like a giant, alien eye. From her wheelchair on her front porch, Nessie watched the light as it swayed unblinking in the breeze.

She pulled the brake up and rolled to the doorway, calling through the screen. "I'm going to make lemonade, do you want some?"

She could hear Henry grunt and push himself out of the chair. Although only forty, he'd grown fat and lazy since his job with the county had been drastically reduced. It was her disability payments that kept them going. She could see him through the screen now. A shadow of the handsome boy she'd begged her parents to let her marry.

"I'll get it," he said.

"I don't want you to trouble yourself," she answered.

"I said I'd get it."

"Well, okay, but not too sweet," she said.

He grunted again.

She rolled herself back into position where the sun didn't quite reach and pushed the brake back into place. Something caught her attention across the street at the old Radley place. They'd been one of the last families to move after the storm. Mrs. Radley had turned the downstairs into a knitting shop while the family resided on the second floor. But with no new babies, no need for knitted booties or caps, the Radleys finally threw in the needles and pulled up stakes. The house and shop had remained empty for ten years, until now.

Now there was movement in a lower window. The driveway sat empty. Debris still clogged the walkway and porch. Nessie leaned left then right. She hadn't noticed anyone enter the house. Nor had she seen Sarah Andrews, the only realtor left in town—part time realtor, truth be told, for she hadn't had a sale in years. So who was it in the Radley house and how had they gotten in?

The screen door squealed. Henry's shadow crossed her lap. He held a tall glass of iced lemonade.

"On the table, please," she said. "No, not there. There. Closer."

Henry pulled the table closer to her chair and hovered. She hated when he hovered. He had never hovered before the accident. Sometimes she thought the accident changed him more than it had her.

"Have you heard anything about the old Radley house?" she asked. He got out more than she did, working the odd job and running errands and such.

"Like what?" he asked.

"Anything. Has it sold? Has someone moved in?"

"Nothing like that. Can I get you anything else?"

"Don't you want to know why?"

"Why what?"

"Why I'm asking about the Radley house."

She ignored his confused frown and pointed. "Look. There's someone in there. Bottom window to the right of the door."

She could tell he didn't see anything. Dusk was falling and she was beginning to wonder if she'd imagined it.

Henry slapped his arm. "Mosquitos are bad. Why don't you come in?"

"You've just brought my lemonade." She picked up the sweaty glass and took a perfunctory sip. The sweetness lay thick on her tongue. It was the ritual she enjoyed, not the drink, which she always ended up dumping in the bushes.

"I'll carry it back in for you. Come on."

"Don't open it until I get there. You'll let the bugs in." She lifted the brake and rolled across the wooden porch. He opened the door and pushed her chair inside with one hand, leaving her at an awkward angle.

"Go put the lemonade down before you spill it."

Sometimes it still surprised her when he actually listened to her. He'd had a peacock's arrogance, which made their marriage difficult before. He disappeared into the living room. She waited, glancing back into the growing dark. A light flicked on across the street then just as quickly flicked off. Henry returned to push her into the living room where the television blared. But her mind was too full to take it in. There was no mistaking. Something was definitely going on at the house across the street.

She was right. Henry went out early the next morning and returned with coffee, bagels, and news. Tom Andrews, Sarah's husband, bought the last sesame bagel, Henry's favorite, and they got to talking. According to Sarah, Mrs. Radley's niece had rented the house to start a business, a beauty boutique of all things, in Culpepper. Mr. Radley jumped at the chance to have someone in there fixing up the place.

It gave Nessie something to watch as the days passed. The sidewalk was swept, garbage was put out on the curb and taken away, and the old peeling white paint was replaced with a lemon yellow. A bit garish for Nessie's taste, as was Bree, the Radley's niece and new tenant.

Any time she caught Nessie staring, Bree waved and flashed a pearly smile. Nessie would pretend not to notice and turn her gaze to the traffic light as though she hadn't seen it a million times before. The frumpy redhead with her inquisitive smile, wide hips, and brightly colored muu-muus didn't sit right with Nessie.

One Saturday she wheeled to her favorite spot on the porch and sent Henry in search of a crossword puzzle. The air was a bit cooler with a hint of rain, a nice break from the humidity. She looked up to see Bree huffing across the street with a small brown bag in her hand.

Nessie fumbled at the brake but she was too late. Bree was already climbing the porch steps with that white grin blazing.

"Hi, I'm Bree," she said, as if the whole town didn't already know who she was. "I thought I'd come over and introduce myself seeing as we're neighbors now."

Nessie had no choice but to shake the pale, plump hand thrust in her face. "Nessie," she said.

"I know, my aunt told me all about you." Bree looked at the wheel-chair, no doubt realizing how rude that sounded. "Not just you," she amended, "but about Culpepper in general. It's a beautiful town."

"It was once."

"Oh, it still is." Bree looked out at Main Street with its rundown buildings and empty sidewalks, then back at Nessie. "You can't always tell the truth of a thing just on appearances."

Nessie frowned. "It serves its purpose."

"I suppose it does. But sometimes that's not enough. People need more—deserve more." Bree's unblinking green gaze reminded Nessie of the broken light. It unnerved her, made her feel naked and vulnerable.

"And sometimes folks like things just the way they are." Nessie looked past Bree to the screen door. Where was Henry with her cross-word puzzle?

"Here." Bree held out the brown paper bag.

"What is that?" Nessie didn't want to take it but had the feeling if she didn't, the woman would just let it drop into her lap.

"I'm an herbalist. I make homemade lotions and soaps and, well, other things. I thought this might help change your, er, situation."

"Excuse me?" Nessie's eyes widened.

"I'm sorry, Mamma always told me I was too bold but when I see a problem, I like to fix it."

"I don't need fixing or changing. Thank you very much." Nessie held the bag out between two fingers. She shook it, a silent demand for the woman to retrieve her belongings.

Bree took the bag. "Perhaps I'll just leave it on this chair here and later—"

"No." The word was too forceful even for Nessie's ears. "Thank you but, no. I don't need your potions. Culpepper doesn't need them. As I said, some folks prefer things as they are." Nessie rolled her chair forward so that Bree had to step back. "I hear Henry calling. If you'll excuse me."

She watched Bree's muumuu blow in the wind as the woman flounced back across the road. Not until she had disappeared inside the Radley house did Nessie turn away.

Henry startled her by opening the screen door. "What was that all about?" he asked.

Nessie shrugged. "Just saying hello to the new neighbor," she said, then rolled past him, ignoring the puzzle book in his beefy hand.

But he didn't leave it alone. He followed her into the kitchen. "She has something to help—I heard her. Why wouldn't you take it?"

She stopped in front of the refrigerator. "Do you really think a few paltry herbs are going to cure what the doctors can't fix?"

"What do they know? They can't even tell us what's wrong with your legs."

"Isn't it obvious?" She spun the chair away from the refrigerator. "I can't walk."

He shook his head. "I don't understand why you wouldn't even want to try to change things."

There it was again. That word—change. She did try to change things. She tried to change *him*. For years she tried with things like marriage counseling and anger management. She even had her father pull strings to get him a county job. But always he'd revert back to his selfish, abusive ways. The accident had been her saving grace.

She pushed forward and stopped in front of him. "I used to wonder the same about you," she said and wheeled out of the room.

* * * *

But despite all her protests, things did begin to change in Culpepper. At first more cars drove down Main Street, slowing as they passed the Radley place. Then a trickle of women appeared. Dour-faced with large sunglasses and dark scarves covering their heads, they'd furtively glance about before slipping inside the lemon house. An hour or so later they'd reappear, sunglasses forgotten, scarves draped haphazardly over one shoulder and small paper bags clutched to their bosoms. The dour expression gone, replaced by something intangible. It took a while before Nessie was able to recognize what it was she saw in their faces. And when she did, she let out an audible gasp. It was hope.

There were other changes, too. Men were smiling again. She even heard one whistling as he walked by. She could see workmen going in and out of the old Coffee Bean. Boards were ripped off a few other shops. Parking spaces were filling up. It was as if the town had suddenly wakened after a long slumber.

But it was the day in early autumn when the traffic light turned yellow and then red that Nessie very nearly jumped out of her wheelchair. Henry was yelling her name from somewhere inside the house. He hadn't done that since before the accident.

She found him in the kitchen, jacket in hand. "I'm going out," he said.

"Out?" She blinked at him. "What about dinner?"

"The boys have put together a card game. It's been ages." He shrugged into the jacket.

"You were supposed to cook the haddock and—"

"I'm not your wet nurse." The sudden rise in volume in his voice shook her. "Cook it yourself."

"You're the one who wanted the fish," she mumbled under her breath.

"What did you say?" He stepped forward.

Her breath caught in her throat and she dropped her gaze to his hands. The hot water heater whistled. Somewhere a dog barked. The screen door squealed open then banged shut. Not until the sound of his footsteps faded did she let out the breath she'd been holding. It was at that moment she knew, her life had once again come to a crossroad. She could either fish or cut bait, as her granddaddy used to say.

Henry started going out more—once or twice a week, then every night. The days were getting cooler and she was on the porch less though she continued to watch the comings and goings on Main from her bedroom window. She was there now, watching the traffic light change— green, yellow, red. She'd always had plenty of time to think but tonight she couldn't seem to shut her thoughts up. Henry hadn't come home yet. The last few nights when he'd helped her to bed, he'd smelled like lilacs. When she questioned him about it he said it was the new soap that Bree had given him. She knew he expected her to be surprised but she wasn't. She'd watched him leave the old Radley place on more than one occasion.

In fact, she was looking at it now. The street lamp sent flickering shadows across the yellow paint. A soft drizzle fell. She was about to let the curtain fall when Henry stepped out of the shadows and into the circle of light. He carried a brown paper bag under one arm. His face, in the soft lamp light, appeared ten years younger. He shrugged the collar of his jacket up and headed towards Main Street.

Nessie found the paper bag the next morning. Henry was still asleep in their old bedroom upstairs. He never came to her room last night to check on her, which was just as well if he'd been drinking. His jacket lay draped across the sofa in the living room, the paper bag peeking out of the left pocket. The stairs creaked and her outstretched arm froze. When Henry didn't appear, she sighed. Just old house noises. But she worked quickly and quietly, pulling the bag out of the pocket and dropping it into her lap. Then she wheeled herself out to the front porch. The air was cool but the sun was up.

She reached her hand into the bag and pulled out a small glass vial. It was filled with a white powder. She turned it over and read the hand written label. "For Nessie."

Her left hand gripped the arms of her wheelchair so tightly she felt something twist inside her chest. On Main Street, the softly swaying traffic light seemed to mock her. In the time it took the light to change from green to red her decision was made.

When Henry left for the bar that afternoon the day had grown unusually warm. An hour later the sun had disappeared and the air turned brittle. Nessie pulled the jacket she wore tighter around her shoulders. She checked both ways, making sure the street was empty, then crossed to the lemon house.

Bree appeared at the door without seeming the least bit surprised. She invited Nessie inside, offered refreshments which Nessie refused, and gave a tour of what she laughingly called her laboratory. Bree was dressed in an orange muumuu—her blond hair braided and hanging down her back. Brightly colored rings sparkled from each finger, mesmerizing to anyone who watched her talk as her hands kept pace with her mouth. She was describing her line of beauty products but Nessie barely listened as she stared at the rows and rows of bottles and vials lining the walls and tables. Some were filled with fine powders, some with colorful liquids, and some Nessie didn't want to venture a guess at the contents.

When Bree stopped talking and began pacing in front of Nessie with a studied look on her face, Nessie had the distinct feeling she was nothing more than a guinea pig. It was the same feeling she'd gotten when she discovered the vial of powder in Henry's pocket. When she demanded to know if Bree and Henry had been drugging her she'd expected a lie, not the eager confirmation and greedy desire to question the results of their experiment. Nessie was struck dumb. Change had happened and not just to Culpepper, but right under her nose.

* * * *

The next day, she woke late feeling tired and achy and called for Henry to lift her out of bed and into her chair. She wheeled herself into the kitchen, Henry on her heels demanding to be fed. She stopped in front of the chair where his jacket hung. Dark stains checkered the right sleeve. She looked at her husband, whose order for a melted ham and cheese sandwich died on his lips.

At half past one, the police arrived.

Nessie sat in her wheelchair in the living room while a visibly shaken Henry brought the detectives in. They introduced themselves as Detective Ryan and Detective Hobbs.

"I went to school with a Hobbs—Vivian Hobbs," Nessie said.

"Yes, ma'am, Vivian Hobbs is my mother." The young detective looked at her wheelchair then quickly away as though by his looking, he would offend her. It was a typical reaction. One she was used to.

The older detective, Ryan, spoke. "If you don't mind, Mrs. Hill, we have a few questions for you and your husband."

"Of course not." She folded her hands in her lap. "May I ask what this is about?"

"Your neighbor, a Miss Bree Radley, was murdered last night. We're questioning anyone who may have seen anything."

Nessie gasped and raised a hand to cover her mouth. She looked at Henry. His brow was beaded with sweat.

"Were you both home last night?" Detective Hobbs asked.

"Yes, of course. I don't get out much." Nessie gestured to her wheelchair.

"And you, sir?" Detective Hobbs looked at Henry.

"Henry doesn't get out much either. I'm afraid I find it difficult being left alone for too long." Henry shot her a glance. "Isn't that right, Henry?"

"Nessie needs me," he said.

"Did either of you see or hear anything unusual last night?"

They both shook their heads.

"We had the television on all night," Nessie said.

"What time did you go to bed?" Detective Ryan asked the questions while Detective Hobbs scribbled in a little notebook.

Nessie looked at Henry. "Around ten?"

He shrugged.

"Is that usual?"

"Yes. Henry will make me a cup of tea and help me into bed before retiring himself."

"You don't share a bedroom?"

She frowned, letting him know she didn't appreciate his line of questioning. "Not since the accident."

Detective Hobbs had the good grace to blush. The detectives rose and thanked them for their time. "If you should think of anything that might be of help, please call." Detective Hobbs handed Henry his card.

"Should we be worried?" Nessie shivered.

"Just make sure you keep your doors and windows locked."

"Of course, and thank you. Oh, and Detective Hobbs, please give my best to your mother."

Henry didn't say much over the next few days. He didn't leave the house. He barely left her side. Nessie was pleased to see that peacock Henry had been sent packing and she was pretty sure, he wouldn't return this time.

The townsfolk stopped smiling. Activity halted around the shops on Main Street. Even the traffic light started blinking. Culpepper was in shock.

She noticed the police talking to a few of the neighbors who hadn't boarded up and moved away. Police personnel wandered in and out of the Radley house for a few days. Then nothing. It was as if Bree Radley had never been.

Nessie let Henry push her wheelchair out on to the porch and park it in her favorite spot.

"I'll go fix your lemonade," he said.

"Not too sweet," she reminded him.

"Not too sweet." He nodded and hurried back inside.

She smiled to herself. Henry had come home so drunk the night Bree was killed he didn't know she'd been the one to wear his jacket—she'd been the one to accidentally get Bree's blood on the sleeve. No one suspected a crippled woman, not even Henry.

Everything had worked out perfectly. Main Street stood quiet. Not even a wind stirred. Nessie's foot twitched. She stretched her leg then quickly moved it back into position.

When Henry brought her lemonade and shuffled back inside, Nessie dumped the sickly sweet liquid into the bushes. What Henry could never know was that she didn't need Bree's potions. If the woman had simply minded her own business she'd still be alive. Whether Henry pushed Nessie down those stairs or not the night of the storm, the truth was the temporary paralysis that followed taught her how to gain control of their marriage. It truly had been their saving grace. And she wouldn't allow anyone or anything to change that.

At the crossroad, the old traffic light stopped blinking and glowed a steady crimson red.

NOVEL SOLUTION

VINNIE HANSEN

Henrietta entered the [ro…

Marvin banged his pudgy hand against the keyboard and corrected the typo to provost. He hated the damn ergonomic thing and wondered how he'd lost that argument to Mary Ellen. She never used the computer except to shop on Amazon or to play Solitaire. The keyboard was one of her passive-aggressive moves to discourage his writing! He'd spent twenty-seven years driving a school bus halfway to insanity. Now that he had retired, Marvin was determined to pursue his lifelong dream of writing even if it killed him. He wasn't about to let Mary Ellen undermine him.

He continued his story.

Henrietta entered the provost's office. Ten years of working as a University of California, Santa Cruz police officer, and she'd never been here before. Provosts usually kept their noses in the world of academia.

A gray-haired gentleman rose from behind a large oak desk to greet her and then indicated a wooden chair upholstered with dark green leather.

"Nice view." Henrietta nodded at the redwood forest outside the…

As Marvin looked down at the keyboard to make sure his ring finger traveled to the "w," he glimpsed the splintered lattice atop their fence. The view was much nicer from the provost's

…window.

Mary Ellen cleared her throat. Startled, Marvin twirled in the black leather chair Mary Ellen had bought for him as a birthday present. He missed his old chair, which had perfectly molded to his body.

"Aren't you going to help prepare the meal?"

"Who went to pick up the fish at New Leaf?" He'd lugged home the mahi mahi, and all the other stuff Mary Ellen had listed—cucumbers, yogurt, curry sauce and chutneys. He'd grilled the fillet on the Weber, too, so she only had to dump it into the sauce. It wasn't like she'd slaved over a hot stove all morning. "I also waited in line for twenty minutes at the bakery to pick up the pie." Key lime, which he detested.

"I appreciate that."

She didn't appreciate it enough to go away.

"What are you doing?" Mary Ellen asked.

She knew damn well what he was doing, so he said, "Googling a recipe for tzatziki."

"It's already made, Marvin."

"I'll be down soon." He glanced up hopefully. Mary Ellen had applied full make-up, so her square face didn't match her neck, and orangey powder collected along her dyed-blond hair. An apron patterned in autumn leaves protected her ruffled, cream-colored blouse. When she turned, her shoulders looked hard as boulders.

Marvin wrote:

Even though Henrietta was wearing her campus uniform, the provost gave her an appreciative once over. With her smooth skin, Henrietta didn't need make-up. She squared her shoulders and pierced the provost with her emerald eyes.

"Thank you for coming, Ms. Marvin."

"Call me Henry."

The provost cleared his throat. "We need a matter investigated with discretion... Henry."

"Discretion is my middle name."

The provost did not smile at her wit, and Henry thought she'd like to pie him. Key lime would be perfect—all that goopy meringue plopping down on his crisp suit, which probably cost more than her month's salary.

"Our Facilities Management has noted a sudden spike in our college's electricity usage on EnergyCAP." The provost tapped the desk with manicured fingernails. The desk, the whole office for that matter, was disturbingly neat, as though it were staged.

"Meth lab?" The university was divided into colleges and Crown would be full of brilliant chemists, not that a person needed more than half a brain to cook meth. The college was also remote, backed up to trails into the redwoods and spots where drum circles celebrated the full moon.

"That's what we want you to investigate. We don't want publicity, especially if all we have are students sucking up electricity for all night raves or secret experiments in their dorms."

"How much longer?" Mary Ellen bellowed up the stairs.

"Just let me finish this scene." These days, between "the change" and his being "underfoot," Mary Ellen slid into crabbiness for no reason.

He sniffed the air. Was something burning? He ignored the smell, reread his last sentence and continued.

"What if the students have set up grow rooms?" Henry asked.

"Grow rooms?"

"For marijuana. Would the university want to pursue that?" This was a university, after all, where on Four-Twenty, Earth Day, the campus police had been instructed simply to do crowd control, while students gathered to smoke cannabis, the fumes billowing from Porter College meadow as though it were on fire.

"Let's take this one step at a time," the provost said. "See what you find and we'll go from there."

Pots banged downstairs. "Marvin!"

"I'm coming!" Marvin longingly reread the last bit of dialog. "Don't get your panties in a bunch!"

Mary Ellen stomped across the kitchen.

As Henry left the provost's office, her boots stirred the redwood duff and she drew in the fresh scent. She worked in paradise up here in the hills above the chaos of Santa Cruz.

Pee-yew! The house smelled like burned farts. Cauliflower?

Even the carpet on the stairs couldn't muffle the anger in Mary Ellen's ascent. Hurriedly, Marvin typed:

Henry leaned against her campus police car. She already had a prime suspect—Bessie Fumes. If a campus party were out of control, if a fight had been reported, Bessie would be involved. An Amazon of a woman, noted for aggressive poetry slam performances, many on the topic of Henry, Bessie Fumes was a very special legacy student, treated with kid gloves. If something were brewing at this college, Bessie would be in it.

Arms akimbo, Mary Ellen occupied the doorway. "I expect a little help."

"They're your relatives!" Inspired by the intrepid Henry, Marvin couldn't stop himself.

"So when your relatives come, I should refuse to cook?"

"My relatives don't visit."

"Oh, that wasn't your long-lost cousin Henrietta who showed up last Christmas? At least my relatives have been invited."

Marvin heaved a sigh. Mary Ellen's sister Susan and her husband Fred were undemanding company. They swilled vodka tonics, plopped on the couch, and gawked at whatever was on the television. "What exactly do you want me to do?"

"Get down the crystal glasses. Put the chutneys in serving dishes. Sharpen the knife and cut the fish."

"Just let me change this last sentence," Marvin pleaded. He couldn't leave his antagonist Bessie cooking in the brew. There were also Henry's eyes, which had popped out of her head to pierce the provost. He'd read the advice: Keep your characters' eyes in their heads!

"No," Mary Ellen said. "You can spend an hour on a sentence."

Marvin stood, defeated, leaving Bessie to boil. She magically took shape in front of him—six foot two, dressed in black leather, a tattooed, Harley-riding dyke. He loved her.

* * * *

In the kitchen, Marvin poured the plum chutney into the crystal dish, a surviving wedding gift. The clotted matter and rich reddish-purple of the chutney offered up a possible simile he might use when he reached the murder in his story.

"What are you doing?"

Why did Mary Ellen always ask that question? It was perfectly obvious he'd jotted a note on his hand.

"That is so tacky. I expect you to wash it off before dinner."

"I'll remove it now." He headed for the stairs.

"There's a sink right here!"

After scrubbing his hand in the closet-sized master bath, Marvin went into the office and scribbled the note on a piece of recycled paper beside the computer: *blood and body matter = plum chutney?* He also wrote a reminder to take Bessie out of the brew and to put H's eyes back in her head.

When he went downstairs, Mary Ellen had set up the folding footstool so she could reach the glasses for the vodka tonics.

"I said I would get those."

"You think you can pull your head out of your story that long?"

The doorbell chimed a perversion of Beethoven. How he'd love to have Bessie Fumes bash it out with a baseball bat. Beyond Marvin's sight line, Mary Ellen cheerily greeted her sister and Fred. At least the occasion allowed him to haul down the Ketel One vodka along with the glasses. He started preparing the drinks as Mary Ellen ushered Susan and Fred into the kitchen, their coats draped over her arm.

Susan sniffed the air, giggled, and said, "Oh, my."

"Cauliflower." Mary Ellen glowered at him. "I wouldn't have burnt it if Marvin had been helping just a tiny bit." Susan followed Mary Ellen down the hallway to put away the coats.

Fred clapped Marvin on the back and said, "How's it hanging there, Marv, my man?"

Marvin grunted and mixed Fred's drink with a triple shot of vodka. The sooner the man was anesthetized, the better.

"You mix a hell of a vodka tonic, my friend."

"Wait," Marvin said, "don't you want your lime twist?" but Fred had blasted toward the living room. Once a college linebacker, the man was still fast in spite of his paunch and jowls.

Marvin mixed a drink for himself and for Susan. Mary Ellen preferred Chardonnay, with her dinner. Marvin tasted his drink, splashed in more vodka, and plucked a knife from its slot in a block of wood. He took the strop from a drawer.

As the two women returned to the kitchen, Fred called, "Mary Ellen, can I turn on the tube?"

"The remote is in Marvin's secret spot," Mary Ellen sang around the corner.

Marvin's grip on the knife tightened. Not only had Fred not asked him—the head of the house—but also Mary Ellen had rooted out his hideaway, and shared the intel with this clod, and God knew who else. He ran the knife fiercely down the strop.

"Are you trying to kill that thing?" Mary Ellen asked. She smirked and glanced at her sister.

Susan tittered and raised her drink. She looked like Mary Ellen with better-proportioned features—a more pert nose, larger eyes, and fuller lips. In high school she'd been regarded as the cuter of the two, but now her butt was the size of two basketballs and her jowls jiggled. Mary Ellen stripped off her apron and hung it on a wall hook by the refrigerator. The sisters were wearing nearly identical cream-colored blouses with long puffy sleeves and ruffles down the front.

"Excuse me," Marvin said. "I don't feel well. Call me when it's time to serve the curry." He picked up his drink and fled toward the stairs.

Marvin sighed with contentment as he plopped onto his desk chair. He wriggled his hips to get comfortable, but the leather felt cold and wrong, like the embrace of a prostitute. Marvin sipped his drink, extracted Henry's eyes from the provost's body and fished Bessie Fumes from the brew. Fortified with another big gulp of the vodka tonic, he continued his story.

Henry sped along the curving two-lane highway, alert for deer or mountain bikers bounding from the redwoods. She pulled the Crown Victoria into a lot and parked far from the apartments situated in a clearing among the trees. These units housed married grad students serving as TA's or student advisors. Bessie's housemate met this criterion except for the married part. However, the university didn't want to appear anti-gay by objecting to the woman's apparent live-in partner. Henry knew that Bessie had no love relationship with her housemate.

Marvin finished his drink, threaded his fingers behind his large bald spot, and tried to lean back in the unyielding desk chair. He mused, and then added the woman's name—*Mary Ellen.*

Henry approached Bessie and Mary Ellen's apartment from the back. If Bessie were home, she would resent a visit from "a pig." Henry did not want to confront the six-foot-two tattooed woman head on.

As Henry slinked through the redwoods, a blue jay squawked at her as though it could sense she was prowling, predatory. When she reached the bedroom window, Henry stood on her tiptoes, her fingers locked like claws onto the window trim. She hoisted herself for a look....

"What are you doing?"

Marvin's hand jerked from the ergonomic keyboard, knocking his empty vodka tonic onto the floor. The glass shattered. Ice cubes and shards sparkled in the watery spray across the worn oak. "Why, why, why do you keep asking that question like a broken record?"

"You need to clean up this mess." Mary Ellen had arrived like a magician—not in a cloud of smoke, but wrapped in the aromas of turmeric and cumin.

Marvin bent over and picked up the largest piece of glass.

"Don't use your hands. You'll cut yourself."

Marvin stood and regarded the wicked point attached to a sturdy chunk of the glass's base. A decision took root. If he wanted to be a real writer, he knew what he had to do.

"What did you do with my chair?" he asked.

"What *are* you talking about?"

"I want my old chair back." He stepped closer to his wife.

"You mean your throne?" Mary Ellen said.

Marvin needed to lean back in its comfortable embrace and to peek in Bessie's bedroom with Henrietta. With Henrietta he would discover a body there. He had not decided yet if it would it be the body of Bessie Fumes or of the housemate Mary Ellen. Could he aptly use the plum chutney metaphor? Might blood and guts look that way?

"What are you doing?" Mary Ellen shrieked.

"Research," Marvin said.

When he finished, he plopped down into the computer chair. It felt better. Much better. He typed.

Over Henry's shoulder, a shaft of sunlight speared through the redwoods into the apartment. The spotlight stretched across the wooden floor and reached the soles of the brown leather shoes. The height of the square heels made them look dressy. Mercilessly, the light illuminated

pale, bare, swollen ankles splayed apart. The creases in tan slacks point-
ed like arrows up the prone body to the stain, bright as plum chutney,
spread across the cream-colored blouse.

CAVEAT EMPTOR

CHERYL MARCEAU

The Hansons stole my dad's house.

I'd never liked the place at Hampton Court Estates, but he'd been thrilled when he found it. "Just think," he'd said, "there's a gym, and a pool, even indoor tennis courts. I'll be in great shape. And no snow here in South Jersey."

That was in June, before two freak December blizzards dumped several feet of snow and kept him barricaded indoors. Just days after the roads were cleared from the second storm, he called and sprung the news that he'd bought a condo in Myrtle Beach, South Carolina. He needed to sell. Now.

"Dad, what were you thinking? How can you buy a place without seeing it?" He was eighty-four, seemed sharp enough but maybe he was starting to lose it. Hampton Court Estates, one of those active seniors' developments that felt as much like a fortress as a haven, gave me the creeps every time I drove through the gates and past the identical beige houses. I wasn't sorry to see my dad leave the place, but I worried somebody was going to take advantage of him.

Turns out I was right. He was so anxious to move south, he grabbed the first offer. The buyers were not nice people. Not even a little bit. They sensed a killing to be made like sharks smelling blood. Dad wouldn't have stood a chance, even if he had let me help, which he didn't.

"I'm your father," he'd said. "I was doing this while you were still in diapers. For God's sake, leave me alone!"

I insisted on coming to the closing, trying my best to protect him in case the Hansons tried to pull something at the last minute.

"Just leave this to me," he snapped as we walked into the conference room at the bank. "I'll handle it." Once inside he smiled and said to those loathsome Hansons, "You deserve the house. I think you'll fit right in at Hampton Court Estates."

"Did you replace that piece of siding by the barbecue grill?" Judy Hanson asked the minute we arrived, not even bothering to say hello first. "I don't want to have to look at that warped bit every time we entertain on the deck."

"Good grief, maybe an inch of that siding got warped from being too close to the grill. Who'll even see it?" I asked.

"I said I'll handle this," Dad growled at me. Then turning deferentially to the Hansons, he said, "The siding is good as new."

"What about the electronics?" Don Hanson asked. The house had been wired for everything by the previous owner—audio and video in every room, controlled by touch panels, and a state of the art security system—or so Dad had boasted when he first showed me around. The system could supposedly do anything. Absolutely anything. Dad never used any of it that I could tell, didn't seem to know how it worked, and never showed any interest in trying it out. I think he just liked bragging rights to all that technology. Like it somehow kept him from geezerdom.

"No idea," he answered, shrinking into his chair a little.

"Everything needs to be in working order. Didn't we make that clear?" Don raised his voice like he thought Dad was hard of hearing. He turned to his wife and in a whisper that could have been heard down the hall, said, "I bet he broke it and doesn't want to make good."

"Don, honey, he doesn't even know what he has," Judy said, only the tiniest bit softer, looking at my dad like he was a pathetic old fool.

Those wretched Hansons demanded one thing after another, while I smoldered. We were there to sign the closing papers, not renegotiate the deal. The non-working instant hot water tap that Don didn't even notice until the inspection, but absolutely had to be replaced. The ugly living room carpet that Judy insisted we repair where the sofa leg had snagged it. The ceiling fan that didn't exactly match the hardware in the guest bedroom that Don insisted we replace with one that matched. The list went on and on. My father agreed to each ridiculous demand looking more and more defeated.

I knew it was childish of me. I really did. But those people needed to be taught a lesson. They had turned my curmudgeonly father into a pushover.

* * * *

Scre-e-e-ek...

"Don, what was that?" Judy Hanson shook her sleeping husband.

"Snrpflrf."

She shook harder. "How can you be snoring with that noise going on?" she whispered, as if afraid to talk loud enough to be heard over his snores.

"Snrpflrf."

She pushed off the covers and reached for the velour robe hanging from the headboard, slid into her slippers and zipped her robe, then grabbed the flashlight from her nightstand and paused inside the bedroom door.

Scre-e-ek...

Judy froze. A moment later she swung the flashlight around the one large room that formed the living room and dining room, finally aiming the beam at the basement door. She inched toward it and jiggled the knob. It didn't budge. She made her way through the great room to the sunroom, and waited. No sounds but Don's snoring disturbed the nighttime silence. That figured. He slept through everything. A motorcycle gang could drive through the bedroom and Judy was certain Don would sleep through that.

Before returning to bed, she circled back to the alarm system panel by the front door. She yawned loudly and stretched, then stopped short.

"System Malfunction. No Power Supply."

She peered out the sidelights next to the door. The street was softly lit and peaceful. There wasn't a living soul in sight.

* * * *

I wasn't proud of myself. I admit that. But I was getting some satisfaction watching her chase around the house, looking for the noises, probably suspecting the worst. When I started to hate myself, I remembered the way they treated Dad. They deserved a little scare.

* * * *

Ka-thunk

Judy leaned toward the kitchen, listening for a repeat of the noise. It could have been the refrigerator cycling on.

Mnmnmnm

The last sound came from the direction of the laundry room, which opened out to the garage. A breeze ruffled her hair and fluttered the hem of her robe. "Eek!" She spun around to see who was behind her, then eyed the vent for the heating system.

* * * *

The next morning was bright and clear, the sky a soft blue that signaled spring in the air. Everything outside gleamed. It was a good day to be alive. I should have felt worse after being up half the night in front of my computer tormenting Judy Hanson. Should have, but most definitely didn't. I hadn't felt so good in weeks. The miserable commute to my office in Kendall Square didn't even get on my nerves.

* * * *

"This house doesn't work right," Judy said at dinner that evening. "I couldn't get the fancy-schmancy video system turned on today, and last night I found out the security alarm didn't work."

"That can't be right. The alarm was set before I went to bed. I checked."

"And I'm telling you, I got up in the middle of the night and the thing said it wasn't working. Something about no power to the system."

Don grabbed the napkin from his lap and walked to the front door, martini glass in hand. "'System Normal.' You must have been looking at it wrong."

Judy nearly flew out of her chair to look for herself. "I know what I saw. I don't know how it got fixed, but it wasn't working last night."

"There's a file in the office labeled Alarm System. I'll see if there's a troubleshooting guide. Just in case it's broken."

"We need an expert. No point in messing around, you might make it worse. That old guy didn't have a clue, probably played with it and un-programmed the controls."

* * * *

I had a late night conference call scheduled with our office in Tokyo, and I couldn't resist keeping an eye on the Hansons while I waited for it to start. I glanced at my computer screen while I tried to read the report from the Tokyo team. It was hard to focus on prepping for the meeting. I needed to review user issues being reported by our Asia service team, and prep for the launch of the next release of our software. I was having too much fun with the Don and Judy show to bring myself back to the task at hand. Like a kid running home after school to play with my toys, I couldn't wait to get home and see what else I could do to the Hansons.

* * * *

The bedroom clock glowed red, the display reading 12:03 AM. Judy tossed and turned. Every floor board seemed to creak and groan. She might have pretended the noises didn't bother her, but her restlessness belied her bravado. She started to get up, then pulled the pillow over her head and squirmed into the blankets.

BANG!

* * * *

I didn't expect that. Must be losing my touch. Hadn't done much programming recently. Well, a little extra drama would be interesting.

* * * *

Judy threw off the sheet and pulled on her robe. It sounded like someone hit the outside wall by their bedroom. Some loose siding near the roof line could have come down in the wind. She peered around the bedroom curtains.

No siding on the grass by the house. The next door neighbor's Marine Corps flag hung lifelessly on the flagpole by his door. No wind, either.

WHOOSH

She tiptoed to the bedroom door and looked out. The house was dark. Nothing moved.

She put her hand to the bedroom's heating vent as if to test it, then felt around on the table for the flashlight and held it out in front of her like a weapon as she investigated elsewhere. Don snored and mumbled, dead to the world.

She stood by the patio slider, looked in every direction, then pulled it open and stepped across the slider track.

WOOT-WOOT-WOOT-WOOT-WOOT-WOOT-WOOT

She slammed the door, scrambling to lock it, and returned to the control panel. Just as she was about to push the buttons, the racket stopped.

"System Malfunction. No Power Supply." Judy read the words aloud, and grabbed the wall for support as she sucked in huge gulps of air.

* * * *

Hmmm, not at all what it was supposed to do. Very odd. I typed a few keystrokes to try something, staring at the screen as I did. All the cameras appeared to be working. The system was on and functioning. I was stumped.

It did occur to me that maybe—somehow, I didn't know how—my father was behind this. I thought about calling him to ask him if he knew anything about it, but there was no possible way he could be meddling with this. Besides, he'd kill me if he had any idea what I was up to.

* * * *

Judy ran into the bedroom, slamming and locking the door behind her. She shivered, although the temperature was set at 70 degrees. "Honey, wake up!" She shook Don's shoulder. "I'm scared. Wake up!" She continued to shake him until he opened his eyes. "Please wake up!"

"Hmmfph. What's wrong?" Don asked when he finally emerged out of his deep sleep.

"The house is going haywire. I swear to God, it's possessed. I just set off the alarm and it worked fine, then it stopped before I could enter the

code, and the message said it wasn't working. There's something wrong with this place."

Don wrapped his arms around her. "Your imagination is running wild. The house just has its own sounds, that's all. You'll get used to it."

Judy sniffled. "I'm not so sure...."

"Trust me. Now let's go back to sleep. I've got an early tennis game in the morning."

Judy climbed back into bed. "I guess you're right. It's good that people have to be buzzed in at the front gate and we have security guards patrolling. We got a decent deal on the house, except maybe we should have pushed the old guy harder on the price. He took our offer so fast, I know we left money on the table. But we did okay. I'll be fine once I get used to it."

"You're right about the price, sugar. Probably could have squeezed another few grand off the deal. But that's water over the bridge, as they say. Now, how about we both go back to sleep?"

* * * *

If I were a better person, I'd have stopped there. But those despicable Hansons had just proved that they hadn't suffered enough. I had a few more ideas that would have to wait until the next night. I desperately needed some sleep. These nocturnal pranks were wearing me out.

* * * *

WSHSHSWSHSHWSHSHWHSHSHSSW

Don rolled over trying to get away from the sound. He burrowed deeper into the covers. He drew his arm up over his ear. Nothing blocked the deep hum that came from somewhere in the house. Finally, he got up to turn off whatever it was. Three nights in their new house and he'd hardly gotten any sleep, what with Judy waking him up at all hours the night before, and now this.

He cocked his head to listen and padded out to the living-dining room. He didn't locate the source of the sound until he bent over toward the baseboard. He held out his hand, only to feel his fingers being sucked toward a small duct in the wall inches from the floor.

* * * *

What the—? I'd forgotten the house was equipped with a central vacuum system. Dad had insisted he preferred the old upright vacuum cleaner Mom had used for years. I poked around the house controls on the screen but I couldn't find the central vac. This was spooky. How could I have turned it on? Maybe I'd read too much science fiction over the years, but for one creepy moment I would have sworn the house had taken on a life of its own.

Nah, that was crazy talk. I typed another command.

* * * *

Don jumped up, coughing violently, enveloped by a cloud of dust.

"Honey?" Judy called from the bedroom. "You all right?"

"I'm fine," her husband answered, hacking.

"No, you aren't." She jumped as the recessed lights came on in the living-dining room. "Oh!" she said, then, "What's that crud doing everywhere?" Don was covered in dust bunnies and unidentifiable gunk. "What did you do?"

"The central vac was running so I tried to turn it off. Then I got blasted with this!" He held out the arm that had been closest to the ducting. It was covered in gray. "The damn machine went into reverse!"

* * * *

I shivered. That was most definitely not my doing. I'd typed a command to turn on all the lights, nothing more. I was absolutely sure of that. Holy hell. What was going on in this house? I started to doubt I could control it anymore. My stomach knotted as that sank in. I watched the Hansons go back to bed and tried to figure out where I had gone wrong. If I'd done it, surely I could undo it.

* * * *

Shoosssssssh

Judy popped up, straining to hear, then wrinkled her nose. The sound might really have been anything, including a car passing by on the street. Or not. Slowly, as if terrified of what she might find, she got up and crept into the living room.

The gas fireplace between the living room and the great room was ablaze, flames dancing to the top of the firebox.

* * * *

Whoa! I wanted to scare the bejeesus out of these people, not burn the place down. What the hell was going on? My hands and feet were cold and sweaty. I couldn't breathe. I'd call the police and confess to the whole thing, but even if they believed me, what would they be able to do?

* * * *

After turning off the fireplace, Judy huddled in a corner of the living room sofa under a throw, sipping from a large glass of wine. Her ragged breathing calmed. She drained her glass, sat back, and closed her eyes.

THUNKA THUNKA SCREEET THUNK

"Help! Someone's in the house!"

THUNKA SCREEEEET THUNKA THUNK

"Don! Somebody opened the garage door!"

Judy pushed herself deeper into the sofa, trembling in fear. Her husband ran to her.

"Did you hear that? Somebody's breaking in!"

"I heard it. Shhh... I'll go out and check the garage."

* * * *

I'd never been so scared in my life. I reviewed the system control panel. The garage door opening and closing would have been a nice ghoulish touch, if I'd actually been the one to do it. I looked at the garage camera view, almost hoping to see some creep actually breaking in. Nada.

* * * *

"Don," Judy called to her husband, "I just want out. The house is telling us to leave."

Silence.

"Did you hear what I said?"

"Don't talk nonsense. The house can't tell us to leave. Something set off the garage door opener is all. The alarm system is—hunh?" He peered at the screen.

"What is it?"

"It says 'Bye.'" He blinked. "I don't like this. Maybe you're right. Tomorrow we'll find a hotel, get somebody to come out here and fix the electronics."

Don ushered Judy back to the bedroom. They climbed into bed, huddled together for comfort, eventually falling into a restless sleep.

PLUNKA PLUNKAPLINK PLUNK PLUNKA PLUNK

Once more it was Judy who woke up first, Don snoring next to her. She shook him furiously.

"Hunh?" Don rubbed his eyes.

"Listen!"

PLUNKA PLUNK PLUNK PLUNKAPLUNK

"What the hell is that?"

"I don't know, and I'm not getting up to find out!" Judy all but shoved Don out of bed. He switched on the flashlight that Judy handed to

him and went to investigate. The sound was coming from the kitchen. He rounded the corner slowly, then stopped dead.

Ice cubes shot from the refrigerator door, bouncing off the floor and hitting the kitchen cabinets. Don pounded on the door, and the ice cube barrage stopped.

A shower of crushed ice poured out.

* * * *

I couldn't control that thing anymore. I didn't know if anyone on earth could control it anymore. A malevolent force had insinuated itself into the electronics system. I was terrified someone might die.

* * * *

"Noooooooo!" A horrible wail came from the laundry room. Don ran in to find Judy pointing at the washing machine. It gurgled, soapy water spilling out onto the floor as it rocked side to side, the tub spinning in a blur. Don grabbed each of the front corners and leaned hard. As suddenly as it had started, the washer came to a complete stop.

"Honey, please, let's go to a hotel right now. I have to get out of here!" Judy sobbed. Don led her to the living room.

"Sit here. I'll pour us both a glass of wine. No place out here in the sticks will even be open at this hour. Let's try to stay calm until morning, and we'll get out while this gets fixed."

WHRRRRR flapppety flappety flap flappety WHRRRRRR

Someone—something?—was out on the patio. Judy and Don seized each other's hands and tiptoed to the slider. Don pushed aside one of the vertical blinds to look. The retractable awning was seesawing out and back. He started to unlock the slider when the awning went slack.

His wine glass shook as he picked it up. "We'll be okay. Daybreak will come soon." He gulped the wine.

SHOOOOOOSSSSHH

The fireplace came alive again, flames licking the outermost edge of the firebox.

"This house is crazy," Judy said. "It's insane! It's trying to kill us. If we stay here they'll find us in the morning with white hair, frightened to death, like those creepy TV shows you watch."

"There's a logical explanation," Don said, his voice quavering. "You saw that old guy, he probably plugged something into the wrong place and screwed everything up. That's all."

Judy trembled. "If one more thing happens, I'm leaving and I'm never coming back."

SSSSSSSSSSSS

Faint rushing sounds surrounded them. "What's that?" Judy asked.

Don strained to listen. "Your hearing always was better than mine. I don't—"

Sprinkler nozzles popped down from the ceiling, spraying water everywhere and drenching them.

* * * *

I didn't know what set off the sprinklers, probably the heat from the fire. At least, that's what I desperately prayed—that it was the heat. I tried every command I could think of. I typed and typed, trying anything whether it made sense or not. By this point I was beyond thinking.

* * * *

"That's it!" Judy said as she ran into the bedroom. She reappeared a moment later carrying an overnight bag. "I'm out of here!"

OUT OF HERE...

"What the hell?" Don looked behind him. He and Judy placed the noise at once as coming from the great room, where they encountered their own faces, drained of color and eyes popping out, displayed double life size on the plasma television mounted on the wall. Their voices echoed through the speakers.

They ran to the front door. Judy grabbed the doorknob and turned, but nothing happened. She pounded on the door. "Let me out!"

Don pushed her aside and tried the knob. When nothing happened, he kicked the door.

* * * *

I watched them on my computer screen, both absolutely petrified. I was as terrified as they looked. I hammered on my keyboard, fervently praying to the gods of hacking to let me come up with something to stop this monster. Nothing worked. Just error messages. There had to be a way. I typed again—hit Enter—ERROR. Again—ERROR. Again—ERROR. ERROR. ERROR. ERROR.

The FaceTime app on my computer chimed. My stomach churned as a wave of nausea crashed over me. My palms were sweaty. I was struggling to breathe.

The monster had found me. I didn't know what to do. If it could torture the Hansons, what could it do to me? Was there any place safe? I shoved against the desk to push myself away as fast as I could.

Suddenly my dad's face filled my computer screen.

"Dad?"

In my terror, all I could imagine was that whoever had taken over my computer and inflicted all that pain on the Hansons was using my father's image to trick me. I couldn't let that happen.

"What the hell d'you think you're doing?" he asked. It was my father's voice without question. That thing was good. I was shaking too hard to answer it.

The monster using my father's voice spoke again.

"Dammit, kiddo, I told you I would take care of it!"

SWIMMING LESSONS

GIN MACKEY

The scream came in the middle of the night, yanking me from a deep sleep. I wasn't even sure at first it was a scream. But something woke me up, something unusual, something bad. I sat up, listening. Then, a second scream, a fear-filled, heart-bashing scream. A child's scream.

Like our Lila's.

As I bolted from bed, I grabbed Harry, a short, hard grab. "There's a kid out there." As I ran down the stairs, I heard Harry stumbling, scrambling.

"Out there" was water, and a twisted river bent on snuffing a child's screams. The cries had been strong, though. The kid's lungs couldn't be filled with water yet. I tried to judge from which direction it had come but I wasn't sure.

Another scream.

Upstream.

In the cold November black, I raced down the lawn and onto the dock, leaped into the back of the boat and ripped the cord. Harry pounded down the pier and in, rocking the boat hard, and I took off, almost throwing him overboard. He steadied himself and sat down. He shouldn't even be out of bed.

"Up this way. A girl," I yelled above the motor.

He grabbed the big flashlight and flicked it on, sweeping the beam back and forth across the water. Nothing.

I throttled back so we could hear. "Where are you?" I shouted into the dark.

"Over here. Hurry."

The voice was still a ways away. "Hang on," I hollered back. Maneuvering the tiller, I moved slowly now in the direction of the scared child's voice. I had to be careful not to hit her. Harry kept scanning with the light. I throttled back once more. "Holler again."

"Please hurry. We can't hold on."

We?

Harry found them with the light—a girl, maybe ten, and a boy, younger—and I eased in their direction. The current was bad here and it fought me. The current had gone after them, too, pinning them to a boulder at the deep end of a rocky outcropping. River riled up downstream, so it might've saved them from something worse. The girl was holding onto the rock with one hand and clutching the little guy by his tee-shirt. His head was down. Unconscious?

I looked at Harry. We knew the current. We'd have to work it. "I'll go below a ways and you can grab the boy on the way by? Then we circle for the girl?"

He nodded that'd work.

"He's stuck," the girl said. "His leg. I can't get it out." Her voice was weakening.

Harry and I locked eyes. Suddenly, things were lots worse. One of us had to go in and no question who it would be. Harry's surgery had been yesterday. The boat end of things wouldn't be any picnic either. We switched spots. He moved us below them and as he made the first pass, I climbed into the water. Frigid, bone-numbing. Gave me precious little time to do what I needed to do and get these kids into the boat.

I thrashed my way over to the kids. The girl was crying now. "We'll get you out of this," I said. "It'll be okay." I hoped like hell it was true. Moving my hand down the boy's leg, I could feel it wedged between the rock and a branch, a ten-footer that must've splintered off in the lightning storm last week. The current had slammed the boy right into it, tangling him up in the mess. I tried easing his leg out. No, it was jammed in there good. I felt around to figure my options. The leg was twisted in a way it shouldn't be. Broken, bad. The boulder wasn't going anywhere, too big. The branch was my only chance. I tried jostling it. There was almost no give. I'd have to go under.

I put my hand on the girl's shoulder, firmly. I wanted to steady her, give her a confidence I didn't feel. "I'm gonna go down and get his leg out." She looked at me, nodded, held him a little tighter.

I dove, snugged my shoulder under one end of the trunk. I heaved but it barely budged. I shifted for a better vantage point and this time it moved a little. I could feel the deadness coming on my hands and arms. I gave it all I had and it slipped from where it'd been lodged, and the current sucked it away. I grabbed the boy as I surfaced, his pain-filled screams piercing the air. There'd be more. We still had to get him into the boat.

Harry was below us and coming our way. "You first," I said to the girl.

"I'm not leaving my brother."

"You have to help get him into the boat." She got it and looked toward the boat, trying to ready herself. Harry sidled up. I could see the terror in her eyes. She'd have to give up her hold of the rock.

"Now!" I screamed. She let go, grasping for the boat, and I managed to give her a shove up toward Harry, and he snatched a hold of her by the shirt and yanked her toward him. Somehow she did a header forward and got herself in. She had to be so frozen she could barely think.

I watched as Harry circled around. The girl's head popped up. She leaned over the side looking for her brother. They got downstream of us and then started up. The boy was whimpering with pain, probably the only thing keeping him hanging on to consciousness. I got ready. I lunged for the boat but I almost lost the boy and I missed it. I couldn't get back to the rock. The current snared us. I'll never know how he did it but Harry maneuvered that boat so it was below us and the current pushed us into it, and Harry's hands and the little girl's hands latched onto us and I knew we'd make it.

The boy shrieked as his broken leg was jostled. I still felt joy. He was alive.

We'd lost our Lila to the river. I still heard it in my dreams, again and again and again, my baby's screams and not being able to get to her in time. Now I felt crazy with the mixed-up grief of my broken heart and the giddy joy we'd saved these two.

That's if the cold didn't get them. That was the big danger now. I pulled the kids in close and huddled with them as Harry raced us back to the dock, tied us on. Blood seeped through his undershirt; he'd ripped his stitches. Harry hobbled to the house and got a blanket. We laid it down on the dock to use as a makeshift transport for the boy. As gently as we could, we raised him up out of the boat and onto it. Harry on one end and the girl helping me on the other, we lugged him up to the house and into the den.

I stripped the girl's wet clothes off her as quick as I could and wrapped her in a blanket nice and tight. Harry snatched scissors and we cut the boys pants off and peeled his shirt off him too, and tucked blankets all around him. Harry'd brought sweats down for me and I pulled them on.

I went over and sat down on the floor beside the little girl. "Okay," I said. "We'll call your folks and get an ambulance to take your brother to the hospital."

She looked up at me, tears spilling from her eyes. "Don't."

"Why?"

Her eyes skittered away, then back, away again. Utterly still, I waited for her, until in a voice tiny, tiny, she said, "My dad's the one threw us off the bridge."

I lost my breath, looked at Harry. And in that moment a thousand thoughts banged into one another, memories of my little girl, my baby, my baby and a wave of deep despair for the loss of her little life snuffed short by the rage of the river, followed by a rage racing through me that a human, a parent, a father, could do to these kids what this girl said he'd done.

My hands shook as I took the face of the little girl before me now in my hands, and whispered, "I'll call the police. We'll tell them together."

A shuddery shake of her head. "They'll give us back like last time."

We heard an engine, followed by the sound of a door slamming. A big vehicle, in our yard. He must have seen our light on the water, followed it here. The girl's hands circled my wrists, tight, tight—I felt the fear-born strength—and I watched her face bloom into total terror. Like the devil himself was going to come into view any second.

"Shhh." I put my finger to my lips.

The boy made a sound, and in a sudden movement, the girl scuttled on her backside over next to her brother. The boy wasn't following what was happening, and moaned from the pain.

The girl leaned over. "Daddy's come," she whispered to him.

His moan turned to a tiny sound of pure fright, then stopped. He latched on to her hand, their white fingers laced together, their eyes wide, fixed on the door.

Harry and I had no time to talk, we couldn't risk it. I put my hands out to indicate everyone stay where they are and I got up, moving quickly out of the den toward the living room where the front door was.

I opened it to a big guy, maybe six foot four. I could see the resemblance to the kids, but there was a mean twist to his face. "My kids fell in," he said. "You seen 'em?"

He was crowding me, trying to look by me.

"I heard 'em out there and went out to try to help," I said, "but the neighbors on the other side got to them first. You want a ride across?"

"Hate to bother you." His eyes took one last sweep of the hall, then landed on me.

"Just take a few minutes, and I'm awake anyway. Besides, the boat's quicker than you could get there in your truck."

"'Preciate it." The distrust I'd sensed in his tone faded.

"This way." I led him around the house and down to the dock. "You go ahead," I said. He got in and sat down in the middle of the boat. I untied us, hopped in the back, revved the motor and we started across.

"They can't swim. Me and my wife neither. Surprised they made it this far. Figured they would've drowned before they got here."

"Someone up above must be looking out for them."

Someone down here was too, but it wasn't him. I thought back to the boy. What kind of dread would make a kid in that much pain shut up like that? What had happened to that skinny little youngster?

We came up to where the current was the worst. I looked toward the foggy shore where we were headed. "Hey, I think I see a kid. Is that one of yours?"

He looked up. "Where?"

"There." I stood up, leaned forward so I was right behind him, pointed past him toward the shore.

"I don't see 'em." He craned his neck, stood up too, staring at the shore.

I shoved him good and hard one way and shoved the tiller in the other and he could deal with one but not with the other and he lost his balance. He grabbed for anything but I backed away and there was nothing to hold but air and he pitched off the side. You'd think a bastard like him would have come back up out of the water like *Jaws* or something, but then again, he'd said something about not being able to swim.

I stuck around, circling the boat near where he'd gone in, just to make sure he didn't get another chance at doing to his kids what I'd just done to him.

DECEPTION

PATRICIA MARIE WARREN

"Jules, I didn't take no money out of your till. I promise you on my sweet momma's grave. Ya gotta believe me."

George Laron looked everywhere but into my eyes. He shifted on the stool, scanned the tables then hunched his shoulders, making himself smaller. Maybe he'd caught sight of Oak Island Police Detective Craig Kearny sipping his coffee and reading the newspaper. "Jules, you believe me, don't ya?"

"George, we both know your momma ain't sweet or dead. She's sitting up in Raleigh at the Women's Correctional Institute for putting a knife in her boyfriend's belly."

I felt Craig walk to the counter. Every nerve in my body started tingling. I closed my eyes and relished the memory of his large hands grabbing my shoulders last night as he pulled me to his chest and kissed me goodnight. I couldn't help running my fingers over my lips.

"Can I help out here, Juliet?" His baritone voice poured through me like warm honey.

"No, thanks, Detective. I've got this handled, don't I, George? He and I are going into the office and look at yesterday's video recording from my new security camera."

"Naw, Jules. We don't need to do that. I gotta get home and feed Momma's dog. I ain't gonna be able to do my shift this afternoon." He pushed his coffee mug across the counter. Peeking from under it was a stack of green paper. He slid off the stool and tucked his chin into his chest as he passed Craig. I picked up the money and counted: one hundred dollars in tens and twenties.

Craig said, "You're going to need a new busboy. Got anyone in mind?"

"It's almost summer. I have a bunch of applications from high school kids looking for work during the season." I didn't mention how overwhelmed I felt at yet another problem… or that having him in my life was the only thing keeping me from running away from this restaurant and the overwhelming responsibilities at home. My cell phone buzzed in my pocket. I pulled it out and looked at the screen. "Sorry, I've got to take this. It's Maria."

Craig's hand covered mine for a second. "I'll see you tonight." He stared into my eyes, his look and touch setting my pulse racing. He winked then walked away. I watched his long legs eat up the space between the counter and the door. When the door closed behind him, I felt like a starving woman. Seven-thirty couldn't come soon enough. The phone in my hand buzzed again.

"Hello."

"Juliet, you have to get home. Lonnie locked me out of the house."

"What were you doing outside without him?" Maria was my housekeeper and daycare provider for my autistic brother.

"He was making a lot of noise and I was on the phone with my sister. I stepped out so I could hear her."

I scanned the cafe and waved Kim over.

"I walked to work," I told Maria. "I'll see if I can borrow a car. Be there in five minutes."

Kim finished refilling a customer's coffee and came up to me.

"What's up, Jules?"

"Can you manage the cash register and your tables while I go home for a bit?"

"Yeah, no prob."

I went into the kitchen.

"Buddy, may I borrow your car? Lonnie locked Maria out of the house."

"Sure, Jules. I ain't gotta be nowhere but right here till after the lunch crowd clears out." He unhooked a wad of keys from his belt and handed them to me. "It's the big one in the middle."

"Thanks. See you in a few minutes." I looked at the clock over the door. Nine fifteen. "The early risers are about cleared out. Should be quiet for an hour or so."

"No worries. Me and the girls can handle things."

"I know you can. You guys are priceless. I couldn't run this place without you."

He grinned. "That's for sure."

* * * *

Maria wasn't out front when I pulled up to our A-frame beach house. The rusted hinges on the porch door screeched in protest when I pulled it open. I crossed to the front door, sidestepping a cracked deck board.

I unlocked the front door and walked into the foyer. "Lonnie? Why did you lock Maria outside?"

I went through the living room to the sleeping porch on the back. My brother had been painting in there when I left for work.

"Lonnie, we talked about answering people when they are speaking to you." No response. Strange. One of Lonnie's habits was to recite the list of rules—as he called them—given by his behavioral therapist. The only thing I heard was a soft, rhythmic thumping coming from my office.

"You know you aren't supposed to be in my office." The door was partially open. I pushed it all the way. The blinds were shut and curtains drawn. It was dim since the sun was still on the beach side of the house. I walked to the desk to turn on the lamp, my foot slipping on some papers as I leaned to it. Annoyance welled up in me as I pulled the chain on the lamp.

The neat stacks of folders on my desk were now all over the floor and what few remained on the desk were no longer stacked. They were covered in bright red liquid and the unmoving body of Ed Spiro, my former boyfriend. Ed's eyes stared straight at me. I smelled the familiar scent of dirty, old pennies.

My annoyance turned to horror. "Lonnie! Lonnie! Where are you?"

My screams nearly drowned out the sound of the thumping coming from the other side of the desk. I hurried around it.

Lonnie was cradling my pink pearl-handled Targus .38 revolver as he sat rocking back and forth, knocking his head against the wall and whispering to himself.

"Oh, Lonnie, honey. What happened?"

I knelt beside him, careful not to get in front of the gun. I slid my hand across his arm and placed it over the revolver. "Let me put the gun away, sweetie. Why don't we go to the kitchen for a drink of water?"

His hands went limp and he dropped his head against my shoulder. I took the gun and pushed the safety on. A hiccup interrupted his chant, but he didn't stop.

I could just make out his words. "Don't go in Juliet's office. Don't touch the stuff in Juliet's desk. No, bobo. I don't want it."

I held him against me. After a minute, he let me help him to his feet and lead him out of the room. I closed the door and put the gun in my waistband.

Lonnie went straight to the kitchen sink and washed his hands, three times as usual. Then he sat at the breakfast bar. I poured a glass of water and set it in front of him.

"Thank you, Juliet."

"You're welcome, Lonnie."

My brain was racing frantically. *What am I supposed to do? I can't let them take my baby brother away. Why is Ed here? Oh, God! Lonnie shot Ed.*

"Lonnie, why did you lock Maria outside?" His reply was a sob.

A dishtowel lay on the counter beside the sink. I squashed the protest in my mind, pulled the gun out of my waistband, wrapped the towel around it, and started rubbing. When I finished, I placed my right hand around the grip and my index finger on the trigger as I put it on top of the refrigerator. Then I called Craig.

"Hey, beautiful. It's been fifteen minutes. Miss me already?"

"Craig, Ed is here... in my house. He's dead. Can you come?"

"What do you mean, dead? Are you sure?"

"He's been shot. Can you please hurry?"

"Did you call 911?"

"N-n-no. I couldn't think...." My heart was beating so fast I could barely breathe.

"I'll call them. I'm coming right now. Stay calm and don't touch anything."

I hit the end button on my phone. Wiping the gun down started me down a path with only one outcome. I needed to think it through before Craig and the other cops got here. There were sure to be plenty show up. After all, Ed was one of their own.

* * * *

Lonnie wandered out to the sleeping porch to his easel. I watched as he picked up a brush then squeezed a glob of red oil paint onto his palette. He swirled the brush in it then slashed at his soft blue and green ocean scene with bold strokes. I should call his therapist to help with the awful things to come, but I could already hear sirens approaching the house. Furious banging on the back glass door startled me. Maria was gesturing to the knob. I let her in. I stood in the doorway staring at the ocean fighting the urge to run down the boardwalk and never look back.

"I've been knocking and knocking. You didn't even look up. Are you angry with me?"

Yes, I was very angry with her. She left Lonnie to face Ed alone. Ed had grown increasingly belligerent since I'd started seeing Craig. It's what first prompted me to ask Craig to walk me home.

I ignored Maria's question. "The police are on their way here. Ed Spiro is in my office. He's dead." I couldn't shake the image of his dead eyes looking at me.

Maria's face went white. "No! I didn't... I never thought...." She shook her head violently. She crossed herself and backed away toward the door to the living room. Her lips moved quickly but silently.

"You need to stay here. The police will want to talk to you."

"I was outside at the end of the boardwalk. I don't know anything. I didn't see anything."

"That's okay. Tell them that."

Car doors slammed outside. I went through the living room to the entry, pulled the door open, and backed up until my legs bumped the console table beside the staircase.

Craig was first into the house. His dark eyes were unreadable, his jaw tight. He put a hand on my arm for the briefest moment then pulled it back when the EMTs and other officers came in.

Craig said, "Juliet, where is Ed?"

"In my office."

"Did you touch anything?"

Trying to remain calm, I stuffed my hands in my back pockets to still their shaking. If I told him what I saw, they would take Lonnie into custody. They might lock him up in an institution. Panic welled up in my throat. I couldn't let that happen. I focused on the scuffed wood floor at my feet.

"The gun... I... I shot him." My voice barely rasped out.

"You did what?"

Swallowing the lump in my throat, I tried again, my voice firmer now that I'd decided to go with my story. "I shot him."

"Where is the gun, Ms. Reese?" Detective Rhea Colson's voice was flat.

"On top of the refrigerator."

Detective Colson walked toward the kitchen.

Craig said, "Juliet, stay here."

My legs felt like rubber. I locked my knees to keep from collapsing. The weight of my lie settled heavily on me. Craig and two uniformed officers went ahead of the EMTs to the door of my office.

He called back to me, "Why did you close the door?"

I could be honest this time. "Lonnie was upset." He didn't question that reason. No one who had been around Lonnie when he was upset would. His behavior could escalate from mildly anxious to over-the-top raging fits and hurting himself in a few moments.

Detective Colson came back to me, holding a bag with my gun in it. "Where is Lonnie?"

"Out on the porch with Maria."

She nodded to the two officers. One of them went to the porch. One of them came back to the entry and stood next to me. She went toward the office.

I dared a look at Craig. He faced the now-open office door with a camera in his hand, his shoulders slumped. I hated that I had to choose between protecting my brother and deceiving the man I had fallen in love with. The full implications of my deception took my breath away. *What will happen to Lonnie if they put me in jail?*

Detective Colson stood next to him, speaking too softly for me to hear. The front door opened, admitting two more people. I recognized the woman, Dr. Karen Trace, the county coroner. I met her two years ago when I had to identify my mother after a drunk driver killed her and my stepfather. Craig and Detective Colson stood aside for them to enter the office that had been the master bedroom when my parents lived here. Craig handed the camera to Detective Colson and she followed Dr. Trace into the room. Craig stood outside the door watching.

After fifteen minutes, Detective Colson came back out and gestured to me. "Let's go sit in the living room. I need you to tell me exactly what happened."

I pushed off the console, walked past her, and sat stiff-backed on the sofa. I braced my heels against the frame so I could balance on my toes in case I needed to run. I almost laughed at the thought of running. How far would I get dragging Lonnie with me? Detective Colson sat on the chair next to me and took a notebook out of her jacket pocket. Nothing in her demeanor hinted that we had been on friendly terms prior to today.

I didn't volunteer any information, so she spoke up. "Ms. Reese, we have a dead man in your office. You say you shot him. I need to understand exactly what happened here today."

"Maria called me at the cafe because Lonnie locked her out of the house."

"When did Officer Spiro arrive?"

I hadn't thought through a timeline. "I'm not sure."

"What was your relationship to Officer Spiro?"

"We dated for a while last year."

"Who broke it off?"

"I did."

"Why was that, Ms. Reese?"

The question should be why did I go out with him in the first place? Ed's boyish good looks had masked a jealous, controlling man. Why hadn't I seen that from the beginning? He was like my stepfather. Like Frank, my nasty stepbrother. I shuddered, nauseated by ugly memories.

I rubbed the decade-old knife scar on my right hand. Something Lonnie said when I found him reminded me of the day I got it. I replayed his words. What was familiar?

"Ms. Reese, you need to answer my question."

"What?" If she'd leave me alone for a minute, I might figure things out.

"Why did you end your relationship with Ed Spiro?"

"Oh. Things didn't work out between us."

"Were you intimate?"

"Why do you want to know that? It's none of your business."

Her eyes narrowed. "This is a homicide investigation, Ms. Reese. Everything about your connection with the deceased is my business."

Homicide. Even though I knew that homicide didn't necessarily mean murder, the word terrified me. My lie was burying me.

"No. We were *not* intimate."

* * * *

More people filed into the house. The cop at the door pointed to Detective Colson. She jerked her head and the newcomers went past us to the back porch. *I should have told Lonnie he didn't have to talk to anyone. Should have reassured him that no one would hurt him.*

"Stranger danger! Stranger danger! Ahhhh! Juliet!" Crashing sounds mixed with Lonnie's shrill screams. He ran through the door. The cop standing there grabbed his arm. Lonnie tore at the man's hand, his eyes flipping wildly around the room.

I jumped up from the sofa. "Let him go! You don't understand. He doesn't know you. You're frightening him!"

Craig's voice rang out above mine, "Perkins, it's okay. Let him go."

Lonnie ran to me. I wrapped my arms around him. When his panicked sobs subsided, I led him to the sofa.

"Sit with me, sweetie." Everyone stood silent, watching.

Lonnie sat perfectly in the middle of the center sofa cushion. I don't know why I let the horror of finding Ed's body blind me to the fact that Lonnie was always accurate. He never said anything that wasn't necessary to explain himself or to reassure himself of his routine. I replayed his chant from earlier.

"Ms. Reese, come to the kitchen with me." Detective Colson stood up.

"But Lonnie is scared. He needs me."

"I'll stay with him." Craig didn't look at me. "Hey, Sport, will you tell me what happened today? It's alright to talk to me, isn't it, Juliet? I'm not a stranger, am I?"

I moved so Craig could take my place on the sofa.

"Lonnie, I need you to tell Craig who was in the house this morning. Can you do that for me?" I had to let him decide whether to talk or not. His quivering hands let me know he was close to a meltdown. I didn't want to push him and trigger his habit of punching himself on the cheek or the nose. The lifelong behavior when extremely agitated showed in bruises on his cheekbones and a flattened nose.

He started speaking as I walked ahead of Detective Colson to the kitchen.

"Juliet woke me up. Juliet gave me my clothes. Juliet went to work. Maria made me breakfast. Maria went outside."

He paused and inhaled deeply, his exhale ending with a hiccup. His voice rose in pitch, his body trembling as he continued in his flat recitation.

"Ed came to the back porch. Ed said what's-up-dummy. Ed locked the door. Ed said go-to-your-room-Lonnie. Bobo said what-the-hell-Ed-what-is-he-doing-in-here. Bobo grabbed my arm. Bobo went into Juliet's office. Bobo said sit-down-now. Bobo said where-is-the-damn-bank-paperwork."

Lonnie put his hands over his ears, rocking back and forth, mewing softly now. "Don't, Ed, that's Juliet's special drawer. Ed said are-you-scared-dummy. Bobo said don't-wave-that-thing-around-give-it-to-me."

Lonnie jerked around and looked at me with wide frightened eyes. "I don't like the bang, Juliet. I don't like the yelling."

"It's okay, Sport. No one's going to hurt you." Craig's voice seemed to calm him down. Lonnie settled back into the cushion, self-soothing by rocking back and forth.

Maria tried to brush past the officer standing at the porch door. She was holding out an envelope. The officer held her arm and took the envelope by a corner.

"What is this?" Detective Colson asked. She walked to Maria, blocking my view.

"That Ed Spiro came 'round this morning. He gave me this. Told me if I left the doors unlocked and made myself scarce for an hour, there would be another one like it waiting in my purse when I came back in. I didn't want to do it, but that there's five hundred dollars." She leaned around Detective Colson and looked at me, seeming to want reassurance. "You know my car needs a transmission." She smothered a sob with the back of her hand.

"What time was that?" Detective Colson asked her.

"I think around seven-thirty or so."

"Stay here," she told Maria. Detective Colson walked to the office carrying the envelope.

I looked from Maria to Lonnie to the office, trying desperately to make sense of everything I'd heard. It slowly dawned on me why my office had been ransacked.

Craig joined Detective Colson, and Dr. Trace next to the office doorway. They tilted their heads in to keep their conversation private. I cleared my throat. They all turned to watch me as I approached.

"Craig, may I speak to you?"

Dr. Trace spoke first. "Ms. Reese, what time did you arrive home?"

"About nine twenty-five."

She nodded. "I'm finished here, detectives. If you have all the pictures you need, I'll take the body now. I'll schedule the autopsy for this afternoon."

Craig nodded to her then looked at me expectantly. I couldn't gauge his emotions by his expression. I wished he would say something.

Detective Colson spoke up instead. "Why did you lie about shooting Officer Spiro?"

"W... w... what do you mean?" Her abrupt question stopped me in my tracks. It's what I had wanted to tell Craig.

"Dr. Trace said Spiro's blood appears to have been congealing for a couple hours. What time did you arrive at the Isle Cafe?"

"Six-thirty, but..."

"Can anyone confirm when you got there?"

"Buddy Harris, the chef. He always gets there before me."

"Where did you find the gun, Ms. Reese?" She wouldn't stop with the questions. I needed to tell them what I thought happened. Time was running out. If they didn't hurry, Ed's real killer would get away.

"Lonnie had it. But I know who did it. Let me explain."

Craig spoke up. "Who is Bobo?"

"That's what Lonnie always called our stepbrother. It was his word for brother. Bobo is Frank Bates."

"Why would Bates be in your house this morning?" Detective Colson asked without looking up from writing in her notebook.

"He threatened to take me to court over custody of Lonnie. But it's all a big deception. He doesn't want to take care of Lonnie. He wants Lonnie's share of the settlement money from the insurance company after our parents died." I looked from one to the other. Didn't they get it?

"Craig, please! Look in my office safe behind the picture of my mother. See if Frank got the court papers. There should also be a thumb drive in there with all the hateful messages he left in my voice mail." I gave them the combination.

"Colson, you go look."

I didn't watch her go into the office. I smelled the copper scent of blood again. My stomach clenched. Now that the adrenaline rush was over, my strength slowly faded away. Black spots danced around my peripheral vision. My knees buckled. Before I could fall, Craig's arms wrapped around me. He guided me to the closest chair. I sat leaning forward with my elbows on my knees, head in my hands, eyes closed.

Detective Colson's voice rang out from the office. "Kearny, I have the papers and thumb drive. Looks like someone tried to pry open the safe. There are scratch marks all over it."

Craig's voice sounded far away. "Perkins and Nelson, find this guy."

"Sure thing, Detective."

I didn't know which officer replied to him. I heard brisk footsteps crossing the living room to the front door.

"You shouldn't have lied to me, Juliet." Craig's breath breezed over my temple.

I opened my eyes. His face was level with mine as he squatted in front of me.

"I know. I was so frightened when I saw Lonnie holding my gun that I could only think of protecting him. It's my job to take care him."

"We will find Frank Bates." He put his hand on my cheek, sliding his thumb over my lips. "It's going to be fine. You're a good sister. It's one of the things I love about you." He replaced his thumb with his lips in a feathery kiss before standing back up.

"Okay, officers, we have a cop-killer to find."

* * * *

The sunset on the ocean was soothing my tired mind. Lonnie and I sat on the porch swing slowly swaying back and forth.

"I love you, Juliet."

"I love you, too, Lonnie."

"I love Craig."

"Me too, sweetie."

"Can he stay here to keep the bad guys away?"

"Well…" Where had he gotten that idea?

A voice from the steps spoke for me. "I think that sounds like a fine idea, Sport." Craig mouthed to me, "We got him."

He joined us on the swing and placed his hand over mine. "What about it, Juliet? Am I staying?"

Finally able to fully relax, I laid my head on his shoulder. "Yes, Detective, I think you are."

SLEEPING IN

TONI GOODYEAR

I lay, unmoving, on Charlie's cheap foam mattress, the kind that shapes itself to your backside, your heels, your elbows, that wraps you up like half a mummy and forces you to keep still. I'd told him over and over that I hated this smotherer, this sink hole. I liked my mattresses hard, but Charlie never cared too much about what I liked and didn't like.

If he was here this morning he'd already have had me up, yanking me to my feet. "Get goin', woman, plenty of time to sleep when you're dead." He thought he was witty as hell every time he said that. For thirty-two years, he'd thought he was the wittiest person in the room.

But this was a day without Charlie, and I'd be the one to decide when to rouse. I could count on one hand the number of times I'd gotten to sleep in. His mattress seemed to tip the scale in favor of staying put, which served him right. Next week I'd go buy a grand new bed and a new coverlet, too, and Charlie could go straight to hell....

I inhaled, letting that thought hover in my mind. Maybe it wasn't right to tell a man you'd just killed to go to hell, not now that it could really happen, might've already happened if you believed that sort of thing. Charlie and I had been raised in the Christian South; somewhere deep down where his mother's tit forever dangled he'd never stopped worrying that hell might really exist. "That's the natural way things are, Charles," she would tell the top of his hang-dog head. So Charlie had always looked at religion over his shoulder, like it was something that might be gaining on him, even while making sure none of the other men ever caught him looking, nor any of the occasional hookers either. Not even that Spandexed redhead over toward Charlotte, the one he'd met on one of those damn fishing trips with Joe Warren, our neighbor next farm over and Charlie's best friend. I knew there wasn't much meaning to them, those five or six weekends a year of tribal debauchery, doing things that made men feel like men. I'd heard Joe talking about it once and Charlie grunting his agreement that the fishing trips were like generators— they cranked enough energy to keep husbands being husbands, fathers being fathers. Somewhere in the heart of all farming men lived a fear of the static earth that would one day swallow them.

I tasted the tang of bitter smile at the corner of my mouth as I thought that. I could feel sympathy for that part of it, at least. Maybe some sliver of me didn't really want Charlie to burn *forever* in hell, maybe just some holding place where he'd get pushed around hard for, say, thirty-two years, with no chance of having anything his own way. No soft mattresses, no sir, you'll get one hard as slate. And none to those damn chili peppers and trial tomatoes that took up all the space in the greenhouse and left no room for your wife's herbs and seedlings, never any room at all. Now you'll be covered in sage and thyme. Now you'll get nothing but smooth ceilings to stare at, Charlie, none of that tacky stippled crap your wife endured all those years when you wouldn't let her take it down. Now you'll plant beds of worthless flowers, money pits brimming with purples, reds, yellows, and stripes, frivolous things that do nothing but call the butterflies. You'll do it for no reason other than the shine it puts in a woman's eyes.

Too bad you forgot about that part, Charlie, the shining part. I remembered him now and again, that boy I'd made up my mind in school to marry, the one who could take me down with a glance or a song when he held his beaten up old guitar or his lap harp. His dark hair had hung to his eyes, eyes so blue you thought maybe an angel had kissed him and turned them the color of sky. Then sometimes those eyes would darken to smoky gray and the muscles in his arms would tighten and he'd press me to him. The first time my inexperienced body felt him on me there was no turning back. I didn't know then that passion, like sweet cream, curdled if not kept fresh. Too bad about that part, too.

I guessed most things between us had lived in that category of too bad. Now I'd have that room I'd wanted for fifteen years, a sun room where I could take my diary and poetry books and the small stereo that had continued to work from the time I was a girl. I'd change that damn sofa in the living room too, that flowery piece from his Aunt Louella that had bulges of fabric knots right where your hips met their comfort. I might even decide to do something really crazy, like raise emus for the hell of it, or maybe start a sanctuary for all the animals that tore at my heart, the ones Charlie had always said weren't worth wasting money on. I could do whatever I wanted.

I could even decide not to get up for the planting of Charlie.

"Martha Lee, you need to get yourself up now."

It was my mother, talking before she saw me, coming up the stairs yakking like she always did.

"You need to get up, honey girl. Put some clothes on. It's not good to stew alone, you need to be among people."

"I don't think I'm getting up today," I said quietly, looking her straight in the eye as she reached the foot of Charlie's bed.

She started to speak again, then stopped. I could see that the younger me had popped into her head, the girl who'd insisted on marrying Charlie no matter how many times she'd warned me he had no room in his heart for a woman. I'd had no trouble staying headstrong in those days. Stubbornness grew down through my toes, anchoring me to the earth like a tap root. I knew she was remembering same as I was how she'd tried to channel that strength in better ways, like the time I'd thought I wanted to dance the ballet, or maybe go to school to become an architect. "Then it's time to hitch up your britches and go after what you want, Martha Lee," she'd tell me, taking my chin in her hand. And my grandfather would lean over with a mischievous grin and whisper, "Shit or get off the pot, Martha Lee," and then he'd slap his knee and howl like it was a special, hilarious truth between us.

But all I'd wanted, finally, was Charlie.

After we were married, Charlie mocked me with my family's words. Whenever I'd threatened to leave or take a stand on something he'd give a nasty little laugh and say, "Time to bleep or get off the pot, Martha Lee," then turn his back to me. Somehow he'd known from the outset that all I'd ever do was bleep.

Only, as it turned out, he was wrong.

It had been ridiculously easy. He had climbed that thirty-foot ladder an idiot's way so many times, propping it against the edge of our high old roof, unroped, no harness despite Joe Warren having gifted him one long ago, telling him to quit being a damn fool and use it. Against the house right below that spot was an old greenhouse, clear glass full of metal stakes inside for the training of vegetables. A single shove of the ladder was all it took. The fall shattered Charlie along with the glass and nailed his chest to a tomato stake. He was gone in an instant.

I'd crushed a couple of the oxys Doc Adams had given me for back pain into Charlie's oatmeal before he'd gone out, mixed them right in with his favorite brown sugar and peaches cut up. Charlie never took oxys, they made him slow, so when the time came to push I'd gotten no resistance, no desperate grab that might've left him hanging from the roof still alive.

Nobody thought an autopsy was necessary, not Doc Adams or Sheriff Bryce. Everyone knew Charlie would kill himself on that ladder someday. He'd almost done it twice before, once when he was trying to trim the big sycamore down near the river, but he'd caught a lower branch as he fell and got off with torn muscles and a broken arm. Another time his foot slipped when he was painting the barn but he was lucky again and fell onto the load of sand they'd brought up to bank the swollen creek. And, anyway, there was no reason for foul play in this marriage, everyone knew. Charlie and Martha Lee were salt of the earth.

He'd been off in the fields the day I'd torn up the shingles at just the right spot to land him on the greenhouse. Then I waited for him to find the problem—in a way you could say I was leaving it to fate. On Saturday, he said he had to fix the roof there because the shingles had gotten damaged and rain would be coming through. I'd offered to help but he'd smirked and said I'd just botch it, I was so stupid about things, it was always up to him to do a thing right.

Pushing that ladder over was like freeing a log jam.

"Folks are waiting for you downstairs," my mother said. "The cars will be here soon. We need to be at the church in an hour."

I held her glance. "I know you heard me. I said I'm not going."

She cocked her head. Unlike the rest of the county, she knew full well that it hadn't been peaches between Charlie and me. She had to suspect that a part of me was at least halfway relieved this had happened. Still, there were the proprieties.

"He was your husband, Martha Lee. What do you expect me to tell people?"

I closed my eyes. "Tell them I'm overcome, that I don't know how I can go on without Charlie. They'll understand, I'm not the first widow in this county who couldn't manage the funeral. Tell them I'll try to come down later, after the burial."

People didn't care, not really, they just wanted drama, blood spilling over the floor like someone had ruptured a colon, circuses that passed for feelings. No husbands were ever hated on death day, nor no wives either. Lies were the only things alive on death days.

She looked at me a moment longer. She knew I was right, people would believe. She gave a final sniff of disapproval, then turned and left without another word.

In a while I heard the cars arriving. I heard the hubbub, my sister Vera's ridiculous laugh that sounded like a sick cat, and Uncle Will's hacking cough that would soon take him from us. I'd always liked Uncle Will; maybe in heaven he could get word of where they'd stuck Charlie and come back long enough to let me know, just for the curiosity of it. I heard more people arrive, doors slam.

A few minutes later my daughter Helene stood before me.

Our only child, married now, she'd always been a good girl, the kind who'd worshipped the ground her daddy walked on, who believed that whatever was wrong in our household had to be because of me. I'd never blamed her, I knew Charlie too well.

"If you don't get up, I'll know it was true all along," she said to goad me. "I'll know it was just like he said, that you were cold and unloving toward him...."

"And hateful," I added softly. "Don't forget that, the part about the anger. Remember? Full of hate and rage. He said I had them in me like genes or infections. That was his word, infections."

Her lower lip quivered. "Please, Mama. Get up."

She could always make that lower lip quiver when she wanted to, from the time she was five. Still, my heart clenched. "You go on down and take care of things, little girl. Leave your sad mother alone."

She narrowed her eyes at me, but there was nowhere for her to go. She'd have to live with the truth of it, that there was no sad mother here. Still, I allowed myself a small twinge of hope. Maybe now, with Charlie gone, Helene could learn to see *me*. Maybe, with time, we could find our own place to stand.

She hesitated, then switched to that rational tone nurses use when they're trying to deal with difficult patients. "Grandma and Joe Warren and I are here to help you get through this, Mama. Grandma's got all the food arranged afterwards, and Joe says to tell you if you don't come down he'll come up and get you himself."

And then she was gone.

I knew that if Joe Warren said he was coming up, he'd do it. I figured he'd be right along, so I struggled up out of my foam prison, put on my robe, and moved to the little sitting area at the opposite side of the room. I sat in Charlie's raggedy old armchair, a relic I'd soon be replacing with a new chaise longue, and looked out the window at the farm.

Five minutes later Joe showed up, carrying a mug of coffee. He looked almost dapper in his black funeral suit, the one with the sleeves just a tad long, and a plain navy tie. His face was leathery from the sun but he looked more like forties than fifties, a strong, striding man.

"Here you go," he said, handing me the mug. "Strong and black, just how you like it."

"It was how Charlie liked it," I said, setting it down on the side table. "I prefer fresh cream but Charlie always said that was foolish nonsense."

Joe said nothing, just stood looking down at me, his eyes dark. "You better drink it anyway, Martha Lee. I think you're gonna need it."

I made no answer to that, though the hairs on my arms raised up like antennae at his tone. He looked around, then dragged a straight back chair from along the wall and sat opposite me. We were practically eye to eye.

"There's something you have to understand," he said. "I know what you did to Charlie. I was coming up from my place to borrow back my hacksaw and I saw it all. I saw you push that ladder. I saw you stand there by that ruin of a greenhouse with Charlie all cut up and stuck like a pig. And I saw you spit, Martha Lee. I saw you spit toward your dead husband before you went into the house to call."

My mind raced back to the day. The woods between our farms came close to the house at that point; it was the usual path to Joe's place. What he said was possible. And it was true—I did spit.

"It was an accident—" I said.

He put his hand up. "Don't even bother with that. Don't even try."

The set of his jaw made it clear there was no further point. I gave it up and sat back as the silence lengthened. Now that the truth was out, my body felt oddly calm.

"I'm surprised," I said, holding his gaze. "You didn't even try to help him."

He shifted slightly in his seat. "Any fool could see he was gone. When you went into the house I took a good look. It wasn't pretty."

I knew the truth of it, of course. Joe had always coveted this spread that met up with his. If he could get his hands on it, it would more than double his holding, make him a man of substance here in the county.

I shook my head. "That's not how people act, Joe. Charlie was your friend. How come you didn't come running?"

His eyebrows arched together into one dark swath and he leaned toward me, looming. "You quit your jabbering about nonsense, Martha Lee, and listen to me carefully while I tell you how it's going to be."

I held my tongue and listened.

"First, you're going to put on your widow's weeds and come downstairs so your mama and I can hold you up during Charlie's service. You're gonna weep and wail and make it look real good. Then, in a few months, you're gonna let folks know it's just too painful to live here without Charlie so you've decided to accept my generous offer for the farm."

"This is my home," I said.

"Well, it's mine now."

"It should go to my daughter."

"She'll have no use for it. It's better off with me."

I studied him for a long moment. "It's your word against mine. What makes you think people will believe you?"

"You're not the only one that's lived here all their life, Martha Lee. I'll tell everyone what I saw, make a big fuss. The story'll grow, and even if it turns out the law can't touch you it'll be like Lizzy Borden for the rest of your life. Everyone will know the truth, that you're a murderer who got away with it. In the end, the law won't matter at all."

What he said was true. His words would climb and claw like thorny vines that had no natural predators, until, finally, they'd strangle my life. I wondered if the suspicions he could raise would give reason for an autopsy. Could they still tell about oxycodone? I didn't know. We didn't embalm Charlie, just put him in a sealed pine box like he wanted, but he'd spent four days in a freezer. Surely the drug would be out of him by now? Doc Adams knew Charlie would never take oxys.

I managed a sad half-smile. "Looks like I've got no choice, Joe. Guess I'll have to do what you tell me."

His lips narrowed to a grin. "Consider yourself lucky I'm only asking for the farm. Now drink your coffee and get dressed—and don't forget to bring along a few handkerchiefs for dear old Charlie."

He stood and looked down at me, challenging. I locked my glance to his as I raised the mug to my lips and took the sip he'd ordered me to take.

He smirked with satisfaction. "Good girl. I'll be waiting for you downstairs. You've got fifteen minutes."

I sat quietly after he left, letting the taste of the coffee fade away. Beyond the window, the farm—*my* farm—lay like a promise in the clear morning light, rows of green and yellow swaying gently in the breeze. The day was too perfect for threats. The rumpled sheets on the bed behind me reflected in the glass, beckoning.

I set the mug down, and stood. There would be other mornings to sleep in.

My widow's weeds were there in the closet, the black dress and shoes I kept for funerals. For Charlie, I'd add my black lace scarf with the single gold thread on the trim and hold it in place with the family cameo he'd given me before we were married. That should look loving and widow-like.

The future would be simple enough. Everyone knew Joe Warren was a daredevil with that tractor of his, always driving the muddy slopes too close to the river, perching on the hillside at ridiculous angles, riding in ways that defied gravity. Sheriff Bryce had told him more than once to quit mucking around, he'd be a sorry sight if that machine flipped over on him like he'd seen happen to the Williams boy, crushed him like a bug, or, worse yet, if it dragged him down the bank and under.

In my dresser were the handkerchiefs my mother had given me when I turned twenty-one—the age, she'd said, when every woman should come to know the feel of silk. They'd come from some far off corner of the Orient, a gentle pattern of lavender and rose, my initials delicately embroidered in one corner. Charlie'd always said they were as phony as a six-dollar bill, a point that certainly would be proven today, I thought with a smile. They would be perfect for the weeping.

I folded two of them into my little black purse and snapped the clasp.

I would be ready in fifteen minutes—just like Joe had told me to.

MIND OVER MANNERS

JIM JACKSON

The only things in his new classroom that looked familiar to Johnny Harrington were the American flag and the picture of President Eisenhower. When the teacher called his name, he popped out of his assigned seat, stood at attention, and drawled, "Present, ma'am." His classmates exploded into giggles and guffaws. The loudest laugh came from the boy who sat directly behind him—a kid Johnny recognized from his bus stop.

"Class." The teacher rapped on her desk to gain attention. The children settled into whispered titters, leaving Johnny red-faced and ramrod straight. Mrs. Wright glared over glasses perched on her nose. "I expect fourth-graders to have better manners. Please welcome Johnny. He's just moved here from…?"

"Georgia, ma'am. Savannah, Georgia." Behind him he heard whispered attempts to match his accent.

"With that tan you have," the teacher said, "I'll bet it's still warm there?"

He considered the question carefully. He desperately wanted to please her so she would give him permission to sit down. "Ah don't know, ma'am. Ah don't know what the weather is today at mah home— Ah mean where Ah used to live—Ah mean…" As her expression turned to a frown, another flush of heat warmed his face. The buzz of twenty-three students sounded like a nest of hornets he had disturbed with his presence.

The teacher clapped her disapproval. Johnny didn't care whether it was for his lousy answer or his misbehaving classmates. All he wanted was to disappear.

"Class, where are your manners? Different parts of the country speak with different accents and have different customs. If you ever move from upstate New York, do you want people to laugh at you because you speak through pinched noses? Of course you don't." The class quieted, and she continued. "We're fortunate we didn't have to waste time moving seats since Harrington fits alphabetically into the open spot right between Patricia Garagiola and Dan Izzo."

That statement caused the students to again burst into laughter, like there was some inside class joke.

"Everyone say hello to Johnny."

They parroted "Hello." The pig-tailed girl directly in front of him turned around. Through clenched teeth she said, "Don't even think of pulling my hair or poking me in the back." She and her pigtails spun into place.

"Patricia," the teacher said, "I'm sure anyone with Johnny's manners won't bother you. And Johnny, you don't need to call me ma'am. Mrs. Wright will do fine." She blinked twice and added, "You may sit down."

"Thank you, ma'am—Mrs. Wright."

* * * *

Johnny was pleased they had Phys. Ed. his first day and would be playing dodgeball, one of his favorite games. Knowing his below average height would count against him, he wasn't surprised that neither captain picked him until only he and an overweight, wheezy kid were left. Dan Izzo had the next turn. "I'll take Fatso," he said. Pointing at Johnny, he added, "You're stuck with Johnny Reb." Johnny took special pleasure in being the one to knock Dan out in three of the four games. The last time his captain even gave him an encouraging slap on the back.

They marched in alphabetical order back to the classroom. When no teacher was looking, Dan shoved Johnny in the back. Johnny whirled around to face his attacker, who stood at least ten inches taller than his four feet four inches. "I'll see you on the bus," Dan hissed.

Several times during the afternoon when Mrs. Wright was at the chalkboard, Dan jabbed Johnny in the back with a pencil. Fortunately, the point was dull and the pokes more annoying than painful. Johnny knew teachers never caught the kid who started things, so he ignored the provocations. It now made sense to him why there had been an empty seat between pig-tailed Patricia and Dan the pest.

Midway through the afternoon Johnny was called to the nurse's office to have his vision and hearing tested. He returned to find the class taking a math test. "Just do the best you can in the time left," Mrs. Wright said. "This is the last practice exam we'll have before the achievement test." He had covered the material in his old school and breezed through the questions.

When the end-of-school bell rang, he opened his desk and returned his pencil to the pencil case snapped into the three-ringed notebook with its five colored sections and fresh white paper. His ruler was missing from the inside pocket. He pulled out each textbook until the only things remaining in the desk were hardened bubble gum blobs and the Hardy Boys book he had brought to read on the bus. By now, the other students had already grabbed their jackets and left.

"Problem, Johnny?" Mrs. Wright asked.

"No, ma'am. Ah mean, no, Mrs. Wright." He removed *The Mystery of Cabin Island* and dropped everything else back into his desk. He grabbed the remaining coat from its peg and raced outside, adding himself to the back of the line for Bus 29.

"Hey, Johnny Reb," Dan Izzo called from partway down the bus aisle. "We saved you a seat." He pointed to the spot next to Fred, another classmate, who sat beside the open window.

Even if Johnny could push past Dan, the ruckus would only bring trouble with the driver. Maybe he could at least avoid being in the middle of those two. "You first," Johnny said.

Dan shook his head. "Good try," he said. "Lose your manners? I invited *you* first."

"Take your seats," the driver called.

Johnny sat. Dan plopped beside him, ramming his hip into Johnny's. Johnny pretended not to notice and opened *The Mystery of Cabin Island* to the folded page. With a lurch, the bus pulled forward. Fred yanked the book from his hand. "Whatcha reading, Reb?"

"Give it back." Johnny made a grab for the book, but Fred held it over his head and toward the window. Johnny leaned over Fred, who elbowed Johnny's chest. Dan applied a headlock to Johnny and gave him a noogie.

"Hey," Johnny exclaimed, "that hurts."

The bus screeched to a halt. The driver shouted, "Knock it off back there. Mr. Daniel Izzo, please take the seat of honor next to me. Mr. Fred Scarano and—I don't know your name, young man—move apart and keep your hands to yourselves."

"Just you wait," Dan said as he stood up. "I'll get you back for this."

The morning bus stop had consisted of Johnny, Dan, six younger children, and three older kids. Johnny figured that he could dodge past Dan while the bus was there, and then run all the way home. He snagged his book from a distracted Fred, slid over toward the aisle, and began reading.

Fred's stop was two before Johnny's. He shoved the book into Johnny's chest as he passed. *Good riddance,* Johnny thought. When Johnny's stop arrived he lined up at the rear door. A voice behind him said, "Where do you live?"

Over his shoulder Johnny saw a smiling older kid. They left the bus together. Johnny gave his new address, pleased he had remembered it. The kid, who sported a flattop just like Johnny's, indicated he lived halfway up the hill on the block before Johnny's. Noticing the book, he said, "Oh, the Hardy Boys. I've got 'em all. Let me know if you want to borrow any."

The two began walking toward home, chatting away about Frank and Joe Hardy. Johnny had forgotten all about Dan's threat until he heard Dan behind him. "Baby's got to have protection to walk home."

Both Johnny and the kid turned around. Before Johnny could think of a reply, his companion spoke, "Pick on someone your own age. Beating up little kids who didn't flunk a grade like you doesn't make you tough."

"Says who?" Dan's eyes narrowed and he clenched his fists at his waist.

The kid handed Johnny his rocket ship lunchbox and puffed out his chest. "Anytime you want."

"Two against one isn't fair," Dan said and walked away.

"I'm Phil." Johnny and Phil shook hands, and Phil continued. "Dan picks on people if they let him. When he starts something, just grab his shirt pocket and rip it off. He'll go home crying 'cause he knows his mother'll wup him. He's supposed to hand that shirt down to his little brother."

"Ah don't want to fight him."

"Won't be your choice, will it?" Phil split off, heading up the hill. Johnny hurried home in case Dan was lurking somewhere.

He followed the smell of fresh-baked chocolate chip cookies to the kitchen. "How was school?" his mother asked.

"Fine." He plucked three warm cookies from the cookie sheet and wolfed them down on the way to his room. Glad to have escaped an interrogation, he flopped on the bed, bouncing the headboard into the wall. Staring at the overhead acoustical tiles he replayed the day's events, flashing back to his stupid answer about Savannah weather, and then to Dan. His parents had told him he should find other ways than fisticuffs to solve his problems.

A rifle like Davy Crockett's "Betsy" would even his odds. But he didn't own one and that wasn't what his parents meant. He did own a pocketknife—not like old Jim Bowie's, but the gift from his grandfather had a three-inch blade. He removed it from the nightstand and lightly fingered his engraved initials. He opened the blade and sharpened it with a whetstone until it could cut a fine line on his fingernail. Then he clicked the blade closed. Opened and closed. Again and again.

Dan was waiting at the bus stop. "Here comes the idjit," Dan said. "You should have heard him. *Yes, ma'am.*" His attempted drawl wasn't close, but it got kids laughing. "And the Pledge of Allegiance? Ah pledge—" He couldn't continue for his own laughter.

Johnny kept his distance and read his book. When the bus arrived, he bent down and made a production out of tying a shoelace whose end he had purposely stepped on to loosen it. He dashed to the bus as the last person got on. Dan was midway back, so Johnny chose to sit near the front with two second graders. When the bus arrived at school, Johnny had a big enough head start that he had hung up his coat and sat at his desk before Dan and Fred arrived.

On the desk was a red folder with his name neatly printed on the tab. It contained his graded math test and some other papers. On top of the test was a circled 97 with EXCELLENT written underneath. "Excuse me, Patricia?" he said to the girl with two long braids who sat in front of him.

Her seat squealed when she swiveled to look at him over her shoulder. "The teacher calls me Patricia because we have another Patty in the class, but I like Patty better."

"What do we do with the red folder?"

"When Mrs. Wright returns our homework and stuff, she sticks it in the folder. Same thing when she hands out mimeoed assignments, like today's vocab and health homework. Every morning, we're supposed to stick our homework in there for her to pick up while she takes attendance."

He felt his stomach twitch. "We didn't have homework, did we?"

"Nah," she said and spun around, her pigtails twirling behind her.

"Thanks, Patty." Johnny placed the Hardy Boys mystery into his desk and looked again for the missing ruler. No luck. He studied the math test to understand his error. From behind him an arm snaked out and ripped the paper from his hand.

"Looks like Johnny Reb is a brown nose, too," Dan said in a low voice.

Johnny sprang out of his chair and grabbed for the test. Dan held it behind him for Fred to see.

Johnny squinted in anger. "Give it to me!"

"What's going on?" Mrs. Wright turned from the chalkboard.

"Johnny was bragging about how he was the smartest kid in the class," Dan said and tossed the paper at Johnny's head.

"Ah did not," Johnny proclaimed.

Mrs. Wright placed her hands on her hips. "Daniel, what have we discussed?"

The opening bell drove everyone to their seats.

Mrs. Wright nodded approval. "While I take attendance, study your vocabulary and then we'll practice our new words out loud."

Great, Johnny thought, *another excuse for everyone to laugh at me.*

* * * *

Johnny completed his health homework on the bus ride home. He should have used a pencil because his answers on the mimeographed sheet illustrating the circulation system had a couple of extraneous lines from when the bus hit potholes. At least he was free to enjoy the late October afternoon.

He jumped from the bus's bottom step. Dan ran over and knocked Johnny's notebook to the ground. Faster than a peregrine falcon swooping on a duck, Dan plucked the homework from the scattered pages.

Johnny stared daggers at Dan. "Hey! What—"

"Is for horses," Dan sneered. "I'll get it back to you before class."

"That's not fair," Johnny said. Fair came out as "feh-eh." He stepped toward Dan, raising clenched fists.

Dan held the paper behind his back. "Just try it, you little feh-ey."

Johnny trembled with anger. He wanted to hit Dan, to knock him down and crack his head. Instead he retrieved his now dirty notebook. His peacenik mother's admonitions to be a good boy and stay out of fights competed in his mind with Dan's laughter. His mother won. This time.

At home, his mother met him with cookies set out on the counter and the question, "How was school?"

"Fine." Johnny hid the soiled binder behind his back. He no longer felt like playing outside. "I think I'll go read." He flopped on his bed, careful to avoid rocking the headboard into the wall. This time he imagined various ways to extract revenge with his knife.

* * * *

"Ah forgot mah homework," Johnny said to Mrs. Wright as soon as he got to class. "If you have another copy, Ah can do it before class starts."

"Just this once," she said. "We expect our students to be responsible for their actions."

He raced through the assignment and tucked it into the red folder moments before the first bell rang.

That afternoon Dan accosted him as they got off the bus. "Give me your math homework."

"Ah finished it at school." Johnny turned his back and walked away.

Dan gave him a slap to the back of the head and grabbed Johnny's book. He flipped through the pages, muttered "no homework," and threw the book at Johnny's head.

Phil, the older kid, stepped off the bus. "Dan, scram. I hear your mother calling."

Johnny gathered the book from a mud puddle. He wanted to kill Dan for messing it up.

"Use your brains," Phil said, "and confront him when it's just you two. That way his friends can't pile on. It'll be less fun for him without an audience, and maybe he won't hit you as much."

Phil's advice did not make Johnny feel better—but back in his room, holding the knife surely did.

* * * *

The next day in gym, he was chosen second and his dodgeball team creamed the one with Dan and Fred. Twice he eliminated Dan by catching balls that Dan threw at him, and he knocked Fred out two other times. The euphoria disappeared while they were waiting in line and Dan grabbed his left forearm with both hands and gave Johnny an Indian rug burn. "That'll teach you, smarty pants."

"Hey. That hurts."

"There a problem over there?" Mrs. Wright called.

"No, ma'am," Johnny said.

"Right answer," Dan said under his breath.

Approaching his seat in class, Johnny had a clear view of Dan's desk. Talk about rotten luck having to sit in front of the big jerk. "Hey! That's mine!" Johnny rushed and grabbed his missing ruler.

"Get your grubby paws off that." Dan yanked it back.

The teacher silenced them both and took possession of the ruler. "We'll talk after school," she said and sent the class back to their seats with the reminder that today was the last day to brush up on their math before the big test tomorrow.

Mrs. Wright stood before them as the buzzer sounded and the remainder of the class left with backward glances at the drama. Johnny, waiting for the teacher to ask him a question, lost the initiative to Dan, who proclaimed that the ruler was his. He even had his name on the back. Mrs. Wright turned the ruler over. Carved into the wood with a Bic pen was a blue "Dan Izzo."

"Liar," Johnny said. "Mah mother bought that for me from the United Nations. It's made of different woods from…" In his fury he could not remember the country's name.

"New Zealand," Dan said. "See, he don't even know."

"Why haven't I seen this before, Daniel?" Mrs. Wright asked.

"I lost my other one. Had to bring this in." He held out his hand.

Mrs. Wright checked her watch and placed the ruler in Dan's hand "This will take more time than we have now. You boys need to catch your bus. We'll talk about this later." She stood at the door and watched them troop down the hall. As soon as they turned a corner, Dan said, "You owe me for that, you little snitch." Johnny walked faster, but Dan kept pace. "On the test tomorrow you're gonna slide your paper over where I can see it so I can copy your answers. Understand?"

"Yeah. You're a liar and a cheater."

Fred stayed on the bus past his stop and got off with Dan. They braced Johnny when he disembarked. "Hey, Reb," Fred said. "Don't look down."

Of course, Johnny did and saw Fred holding his pointer finger and thumb in a circle. "You saw the sign," Fred crowed. "Now I get to slug you."

"Those are the rules," Dan said, and before Johnny realized what was to happen, Fred slammed his fist into Johnny's left arm, almost causing him to drop his books. "You don't help Dan out on that test, and that'll feel good compared to what we'll do to you."

Johnny was determined not to cry, but once he got home he pounded his pillow. Two against one wasn't fair. And the teacher was against him. Even Phil hadn't interfered when Fred hit him. "Those are the rules," was all Phil said. "Don't look down next time."

Tomorrow was it. He could either give in, let Dan cheat, and then just try to stay out of his way, or he was going to get pounded. Maybe not at the bus stop, but he was sure Dan and Fred would catch him somewhere where they could do what they wanted.

He could convince his mother he was sick. Stomachaches were good for that. She couldn't disprove it. Of course, that would only put it off. He wasn't going to win with his fists, even if he did fight. The only way he was going to win was with the knife.

It could work—unless they wrestled it away from him before he could use it.

He begged off dinner, in case he wanted to use an upset stomach as an excuse for tomorrow. He couldn't go on living like this; he knew he had to make a decision. Too exhausted to even read, he fell asleep to the confused dream of Davy Crockett fighting river pirates at the Alamo.

* * * *

Johnny left his house at the normal time so his mother wouldn't get suspicious. He patted his front pocket. The knife was there. And he had a plan. He hid behind a leafless lilac bush and made a last minute sprint when the bus arrived. The driver saw him and kept the door open. Johnny dropped into the "loser's" seat in the front.

First off the bus at school, he raced inside and was sitting at his desk with his hands folded in front of him when Dan walked past, bumped his shoulder, and whispered, "You know what to do."

Johnny's neck and head ached. He closed his eyes and pictured Davy Crockett and Jim Bowie at the Alamo. They hadn't chickened out against a whole army. Of course, they had died.

Mrs. Wright took attendance and handed out the tests. "One hour," she said. "Ready? Start."

Johnny slowed himself down, checking his work as he went, making sure to completely fill in the ovals. He finished with fifteen minutes remaining and, seeing Mrs. Wright was not looking, he slid the paper to his left, leaned over the pad on his right, and pretended to work hard on a problem. When the teacher said pencils down, Johnny pulled the answer sheet back in front of him.

On the way to lunch, Dan followed Johnny into the bathroom.

"You saved yourself a beating today," Dan said. "I got you something to show my appreciation." He reached into his pocket. Naturally, Johnny looked. Dan pulled out his hand formed into the circle sign and said. "Ha! You saw it," and belted Johnny on the left arm.

Johnny couldn't help his eyes tearing up. He reached up, grabbed Dan's pocket, and yanked as hard as he could, ripping it nearly off and tearing a hole in the shirt. Dan started bawling like a baby.

Johnny didn't wait for Dan to recover. It was time to finish him off with the knife.

* * * *

As directed, Johnny sat on his hands in the chair before the principal's desk. Mrs. Wright sat beside him, knees together, hands clasped in her lap. The principal leaned in. "Tell me in your own words what happened, young man."

Johnny's hands shook even though he was sitting on them. His legs wouldn't be still either. It was like he was already in the electric chair. But when the principal used that stupid adult phrase, "in your own words," Johnny almost laughed.

"Dan's a bully. He sits behind me in class and pokes me with his pencil. He's at my bus stop, too. Ah can—I can show you the bruise on my arm where he hit me." He peeked at Mrs. Wright, but didn't get anything from her. The principal had crossed his arms and was glowering.

"He stole mah—my ruler, and my homework, and today he has my knife. And he told me to let him cheat on the math test or he'd beat me up."

"Why didn't you tell Mrs. Wright?" the principal asked.

"She didn't believe me when I told her Dan stole my ruler." He glanced at Mrs. Wright, but couldn't read her expression and rushed on. "So, I let him copy my answers. I knew he wouldn't get to the third column on his own, so he wouldn't discover that I moved all those answers by one. If the right answer was 'A' I marked it 'B.' 'E' became 'A.' I planned to tell Mrs. Wright at the closing bell." He turned to Mrs. Wright. "Did you check the papers?"

"Just tell us your story, young man," the principal said.

"When Dan hit me in the bathroom… well, my parents would kill me if I hit him back. But I had to do something, don't you see? So I ripped his shirt pocket."

"Why?" the principal asked.

"Ah—I knew we'd both get sent to your office, and that I could prove he cheats. Mrs. Wright knows I wouldn't get all the answers wrong on the last column, and Dan getting the same answers had to be cheating." Johnny again turned toward Mrs. Wright. "Did you find my knife?"

"I did believe you about the ruler, Johnny," Mrs. Wright said. "But with Dan's name on it, I didn't have time to resolve the issue. I hoped you would be able to deal with Dan on your own. Your knife was where you told me it would be." To the principal she said, "Dan denied ever having seen it before. It's engraved with Johnny's initials, JH, and was hidden in Dan's desk next to the disputed ruler. Dan definitely copied Johnny's answers." She patted Johnny's knee. "I don't condone Johnny's actions, but Dan has been a bully and he needs kids like Johnny to stand up to him. I think Johnny's going to fit in fine. Already his accent is fading along with his tan."

The principal sat back in his chair. "Johnny, do you have anything to add before I determine your punishment?"

"Yes, sir. I'd like to be called John."

TOYING WITH A FORTUNE

NICOLE MYERS

Yesterday, at a little after noon, I'd dropped my son off at his kindergarten class and stopped at an elderly neighbor's house. Mrs. Anderson had promised me a donation to Alcott Elementary's first annual rummage sale and silent auction fundraiser. After ringing the doorbell, I rubbed my hands together for warmth and pulled my pea coat tight. This was the coldest January I could remember and I'd lived in the Seattle area all my life. I rang the doorbell a second time and finally heard Mrs. Anderson fiddle with the deadbolt.

"Lucy," she said. She wore a polyester sweat suit in the style made popular by old ladies everywhere. "It's so good to see you again. Come in. Let me show you where the boxes are." Leaning on an ornately carved wooden cane, she led me through her house to the basement door.

"I'm so glad to be getting rid of them. I can barely move around down there." She swung a heavy wooden door open to reveal a dark pit.

I peered uneasily down into the hole. I've never been a fan of basements, and from my first view of it, the lower level of this circa 1900s bungalow would not be an exception. What I wouldn't do for my kids.

"Are you sure you want to go down there?" I asked.

"Of course I'm sure. I may not be a spring chicken, but I can still get around in my own house," she said, reaching in to flip the light switch. A bare light bulb dangling from the ceiling illuminated a set of steep wooden stairs. Clutching the railing, she picked her way down the steps. I followed behind her and kept a few stairs between us.

She wasn't kidding about the amount of stuff in the basement.

We threaded our way along a narrow path lined with canvas-covered furniture, rusty old tools, and faded floral luggage. She stopped in front of a row of boxes threatening to crowd out the harvest gold washer and dryer.

"Here they are," Mrs. Anderson said. "I'm not really sure what is in these anymore, but you are welcome to them for your school rummage sale."

I hadn't expected so many boxes. Mrs. Anderson noticed my surprise.

"I'm the last of my family. Most of these belonged to my father's best friend, or as we knew him, Uncle Henry. Because he didn't have room in his bachelor apartment, he stored them in the attic of our family's cabin at the lake. After my husband died, I sold the lake property and moved all the furnishings and boxes down here." She ran her finger under the packing tape to break the seal on the first box. "Uncle Henry was a salesman and always on the road. These are some of the things he collected in his travels."

"Didn't he have any family?"

"No, he never married. He died fairly young."

"What happened to him?" I asked.

"He was killed in a burglary at his apartment. The burglar must not have known he was home and Uncle Henry surprised him. They never did find who killed him." Mrs. Anderson gazed off in space for a few seconds before refocusing her attention. "Well, that was a very long time ago."

She removed several leather bound books from the cardboard box, placed them on top of the dryer, and opened another box. "My, this is pretty," she said as she unwrapped a beautiful glass vase painted with cherries. "I'm sure someone would want this."

I picked up a dusty book from the pile. I flipped open the cover carefully and read the copyright date—1850. Wide-eyed, I gingerly replaced it.

"Mrs. Anderson. These might be antiques. Are you sure you want to donate them? They could be worth quite a bit of money," I said.

"Oh, no dear, don't worry about it. When my husband died, his life insurance policy left me with plenty of money to live on. All of my assets will be going to charity when I pass on."

"Are you sure?" I asked again. This donation could be a huge boon for the school's playground fund. My seven-year-old would be thrilled if we could raise enough money for a new swing set and big toy structure. Maybe there would even be enough left over for some new soccer balls.

"Yes, I'm sure." She smiled, and her eyes grew misty. "Darrell and I wanted children, but we were never blessed with them. I've spent many happy afternoons looking out my living room window and watching your little ones and the other neighborhood children playing and laughing. I can't imagine a better place to donate these things."

"Would you mind if I take these in for an appraisal? We can probably get more money for the school by selling some of these to antique dealers or collectors."

"That's fine, dear. You could try that antique dealer next to the library downtown. I seem to remember my uncle mentioning him, but I've never been in there myself." She repacked the books and vase in their boxes and pressed the packing tape back into place.

"Would you mind carrying the boxes upstairs?" She gestured at her cane. "It's hard to manage with this thing."

"No problem," I said. I carried all seven boxes upstairs and brought them back to my house across the street. Before leaving with the final box, I impulsively gave her a hug.

"Thank you so much, Mrs. Anderson. This will really help."

She blinked back tears, murmured a goodbye and softly closed the door.

After lugging the last box home, I sat down amidst them on the living room floor to investigate their contents. Box after box revealed antique books and other collectibles. Wedged down the side of a carton, I found a bundle of postcards, tied loosely with yellowing string. I untied the neat bow and sifted through them. All of them were from Henry Ziegler to a Richard Dennis, who I assumed to be Mrs. Anderson's father. Uncle Henry had traveled extensively across the United States, mailing postcards from New York, Boston, and even Nebraska. I hoped I'd someday get to visit some of the more interesting locations.

I wrapped the postcards back up and chose ten of the oldest books to take to the antique dealer downtown. How exciting would it be if one of these was worth a couple thousand dollars?

I parked in front of Haverstone's Fine Books and Antiques. An octogenarian with a precisely trimmed gray beard looked up as the bell above the door rang.

"Welcome, I'm Albert Haverstone," he said. "How may I help you?" He stepped nimbly around a brass coat rack and eyed the books in my arms.

"Well," I said, "my kids' school is having an auction and a neighbor donated these. I'm not sure if they are worth anything, but I figured I should check before we sell them. Could you take a look?"

"Of course. I would be pleased to do so. Come over here," he said, motioning to a chair across from where he took a seat behind a mahogany desk. He pulled a pair of glasses out of his suit pocket.

He went through the books, consulting a thick manual as he went along. Several times I thought I saw an avaricious gleam in his wizened eyes, instantly replaced by stoic ambivalence.

"So what do you think?" I glanced down at the books. The oldest one, *Tamerlane and Other Poems*, was published in 1827. The only author listed on the book cover was "A Bostonian" but I figured any book that ancient had to be somewhat valuable. I tapped my fingers lightly on the chair's edge as I waited to hear the verdict.

"Most of them appear to be in fairly good condition and some of them may even be worth upwards of a few hundred dollars apiece," he said, not even glancing up at me as he furiously scribbled what looked like hieroglyphics in a spiral bound green notebook. I felt like my eyes were going to pop out of my head.

"What about that one?" I regained my composure and pointed at the Tamerlane.

"Well," he said, "it is indeed quite old and if it went to auction, it may go for three hundred dollars or so. If you would like, I can buy it and the others from you and save you some time. I don't usually buy things like this without closer examination, but I would like to help you and the community with your fundraising efforts."

"Oh." I hadn't considered that he might want to buy them outright. If they were each worth a few hundred dollars though, that would be fantastic for the school. "I have more at home, several boxes in fact, but I would need to clear any sale with the auction committee first."

"That is quite all right, my offer will be still be available after you speak with them. Would you like me to appraise the other books?"

"That would be wonderful." We set an appointment for the next day at two o'clock in the afternoon.

The next morning, I scrambled to get the kids to school on time. I had forgotten that my son had an all-day field trip to the Aquarium and needed to be to school early. On the way home, I swung by the supermarket for dinner fixings and dropped off the dry cleaning. When I got in the door, I chugged a cold cup of coffee and grabbed the overflowing laundry hamper to take it downstairs. As I propped the basement door open with my foot, the stack of antique books seemed to call out to me. I put down the laundry at the top of the stairs, picked up the Tamerlane book, and reverently ran my fingers over the cover. The book was almost one hundred-ninety years old. I needed to know more about it.

I opened my laptop and typed the book's title into the browser's search window. I almost fell out of my chair when I realized I was looking at an original copy of Edgar Allan Poe's first work. I added "value" to the search and clicked on a link to the *Antiques Road Show*. The small blurb listed the book as rare and gave a recent auction price of $198,000. Blood pounded in my ears and my vision blurred. Albert Haverstone had told me it was only worth a few hundred dollars. That lying cheat! Were the other books worth more than he'd let on as well?

I clicked on the next link. It was a 1960s newspaper article from the archives of the *Omaha Times*. Not much help for a current valuation, but it would be interesting to find out how much the price had gone up in value over the years.

"A first edition of Edgar Allan Poe's *Tamerlane and Other Poems* was among the items stolen from the house of local millionaire Edward T. Grimes. It is valued at $15,000. Police suspect that the thieves were two men Mr. Grimes had recently befriended."

The article went on to describe the other stolen assets, including a three volume set of Jane Austen's *Pride and Prejudice*, a first edition of *Walden; or Life in the Woods* by Henry David Thoreau, a vase and other collectibles.

I sat back in my desk chair. Wow. An image on the screen of one of the stolen collectibles caught my eye. It was a glass vase with cherries painted whimsically around the base. For a few seconds, I couldn't breathe. I was pretty sure I'd seen the two other books referenced in the article.

I grabbed the bundle of postcards and rifled through them until I found it. *Greetings from Nebraska!* By squinting a little, I could make out the postmark city and date—June 26, 1962. Uncle Henry had been in Omaha just one day before the theft occurred.

With a feeling of dread, I went through the other two boxes and entered descriptions of their contents into an Internet search engine. Unfortunately, most of them had corresponding stolen item reports and correlated with dates and places from Uncle Henry's postcards.

When I finished listing the values on my notepad, the total came to over a million dollars. One item, a cast iron children's toy bank in the shape of the "Old Lady Who Lived in a Shoe," appeared to be worth almost half of that sum.

If it were true, everything had been stolen in the late 1940s until the early 1960s. Odds were, Uncle Henry had lied about being a salesman. His business travels had been nothing but a cover for thievery.

I got up from the computer and rubbed my strained eyes. The contents of these boxes were worth more than my mortgage.

I looked out the window at Mrs. Anderson's cheery yellow house. The thefts had happened so long ago, would it really hurt to keep the items and sell them for the school? The money raised from the sale of these antiques could provide so many things—books for the library, classroom supplies, and safe playground equipment. I cut off the fantasy before I could get any further.

Great. If I couldn't sell these books, what was I going to do with them? If I reported the items to the police, they would be at Mrs. Anderson's door in a second. I didn't know if she could take the inevitable barrage of questions regarding the items' provenance. Could she be implicated in the crime somehow? Worst of all, Mrs. Anderson would be devastated to find out her beloved Uncle Henry was a master thief. But if I knowingly didn't report the stolen goods, I would be just as bad as Uncle Henry.

The boxes seemed to have multiplied, fighting for space on my grape juice-stained carpet, sandwiched neatly between a Lego castle and a Barbie tea set. My gaze caught on the shoe bank poking out of a box. Had the rightful owner played with it as a child? Was it a cherished family heirloom? I hadn't found a report of the toy being stolen, but the theft might not have made the papers. My stomach clenched into a tight knot as I carefully pushed the shoe bank back into the box and shut the lid. I knew it would cause Mrs. Anderson pain, but I needed to notify the police.

Desperate for a distraction, I dragged the dirty laundry down to our finished basement, transferred a load out of the washing machine and into the dryer, and began to sort clothes into piles. The mundane task couldn't stop my brain from spinning even faster than the dryer humming along beside me. Should I call the police immediately, or should I tell Mrs. Anderson myself and give her some time to process the news before they arrived to question her? With a crime this old, was there any harm in waiting another few hours?

When everything was sorted, I picked up the hamper and plodded up the stairs. Something in the dryer clanged loudly with every spin. I probably should have clasped the straps of my daughter's Osh-Kosh overalls before drying them.

Still lost in thought, I opened the basement door and saw a silver-haired man standing in my living room. I looked at my watch. It was only a quarter to noon. Why was Mr. Haverstone here already? And more to the point, why was he in my house, shoving books into one of many oversized canvas satchels?

If I could get back to the basement without being seen, I could use my cell phone to call the police. Just before I could fully close the door, it creaked. Mr. Haverstone looked up.

"Oh, there you are," he said, smoothly masking his shock. "I knocked, but no one answered. The front door was unlocked, so I thought I'd wait in here, out of the cold."

"Our appointment wasn't until two o'clock." I narrowed my eyes at him. "And why are you taking those books?"

"I thought I would bring some back to my shop to do further research. If I can find the right buyer, some of them may be worth more for your school."

I highly doubted he was trying to help me or the elementary school. He glanced over to the computer, which still showed an image of the stolen Tamerlane and vase, with the headline, "Theft at Grimes Mansion."

"So you know we stole them." His voice chilled me more than the brisk winter air outside. From underneath his blazer, he pulled out a handgun. "I'm a little rusty at the burglary gone wrong scenario, but I'll try to remember how it goes."

I finally connected the dots. Mr. Haverstone had been Uncle Henry's accomplice.

"I always wondered where Henry had left the goods. I never did find them in his apartment. How fortunate that you brought them into my shop." He waved the gun at me and pointed at the wall opposite the curtained windows. "How about you stand over there while I pack up the rest of these things? If the neighbors hear the gunshot, they may call the police before I can get everything back to my car."

I set the laundry hamper down and stood in front of the plastic toy kitchen I'd often complained took up half the wall space. He was going to kill me, right here in my own living room. Mr. Haverstone deftly transferred the remaining books into bags while still training the gun on me. I reached behind me blindly, searching for anything to use as a weapon.

"Beep, Beep!" From across the room, an orange plastic car rammed into the heels of his leather shoes. Startled, Mr. Haverstone stumbled forward and braced himself on the desk with the hand holding the gun. I removed my left hand from the car's remote control and whacked him in the head with the cast iron frying pan my daughter loved to use on her toy stove. He crumpled into a mass of khaki and tweed.

I picked the gun off the floor, ran outside, and called the police on my cell phone. With the front door open, I waited on the porch, shivering and keeping a close eye on the unconscious man in my living room.

When the police arrived, I told them everything, including the part about the stolen goods. Uncle Henry's treasures had affected so many lives, but I hoped returning them would heal some wounds. Maybe even the toy bank's owner would be found.

The police knocked on Mrs. Anderson's door, but she wasn't home. They said detectives would follow up with her tomorrow and they confiscated the boxes.

A few hours later, I saw a light on in her house. I decided it was best for me to break the news to Mrs. Anderson.

"Lucy, I wasn't expecting to see you," she said. "Did you forget something?"

"No." If only it were that simple. "Mrs. Anderson, I have something I need to tell you."

"Well, what is it dear? Oh, where are my manners? Come in, sit down." She motioned to a floral sofa and sat down in a wingback chair.

"Those antiques you gave me yesterday, for the school auction…"

"Yes? What about them? Have you had a chance to look at them yet? I had hoped that there would be at least one item in there that would be worth something." Her face fell.

"Um." I bit my lip. "Most of the items in there were worth something. Not just something, they were worth a lot. That's the problem. I looked them up on the Internet and I found reports of stolen items that matched their descriptions. I think your father's friend may not have been the salesman you thought he was."

"Oh!" Mrs. Anderson exclaimed. She sat back in her chair and stared straight ahead. I hoped my news wasn't too much of a shock. "My mother and father always said he was a salesman. Do you really think he stole all those items?"

"It seems strange that almost everything I researched online had a matching theft report," I said gently. "Maybe he just got them from a friend?"

"I guess we'll never know. It wouldn't have crossed my mind that he was a thief," she said. Her face was much paler than when she'd answered the door. "So what are you going to do?"

"That's kind of why I'm here. I wanted to let you know that I've notified the police about the items." I told her about the day's events.

"Oh. This is too much." She got up and I heard her fumble around in the kitchen.

The adrenaline rush from the last twenty-four hours had vanished and I felt drained. I leaned back in my seat. I never imagined I could raise over a million dollars in donations for my kids' school, but for a while it had seemed possible. The other donations the PTA received for the rummage sale should be enough for new playground equipment, but I doubted some old sweaters and jeans would earn the playground fund much more than a thousand dollars. Still, it was better than nothing.

"Here," she said, returning with two steaming mugs. "Mama always said a cup of tea makes a person feel better, and I think the two of us could use it. Lucy, I feel so awful about placing you in harm's way. I never would have given you the antiques if I'd known where they really came from."

"Thank you." I took a small sip. "Don't worry about it. I know you didn't know about Uncle Henry. It was disappointing to hand everything over to the police, but it was pretty cool to hold something worth a million dollars. Do you know one of the antiques was worth almost half a million all on its own?"

"Really, what was that? I still can't believe those were in my basement all these years," Mrs. Anderson said, setting down her teacup on a crocheted coaster.

"It was a children's toy bank from the nursery rhyme, the 'Old Lady Who Lived in a Shoe.' It's from the mid-1800s and could be worth upwards of $450,000. I couldn't find any indication it was stolen, but I'm sure the rightful owner will be happy to get it back." I looked at my watch and stood to walk to the door.

"It's later than I thought. I've got to get going. I'm so sorry about all of this. I really appreciate your donation, even if it didn't turn out to be anything big." My hand was on the doorknob when she called out to me.

"Lucy." Mrs. Anderson disappeared down the hallway. When she returned a few minutes later, her face was flushed and she handed me a black and white photo. A small, fair-haired girl smiled into the camera, her hands wrapped around a shoe-shaped toy.

"I don't understand," I said, handing the photo back to Mrs. Anderson. "How did you get this picture?"

"That's me in the picture. The toy never belonged to Uncle Henry. It was my mother's and she gave it to me to play with when I was a small child. It was one of my favorite toys." Mrs. Anderson lightly stroked the photo and smiled. "I put it in the box with the other antiques because it was just floating around down in the basement and I didn't want it to get broken. Please take it. I can't think of a better use for it than to help with the children's playground fund."

BLINDED BY MURDER

KELLY COCHRAN

Woo-OO-oo-oo-oo. Woo-OO-oo-oo-oo. The cooing of mourning doves captured my attention. The doves were an integral part of spring around my home and their return brought a sense of comfort. The sound of their wings fluttering signaled someone's arrival. I put my sunglasses on, sat in the chair, and waited.

The door opened. "It's Jimmy. Are you ready, Miss McKinney?"

"I wish you'd call me Ava."

"I don't want to disrespect you, ma'am."

"Ma'am? Talk about disrespect. It makes me feel like a little old lady."

"I'm sorry. I didn't mean—"

"I'm kidding!"

Jimmy cleared his throat. "You need me to help you… Ava?"

"Finally! How long have I've been asking you to call me Ava? Two years?"

"Yes, Ava, it's been a looooong two years since I started working for you."

"You're feisty today." I picked up my cane, moving it back and forth as I walked toward the door. I made my way to the end of the walk where Jimmy took my hand and led me to the back seat of his car.

After being diagnosed on my thirty-fifth birthday with vision loss of an unknown origin, I'd hired Jimmy as a part-time driver. He took me to the grocery store, the library, and lately, north to Arlington, Virginia where I'd been seeing a holistic doctor who specialized in treating chronic headaches.

* * * *

"Dr. Trenton is ready for you."

"I'll be back, Jimmy. I'm sure they must have the *Sports Illustrated* swimsuit edition, so you can catch up on your sports news." I chuckled.

"You are in rare form today, ma'am." A small laugh escaped Jimmy's mouth.

The assistant took my arm and led me back to the exam room where she took my blood pressure and left me to wait for the doctor. The longer I waited, the more restless I became.

"Ava. How are we doing?" Dr. Trenton sat down in the chair near me.

"That blue tie really brings out the color in your eyes."

"Was that just a good guess or can you really see?"

"Surprise! Yes. Yes, I can." I took my sunglasses off.

Dr. Trenton patted the exam table. "Hop on up here and let me take a look! How are your headaches?"

I jumped up onto the table. "Completely gone. You're a genius."

"Now, Ava, we don't know if it's permanent. How long have you been able to see?"

"I started seeing blurry shapes, like trees and cars, a week after my last appointment. It's improved every day."

"Have you told anyone else?"

"No. You said you wanted to be the first to know. Plus, I wasn't sure if it was a fluke, but it's been almost a month now. I can't wait to tell everyone! Do you know how hard it is to pretend you are blind?"

Dr. Trenton placed his hand on my arm. "Ava, it's really important you not tell anyone. I could lose my medical license."

"Why?"

"Remember when I told you not to talk about the medication I'd been prescribing? About how I am having you take more than the dosage written on the label?"

"I remember."

"I've been prescribing the medication for off-label use. Normally that isn't a big deal, but I'm having you take a dosage above the maximum approved by the FDA. I should have filed an application as if it was an investigational drug, but I didn't want to wait for the red tape to clear. Your mother wouldn't have wanted that either."

Dr. Trenton had been in love with my mother. He'd been as devastated as I had when she died three years ago. "So, I can't tell anyone?"

"No, Ava, you can't. I really could lose my license. If that happens, I won't be able to prescribe the medication and you'd have a hard time finding another doctor who would."

"How long will I have to keep this secret?"

"It may feel like an eternity, but it won't be. We need to be careful how we proceed. If you agree, in another month, we can reduce the amount you take and see how it affects your vision. If you begin losing your sight again, we'll increase your dosage. Once we're sure of the protocol necessary to keep your vision, then I'll file. Be patient."

The sincerity in his eyes was unmistakable. "Mom would have been so proud of you, Dr. Trenton."

"I keep telling you to call me Mark, like you did when your mother and I were dating. In a way, it brings her back to me. I still miss her, you know?"

"Me, too. Thank you for everything, Mark." I got up from my chair and hugged him. "And thank you for making the last days of my mother's life her happiest."

Mark hugged me back.

* * * *

My supply of Haagen-Dazs Chocolate Chocolate Chip ice cream was now depleted. I dropped the empty carton into the trash. Pretending I was blind had become stressful since finding out Dr. Trenton's livelihood and my vision were at stake.

The phone rang. I'd been ignoring it all week. If I couldn't let anyone know I could see, then I didn't want to see anyone. But, I was smart enough to know that at some point someone would send the police to my door to check on my well-being. Was she dead or alive? I picked up the receiver. "Hello."

"Miss McK… I mean, Ava. You missed the library last week. I thought you were tired or busy, but when you didn't call yesterday I knew something must be wrong. Are you okay?"

"I'm fine Jimmy. I'm just feeling down."

"I ran into Miss Alter and she said the library was going to be closed today because she's attending a seminar. And, well, I know how much you like going to the library when you can have it all to yourself."

Olivia Alter was the librarian of our tiny library and she'd given me a key so I could come and go whenever I wanted. She'd taken it upon herself to look after me when I lost my vision, even purchasing some special headphones for me to use.

"No, I don't feel up to it."

"I'm not taking no for an answer."

"You do know that no means no, right? I don't want you to end up in jail for misunderstanding what one of your dates says." I tried holding in my laugh. Jimmy was newly divorced and had recently started dating. The stories he'd told me had been more comical than anything.

"That must be a yes. I'll pick you up in thirty minutes."

"Yes, sir."

I went into the bathroom and looked in the mirror. If anyone saw me this way, they'd wish they were blind. I had chocolate chocolate chip ice cream in my hair, smudges of chocolate on my left cheek and I hadn't bathed in over a week. After a quick shower, I blew my hair dry and threw on a pair of jeans and a t-shirt.

Being able to see again meant I was almost guaranteed I wouldn't end up with lopsided lipstick or big, bushy eyebrows. When the doorbell rang, I hurried to put a light coat of tinted moisturizer on my face.

I put on my sunglasses and opened the door. "I'm ready to go!"

"Where's your cane, Miss McKinney?"

Oh no. Sequestered in my home I hadn't needed my cane. "Oh, yes, my cane! I've gotten so good at walking around my house. It's like I've developed navigational sonar. But outside is different. I think my purse and cane are in the kitchen."

My heart rate settled down once I saw Jimmy walk toward the back of the house.

"I see your purse, but not your cane," Jimmy yelled from the kitchen.

I hurriedly looked around the room and spotted it leaning against the living room chair. "Maybe I left it in the living room," I yelled back.

"There it is." Jimmy picked up my cane and handed it to me along with my purse.

I let Jimmy guide me out of the house and into the back seat of his car.

Jimmy backed out of the driveway. He checked his rearview mirror and I caught him looking at my reflection.

"Thank you, Jimmy."

"For what?"

"Because you cared enough to make sure I was doing okay, and you even went a step further. You got me out of the house."

"No need to thank me. You've become like family."

* * * *

"Here's the key to the library." I handed it to Jimmy.

"Going to the back like usual?" Jimmy asked.

"Yes. Once you pick an audio book for me, you can go if you want and pick me up later."

"I wouldn't think of leaving you here alone."

I walked to the back where my favorite chair was located, being sure to feel my way with my cane.

"Are there any new mysteries?"

"Two. *The Gods of Guilt* by Michael Connelly and *Daddy's Gone A Hunting* by Mary Higgins Clark."

"I'll listen to Mary Higgins Clark."

I sat down, reached into the drawer of the side table and grabbed the special headphones. Jimmy loaded the CD and placed the player on the table next to me. I took the headphone jack and plugged it into the player.

"How are you doing that? That's amazing! You just plugged that right in. Are you sure you're blind?"

My heart rate ticked upward. Ever since I told Dr. Trenton I could see, I was having a much harder time pretending I couldn't. "I'm just really good. Watch this!" I took a bottle of water out of my purse.

"It isn't going to be impressive if all you do is unscrew the top."

"No, I'm going to set it on the table in front of the chair." I leaned forward and dropped it on the floor.

"Amazing accuracy!"

"What'd I tell you?"

He laughed and bent over to pick up my bottled water. "Here you go."

I waved my hands in front of me trying to find it. I made sure my hands were everywhere but near the bottle.

He placed the bottle into my hand. "I'll be here if you need me."

Pressing play, I snuggled into the chair and closed my eyes. One deep breath and I was transported into another world. One of mystery and suspense.

The narrator's voice rose and fell, lightened and deepened as she assumed the roles of the characters in the story. I began hearing voices in the background and wondered if there'd been a mistake in the audio book production. The background voices got louder and angrier. I opened my eyes and found Jimmy yelling at a man. I turned down the volume on the CD player. It was difficult to hear what was being said, but I kept my headphones on so Jimmy wouldn't think I was eavesdropping.

"…owe money—"

"I told… son… leave…"

Everything was muffled. I missed nearly every other word, but heard enough to know that someone owed someone else money.

"She's blind. Don't… alone!"

With or without the headphones, there was no mistaking the sound of a gunshot. Fighting my instinct, I sunk deeper into my chair. Jimmy fell to the ground. I had to stop myself from screaming. The other man was still standing and holding the gun.

I pulled my sunglasses down my nose a tiny bit trying to get a visual. The man wasn't facing me. The only thing I could make out was the color of his hair and a large birthmark covering the lower right side of his face and neck. He wiped off the gun with his shirt and then dropped to the floor. Both Jimmy and the man were obscured by a table, so I pushed my sunglasses back into position.

The man stood back up without the gun in his hand, then walked out of the library calmly, as if he'd just been there to check out a book. When I could no longer see him, I ran toward Jimmy. "Can you hear me?"

Jimmy didn't answer. He'd been shot in the face. A burning sensation in my throat signaled there might be some vomiting in my future. I kneeled, took the gun out of Jimmy's hand and threw it a few feet away. I found no pulse in Jimmy's wrist. I moved my hand up to his neck to his carotid artery, but there was no pulse there either. Jimmy was dead.

I ran to the front desk and dialed 911.

* * * *

I collected my cane and purse, sat down on the floor next to Jimmy, and waited. Less than ten minutes passed before the police and ambulance arrived.

"Are you okay, ma'am?"

Hearing the word ma'am, I wanted to cry. I wanted to hear Jimmy say that word again, but this tragedy rendered it impossible. I wanted to clean Jimmy's blood from my clothes, but I couldn't let the officer know what I really wanted. "I just want to go home."

"I'm sorry, but we need to ask you some questions. Can I help you into a chair?"

"Yes, thank you."

"Here you go." The officer grabbed my arm, helping me up.

"The library is closed today. How did you get in?"

"Miss Alter gave me a key so I could use the library even when she wasn't here."

"Did you lock the door behind you?"

"Jimmy opened the door. He must not have locked it."

"Can you tell me what you saw? Uh, I mean heard? Sorry about that."

I was about to lie to an officer of the law. Maybe it wasn't really lying if I answered truthfully using my other senses.

"I heard Jimmy yelling at someone. Both of their voices were muffled because I was wearing headphones. Jimmy saved my life."

"What do you mean by that?"

"The two were arguing. It sounded like a man. He must have said something to Jimmy about me because I heard Jimmy telling him I was blind. If the man hadn't known, he would have killed me. Why leave an eyewitness? Right?"

"Did you recognize the other man's voice?"

"No. I heard a few words here and there, like money, son, and blind, but the sounds and tones were muffled."

"Do you know if it was Jimmy's son?"

I knew it wasn't Jimmy's son even though I'd never met him. This man appeared much older. "Like I said, I couldn't make out the voice, but he might have been older. And from the way Jimmy talked, his son would never hurt him."

"How did you know Jimmy was the one who'd been shot?"

Now, I had to lie. There was no other way. "After I heard the gunshot, I waited until I thought it was safe to move. I took off my headphones and called Jimmy's name. He didn't answer. I got up to look for him and ended up hitting him with my cane."

"You took a risk. The man could have still been here."

"Yeah," I said softly.

"Not sure why the man shot upward through Jimmy's chin. It's an unusual place to shoot someone. And he left the gun." The officer scratched his temple.

"Maybe he wanted to make people believe Jimmy committed suicide," I offered.

The officer gestured toward the gun on the floor. "But the gun is two feet away."

I didn't look at the gun. "It was in his hand. I tossed it after I found it."

The officer raised his brows. "How'd you know it was in his hand?"

"I was feeling around trying to find out if Jimmy was alive."

"Uh huh. You sure you didn't shoot him? I mean, that would make sense seeing that you are blind and he was shot in an awkward area. Maybe it was an accident?"

"No! I would never hurt Jimmy."

"Why'd you compromise the evidence? You may have destroyed the killer's prints and the only evidence that might help clear you."

I wished I could tell him the killer wiped off the gun. "I just wanted to get the gun away from Jimmy."

"We're going to need to take you to the station for fingerprinting."

"Am I in trouble? I just want to go home." I felt a tear slip.

"You were the only one here with him. You said you moved the gun. If you didn't kill him, then we'll need your fingerprints for elimination purposes. It won't take long." He turned to the other officer, "Please take Miss McKinney to the station and then give her a ride home."

* * * *

Jimmy had been dead five days. I sat in the living room waiting for Jimmy's son, Criston, to pick me up.

The police had no firm suspect. I'd helped them the best I could, providing information about everything I heard, touched, and smelled. Criston had been eliminated as a suspect, but I was still in the running. No one had seen the man at the library, coming or going. The killer was a mystery.

The doorbell rang. "I'll be right there."

When I opened the door, Jimmy's spitting image was standing in front of me. Though I'd never met Criston, I heard so much about him from Jimmy.

"Thank you for giving me a ride."

"No problem."

Criston led me to the front seat of his car and placed my cane in the back.

"Your father was like family to me. I don't know how I'm going to replace him."

We talked about Jimmy as Criston drove. He became quiet as he pulled into the cemetery, following the road to the right where a white tent had been erected and a hole dug for Jimmy's final resting place.

As we walked toward the chairs, I noticed the family sitting in the front row and in the back, the detective working the case. He stood and observed the crowd, as though he expected the killer to come pay his condolences. Criston sat me down in an aisle chair, in the second row, behind the family members.

A chair in the front row remained empty. I thought about Jimmy and wondered if the chair had been left vacant for Jimmy's soul. I bent my head down as I listened to the pastor offer a final prayer, blessing Jimmy and asking the Lord to watch over Jimmy's family.

"I'm glad you finally made it," a woman whispered.

I opened my eyes and saw a woman leaning into a man sitting in the once empty seat.

The pastor ended his words of sympathy. The woman spoke to the man again. "Since you missed the funeral home, Sammy, why don't you say a few words now?"

The man grunted as he got up off the chair and walked toward the casket. His head was down. I could feel his pain.

"My brother was a good man," he said as he turned to face family and friends.

The family turned to look at me, confirming the gasp I'd let out had not been silent. I began crying and gasping, crying and gasping, in a desperate attempt to explain my behavior.

"Are you okay?" the woman asked.

"I'm so sorry. It's just that he's right, Jimmy was a good man."

The port-wine stain blazoned across the side of Sammy's face continued to cause me distress. My hands were shaking, even though Sammy didn't seem alarmed by my outburst. After everyone turned back toward the casket, Sammy continued on about how wonderful Jimmy had been, a true saint, a man with no enemies.

No enemies, except one. It was eerie how Sammy stood there as though he didn't have the blood of his brother on his hands. I listened intently, waiting for the end.

"God rest your soul, Jimmy." His brother touched Jimmy's casket before heading toward the chairs.

The woman stood and thanked everyone for coming. I swiveled around on my seat in order to get up and saw the detective walking back to his car. With every step he took, I searched for a reason to justify my silence.

* * * *

I grabbed the weekly newspaper off the front stoop and headed for the kitchen for a cup of coffee. It had been two days since I'd run after the detective and confessed my ability to see, so I wasn't shocked to see the newspaper article about Sammy's confession.

The article reasoned it was Sammy's gambling habit that had gotten him into trouble. Details about how Sammy had followed Jimmy to the library that day, how he'd become angry and shot Jimmy when Jimmy had refused to cash out his son's college fund so Sammy could pay off his debts, seemed unfathomable. How could someone shoot their own flesh and blood?

I took a sip of coffee and continued to read. When the focus of the article changed from Sammy's confession and the killing to the blind woman who could see, I knew I was in trouble. I threw my clothes on and ran out to my car.

The drive seemed to take forever, but when I pulled into the parking space, the clock in the dashboard confirmed it took exactly one and a half hours. I took the paper and headed up to Dr. Trenton's office.

"I need to see Dr. Trenton. It's an emergency!" I ran through the door and into Dr. Trenton's office.

"You can't just barge in."

"Tell him I need to see him right away!"

A few minutes passed and Dr. Trenton entered. "Where is your cane? Your sunglasses?"

"It's out. The story is out." I handed him the paper.

He read the story. The deep furrow in his forehead was all I needed to see to know that I had ruined his life.

"The story is about you. A blind woman sees the killer. I don't see my name in here."

"Mark, I'm so sorry. I had to tell the detectives I could identify Jimmy's killer, because Jimmy deserved justice."

"So, you told him about me?"

"The detective threatened to arrest me unless I told the truth, but I knew I had to protect you. I told him I was seeing you, but that my eyesight came back for no reason, the same way it disappeared."

"If you didn't mention the medication, I should be okay. But we ought to decrease the dosage of your medication to meet the FDA guidelines, just to be safe."

"What if I lose my vision again?"

"Please try not to worry. I'm going to file the application as soon as possible so I can legally prescribe the necessary dosage. While it's being processed, I'll monitor you to see how much vision you lose, if any, and when. I promise you I'll do everything possible to make sure your ability to see is permanently restored."

* * * *

The doorbell rang. I grabbed my cane and made my way to the door.

"Hi, Miss McKinney!"

"Please call me Ava, Criston."

"Yes, ma'am."

I smiled. He was just like Jimmy.

"Are we ready to go?"

"Yes, Ava."

Though my headaches continued to be controlled, I'd lost my eyesight one month after lowering the dosage of my medication. Criston was taking me to Dr. Trenton's office because the application had been approved. I couldn't wait to get my vision back.

The ride to Arlington went quickly as Criston and I talked about his father. When we pulled into the parking lot across the street from Dr. Trenton's building, I turned to Criston. "I can find my own way."

"No, ma'am, I'm going to escort you and make sure you get there safely."

"Ma'am, again? Are you looking to get fired?"

"Um, no ma..., uh, I mean, Ava."

"I'm kidding, Criston!"

He smiled. "Let's go then. It takes time to help little old ladies across the street."

JUST MY TYPE OF REVENGE

CHELLE MARTIN

Susan Bass adjusted her oversized tortoiseshell eyeglasses, picked up her steno pad, and tapped gently at her boss's door. She'd been watching him through the glass, gauging the amount of time it would take him to finish reading a proposal delivered by FedEx thirty minutes ago.

"Mr. Miller, are you ready to continue this morning's memo?" she asked softly. Despite being invited to do so, Susan could not address upper management on a first name basis. It didn't seem professional.

John squinted at the document in his hands, mumbled aloud the last page under his breath, then motioned to Susan to take a seat opposite his enormous and intricately carved mahogany desk. Shorthand might be a bit outdated, but once her boss had learned of Susan's skill, he took advantage of it.

As Susan carefully gathered her long plaid skirt beneath her and sank into the sumptuous leather chair, her co-worker Barbie Stockwell knocked loudly, then rushed into the room without an invitation. Dressed in a black power skirt suit, stilettos with gold-capped heels, and sporting enough Chanel No. 5 to turn every man's head within a fifty feet range, Barbie commanded attention, even though she, like Susan, worked as administrative support.

"John," Barbie said forcefully, "this financial report just came in to Douglas and I noticed some blatant discrepancies in the figures. Some items were transposed or left out altogether." She looked accusingly at Susan, then back to John before she held up a hand. "Don't worry. I caught the errors and corrected them before the papers went out in the mail, but Douglas wanted me to bring the matter to your attention. You know how he is about accuracy."

Barbie handed John a copy, then continued. "He's still pretty angry about not getting that memo last week. Can you remind Susan to place future memos directly on his desk?"

Susan gritted her teeth. *How dare Barbie talk about her like she wasn't in the room!*

John Miller nodded. Barbie ended the one-sided conversation with, "That's all." With a toss of her platinum shoulder-length, precision-cut hair, she turned and exited the office. Her perfume lingered behind like a nuclear cloud.

"I'm sorry for the interruption," Susan said. "I should have stopped her."

"No, what you should have done was checked this financial report," John said, holding it out to her. "We can't afford mistakes around here, Ms. Bass."

"Mr. Miller, I can assure you, I double-check everything for accuracy. My files are up to date. And I keep detailed records of everything that transpires in this office." *You know that*, she wanted to add. She'd been with the firm for the last five years and from the neat little bun that sat atop her head to her sensible loafers, Susan had always worked above and beyond. From day one, she had never complained about overtime or taking work home with her. Never complained about missing office birthday parties in the break room because she'd been asked to pick up dry cleaning or gifts for her boss's wife. Never complained about the first time she'd been passed over for a promotion. Or the second.

"I'm also certain that message was on Douglas's—I mean, Mr. Brewer's desk."

"See that it doesn't happen again," John said, then quickly changed the subject. "Read to me where we left off in the memo."

Susan wanted to argue the point, but knew it was futile. She absently read aloud the words on her pad, then waited for him to continue dictating. *That's another thing*, she thought. *I'm the only administrative assistant who knows shorthand. And I can type faster than any of the other girls can talk. And....*

John swirled in his executive high-backed leather chair, then began speaking. "Which brings us to the matter of departmental promotions. It is with great pleasure that I award Benjamin DeStefano the position of Human Resources Manager, where he will continue the work of Robert Bingham, who is retiring. Secondly, I am laterally promoting Miss Barbie Stockwell to the position of Assistant to the Human Resources Manager where she will continue the work of Millicent Wallingford, who is likewise retiring."

"Excuse me?" Susan said.

"What part didn't you get?" John asked. His chair had stopped moving and he'd positioned his arms on his expansive desk, leaning toward her.

"I got all of it," Susan said. "I just don't understand it. I've been passed over twice for promotions. To girls who haven't been here as long as I have. Even Barbie. She's been here less than three months. I've been here five years. And—"

His desk phone rang and he quickly reached for it. "That'll be all," he said. End of discussion.

Susan left his office with tears blurring her eyes. Crying was so unprofessional. She left her memo pad on her desk, grabbed her purse, and went to the ladies' room.

She found a pack of Kleenex tucked into a side pocket of her bag and dabbed at her eyes. Without makeup, there wasn't any runny mascara to fix or blush to repaint. No, just a little Visine and she'd be good to go. She was about to pull the bottle from her organized little carrier when the toilet flushed. She hadn't bothered to check to see if she was alone when she entered the ladies' room and didn't want to be seen crying.

"Susan? Are you okay?"

It was Anna Chang, an older woman from the accounting department.

"Yes, yes, I'm fine," Susan lied. "I think I got something in my eye."

Anna stood beside her at the double sink as she washed her hands, but her gaze never left Susan's face in the large mirror. "You don't seem fine. And if you have something in your eye, why are they both red? What is really going on?"

"Nothing you can help me with, Mrs. Chang."

"Is it that Mr. Miller?" Anna asked, narrowing her eyes. "You didn't lose out on another promotion, did you?"

Susan's shoulders slumped as she nodded in defeat.

"What was his reason this time?" Anna asked as she dried her hands on a paper towel.

"He didn't say. But something fishy is going on. Barbie Stockwell brought him a financial report and claimed that I'd submitted it with errors. She conveniently took the credit for correcting it. She's also the one getting the promotion." She stopped to blow her nose. "There was another day she claimed her boss never got a memo, which I specifically remember leaving on his desk. I had to retype the entire thing and then, of course, he complained because it was late."

"You remind me a lot of myself when I was your age," Anna said. "I wasn't in this country for very long, so my English wasn't very good. I didn't have money to buy the latest fashions. And I was very timid." She took Susan by the shoulders and turned her toward the mirror. "Look," she said, "and tell me what you see. Is this a woman who is confident? Is she someone with a take-charge attitude or does she blend into the background? That is what you need to be asking yourself, Susan."

Before Susan could ask Anna for suggestions, the bathroom door opened and Barbie Stockwell tottered past them on her heels. She threw a cigarette into her mouth and flicked her lighter, then settled onto one of the nearby lounge chairs and inhaled deeply.

"You aren't supposed to smoke in here," Anna said.

Barbie snorted, "Are you going to report me?" She exhaled a large plume of smoke, then waved dismissively at the two women. "It's not worth the bother. I'm sure Susan has told you I'm going to Human Resources, so I'll be out of your hair." She threw her cigarette butt down on the tile floor, then snuffed it out with her stiletto. "Crushed like a bug," she said, as she moved to leave. "I'm sure Susan knows what that's like." Her laugh followed her out the door.

Anna turned to her friend. "I wish I could help you." She touched Susan on the arm, then left the ladies' lounge.

Susan decided then and there that she was through being a doormat. If she didn't do something now, she'd never better herself.

She was about to enter one of the bathroom stalls when she noticed Barbie had left her pack of cigarettes on the little side table. She picked them up and discovered only a few were missing, but the pack had an odd bump. Susan tilted the pack onto her hand and several white pills rolled out. Ketamine? She'd have to check to be sure, but the pills sure looked like the ones she saw on a recent news broadcast about club drugs. A plan started forming in her head as she stuck the pack into her purse. She had just about closed the stall door when she heard someone enter the room.

"I thought I'd left them here, but I guess I was wrong." Barbie, looking for her smokes.

"Maybe Susan took them," another voice said.

"Are you serious? Can you picture Susan with her little bun and sensible shoes doing anything as scandalous as smoking?"

Both women laughed, then the door closed and the room was silent again.

Susan finished up in the bathroom, thinking to herself. *Scandalous, huh?*

* * * *

The next morning Susan had a hot coffee—black, no sugar—waiting for John Miller when he arrived. "Just the way you like it, sir," she said, handing it to him as he passed by her desk on the way to his office.

"Is my reservation ready for today?"

"Room 111 at the Hilton on Park," she said in her sweetest voice. It was nearly a standing reservation in a busy hotel conference center across town. Meetings almost always ran late and he liked having a room to crash in.

As soon as her boss finished his coffee and left the office, Susan put her plan into work.

John may not think she kept detailed records, but Susan opened her telephone memo book and began thumbing through her list of all incoming calls. A woman named Sandra McMillan called every few weeks. She never gave a company name when asked, just "He'll know what it's in regard to."

Susan felt she knew what it was in regard to as well. The calls more or less coincided with the hotel bookings. Well, it really was none of her business until John (formerly known as Mr. Miller) made it her business. She entered the woman's number into the reverse directory website and up popped a name. Not for Sandra McMillan, but for Arlene Steadman. Interesting. Susan dialed the number and Arlene answered on the second ring.

"Sandra McMillan?"

"Y-y-yes." She hesitated. "Do I know you?"

"This is John Miller's administrative assistant. John asked me to give you a call regarding today's business meeting. His cell phone isn't working, so you can't reach him. But he left an address where he'll be after the meeting and would like for you to meet him there. Oh, and he said to be sure and tell you to wear the emerald bracelet."

Sandra/Arlene took down the address and thanked her for calling.

Next, Susan dug through the copies of receipts she had kept for gift purchases for John's wife. She found the invoice for the beautiful emerald bracelet, dialed Goldman's Jewelers and asked to speak with Charlene.

"Charlene, this is Susan Bass. Remember that emerald bracelet I bought a short while ago for Mr. Miller's wife? Could you please call his wife at home? She's very upset that the clasp has broken. I tried reassuring her you'd repair it quickly, but I know she'll feel better hearing it come from you. Thanks so much."

Susan hung up the receiver and leaned back in her chair. She had to admit that no longer being a doormat felt pretty good.

* * * *

Susan arrived early for work with a spring in her step. She ran into her friend Anna Chang in the break room where they both grabbed a morning coffee to start the day.

"Susan, you aren't going to believe this. Your boss's girlfriend showed up at his house. His wife shot her, then waited for him and shot him, too. She'll survive, but he's in critical condition. Doesn't look like he'll ever be back to work."

"Oh… wow." Susan had known that John's wife had caught him cheating before and would react badly to another woman showing up looking for him, but she had no idea the Millers owned a gun. *Still… John brought this on himself. He and Barbie. If they'd only been nicer to me and I'd gotten the promotion I deserved, none of this would have happened.*

Barbie walked in waving her mug adorned with a big letter B. "Oh, Susan, I just heard about John. Are there any guys who aren't cheaters? Well, I guess he got what he deserved."

Anna said to Susan, "I'm sorry about your boss. We'll talk later." As Anna brushed passed Barbie on her way out, she couldn't resist muttering, "What an appropriate initial."

Barbie ignored the comment and poured herself a cup of coffee. She grabbed the carton of milk, but only a few drops trickled out. She sighed dramatically and waved the empty box at Susan. "Well?"

"Well, what?" Susan said. *Did Barbie expect to be waited on?*

"Never mind. I'll get it myself." Barbie plopped her mug down, splashing coffee on the countertop. She moved to the small refrigerator and complained because the milk wasn't on the door where it should be. Someone had hidden it behind several lunch bags, cartons of yogurt, and soda bottles.

The delay gave Susan the opportunity to slip a small white pill into Barbie's coffee. Her research on the drug confirmed her suspicion that it was Ketamine. The club drug had all sorts of psychiatric effects so, most likely, Barbie had never taken them at work.

* * * *

Susan fielded call after call from clients who inquired about the tragic news that had befallen her boss. She did her best to reassure them that their accounts would still be given the attention they deserved.

Hardly an hour had passed when a commotion erupted in the main office. One by one, workers left their cubicles to investigate the loud music and even louder voice of Barbie.

"I just love this song!" Barbie said. She clutched a small battery-operated radio in one hand, while trying to grab onto a few male co-workers. "Come on, you have to dance with me."

The audience's reactions ranged from laughter to disgust, but Barbie seemed oblivious. She started a strip tease. By then, Security had been called and Barbie was escorted from the premises. It was doubtful after that performance that she'd still have a job, let alone a promotion.

Later that day at a departmental meeting, Douglas Brewer presented a new organizational chart. "Due to unforeseen circumstances, we will be looking for some new hires to fill John and Barbie's positions. And I'm promoting Susan Bass to Assistant to the Human Resources Manager. Her work has always been very detailed and she deserves to be rewarded."

Douglas was complimenting her. Susan beamed, happy that Barbie's plan to damage her reputation had not gone beyond John Miller's office.

Benjamin DeStefano approached and offered his hand. "I'm looking forward to working with you, Susan. I hear you have a gift for detail and we can use that in Human Resources."

"Thank you, Mr. DeStefano."

"Please, call me Ben."

Susan smiled and shook his hand. "Okay, Ben."

HERBS TO YOU

NORMA HUSS

Lily shoved the shiny brochure in my face. "Burl, did you see this?"

By the time I'd looked up from the newspaper, she'd grabbed my hand. "Come on, Burl," she said. "Look at it."

It was another one of those ads for new communities. "I'm looking. Why am I looking, Sweetheart?"

"You know perfectly well," she said as she curled up on the settee beside me, her snippy voice changing to a purr mid-sentence.

After nearly twenty years of marriage, I knew what that meant too. "There's nothing wrong with this house or this neighborhood. It's a friendly place, and there's plenty to do. You've said that yourself. Great library around the corner. Not far from the theater with live shows. The mall only a mile away. Certainly you don't want to move away from your garden, your little shop, and your incantation friends."

"Do you see the words? Vibrant, night life, tennis courts, bistro—expect the unexpected."

I had to smile. The unexpected. I whispered, "Remember when we feared the unexpected?'

"That was you. I was never afraid." She drew away from me, leaned back, and toyed with a lock of hair near her ear.

"No." After she stood up, I added, "And fear isn't the right word, is it?"

No, fear wasn't the word. Neither was unexpected.

Except for the twenty years. Never thought we'd last that long. Our wedding anniversary—coming up in three days. Lily, so young, marrying a crusty old shrimper who spent his days on a smelly boat in the Atlantic. Her idea to marry on her birthday, and not much I could have done about it, even then.

Lily was quick-silver, darting here and there. While I sat thinking, she'd gone out into the back yard where her garden had taken over nearly all the space.

I followed and watched her snip herbs like she did every morning. Herbs for love, friendship, spice, health, who knows what all. Each one meant something to her. She caressed them as she clipped, murmuring her incantations. The words were the important part, she always said.

She knew I stood behind her, but she didn't turn. I said, "Lily, my enchanting love. I was the fearful one, more afraid of you than you were of the world. Me, an old codger, married to the most beautiful girl in the world."

Lily carefully examined the bush for exactly the right leaf to cut. "You used to say, 'the most beautiful girl on the street.'"

"And you are the most beautiful girl on this street, hands down."

She turned those bewitching eyes on me disdainfully. "Besides me, there is no one on this street under sixty. No woman under forty, actually. And I will not be living here when I turn forty."

I pulled at the stubble on my chin. "Guess that gives us a year and three days to think about it."

"Oh, make a joke of it. Silly Lily, got her head in a snit." She snatched her basket of herbs and ran into the house.

After twenty years, I should know what's going on with the woman, but I don't. She confuses me more every day. Move away? Since she'd gone into her work room where she mixes up her charms and talismans with herbs and incantations, I returned to the lanai where we ate breakfast every morning. The sunshine filtered through the trees, illuminating the brochure she wanted me to see. I picked it up.

The whole dang message was youth. Young professionals sipping drinks, diving into the pool, and cuddling on a garden bench. Standing around in rooms with chairs too fancy to sit in. Looking at each other instead of the crazy-colored walls. Young people having fun. Not a single retiree in sight.

When she set her cap for me, I'd warned her. I would be old long before she was and retired while she was young. But she'd wanted marriage and she'd wanted me. Mostly, she'd never been sorry. Not after the first few years, anyway. There had been another time. She'd wanted out once. Then it was too late.

I wasn't surprised when Lily came into the room, striding with purpose, to face me.

"Okay, it's major, life-changing decision time," she said. "You're always saying, fish or cut bait. Now it's me saying it. I'm leaving this place with its 'mature trees' and old biddies. Nothing to talk about but cats and grandchildren." She hesitated, then added, "With you, or without you."

"Twenty years... means nothing?"

Her eyes widened for a moment, but then closed to reopen with the same determination. She'd made her decision. It wasn't the house Lily wanted to leave.

Sixteen years ago, I'd faced another decision and I'd cut bait. Could our lives have been different? Now I had no choice.

I patted the cushion beside me. "Sit with me. I want to tell you how much I love you, and how I've loved you through the years. Will you listen? Let me tell you a story. Will you give me that?"

"A story? You want to tell me a story?" But she sat down—on the wicker chair across the room.

I couldn't look at her as I began. "The ocean was a little rough, nothing we hadn't seen before. All the shrimp boats left before sunup. Four of us. Me with my crew. Raymond and Marty with their boats and crews. And Caleb with two good men on the *Mary Belle*."

Lily jerked forward. "Oh, God! You're not going to drag that up."

I sat, staring at my knees, still not ready to face her. "I know you took it hard, but hear me out."

She flounced and glared, but she leaned back into the chair where the sun played across her face.

"Do you remember what the shrimp boats reminded you of? With the outriggers on each side holding the dark, heavy nets out of the water, you said they were like huge bats with their wings all folded up, ready to go to sleep. I couldn't see it at first, but after a while, I decided you were right. Bats. Scary things if you aren't familiar with them. You took one look at my shrimp boat and decided that was enough for you. But that day, you came to see me off. Three in the morning, and you came along, brought my lunch pail, kissed me and told me you loved me.

"Remember those black lunch pails? We all had them. Big, with a pint and a half thermos of hot coffee, two sandwiches thick with slabs of ham, a pile of your lemon twist cookies. That was the fruit of the day. Remember how you used to tease? 'Take an apple, at least,' you'd say."

I glanced at Lily and waited for the reluctant smile before I continued. "Remember those little dolls you used to make? Special for tourists. You were a go-getter. Sold them to the tourist shop. They couldn't keep them on hand. 'Happy Voodoos,' you called them. You sewed stuff into the bodies, little bits of spices and weeds you gathered along the road out front. Then you'd hold each one in your hands like you were praying over it. 'Adding the spirit,' you always said. I guess that's what you did, making each little doll into a happy voodoo."

Lily crossed her arms over her chest and leaned back. "Is this story going anywhere?"

I licked my lips. Hesitated, but I had to continue. It would only get worse. "You hadn't come down to the boat with me before, not that early. Back then, that's when we went out shrimping, getting to our grounds as the sun came up. Wasn't until later someone decided the shrimp were closer to the top at night."

Finally, I looked at her directly. "When they started shrimping all night long, that's when I knew I was too old for it. I couldn't leave you every night, night after night."

"Is that your point here?"

"No, there's more." I'd only begun. And I'd tell her. I'd kept it in for so many years. She'd been hinting about that fortieth birthday coming in a year. About her youth fading away. I had to tell her now. Reliving her twenties, after they were gone? Wouldn't work.

"You came down to see me off that night. You seemed so happy, even excited. Not like you had been. I figured our troubles were over. Something told me that, you know? That's why I looked inside the lunch pail and saw one of your little voodoo dolls. I was a happy man.

"But, then I saw Caleb walking toward the rest of us. He'd been your sweetheart once. He left, we married, then he came back, thinking you were still waiting. I had you. My Lily. He had nothing. I felt a little sorry for him, you know?"

Again I glanced at her. Alert, but no reaction. Waiting with her eyes glowing, her hands now relaxed in her lap.

"We didn't know the storm was coming. Maybe no one did. Didn't matter. We thought we were invincible. Weather report? Bah. That was for sissies. No weather could beat us, no how." I knew my tone had taken on that "good-old-shrimper-boy" sound that she never liked. It fit, somehow.

"After we got out there, one of the other guys listened in and heard the small craft warning. We radioed back and forth, but we were tough. All the way out there? We weren't going back without a full load of shrimp. Didn't matter that we were spread out for a few miles, that we couldn't see each other. Never could, even on a bright day. We saw even less with the squalls building up, but we were together.

"I lowered my net on the right side, steamed along a tad, then pulled the net tight. Usually, I'd pull that net up right away, unload, but the wind was kicking up pretty fierce. I lowered the other net. It was raining like stink and I couldn't see more than twenty feet. Still didn't matter. We knew there were shrimp in that net. We'd have to wait for a lull to pull them all in, dump them on the deck, toss out any fish, and chuck the shrimp into the hold with the ice."

Lily jumped up. "Okay, I get it. You slaved away earning money so I could spend it. Is that how you show your love?"

I dipped my forehead into my hand, rubbed my brow, then looked up, pleading. "Lily, what gave you that idea? Did I ever say anything like that? I worked. That's what I did. I've never—"

"No, you haven't." She shook her head, stared off into space before turning those vivid eyes back toward me. But she didn't leave it alone. "Men—I know what you really think. You have your fun. You go off, have your adventure, come back to... Let's just forget this story, shall we?"

She'd never been quite so... so harsh. I would not be goaded into a fight. Instead, I said, "Please?"

Eventually she plunked back into the chair, chin thrust out, eyes glued to her toes.

At least she listened. It wouldn't get easier, but I continued. "The wind must have hit thirty, forty knots. My crew and I had been through it all before. Caleb was the newest shrimper, but I knew he'd be okay. He didn't have you, but he had the lucky charm."

"What are you talking about?" Her voice was steely cold, her eyes that nearly black shade they got sometimes.

Could she take the rest of it? But the rest of it was my proof of love, despite what I'd known all these years. "One of the other boats caught a glimpse of him. He'd pulled his first net up and the boat was heeling. You don't know how that is when you've got a full load of shrimp hanging in that net on one side—ten, twenty feet off the boat's center, but it's a bad moment. A big wave can knock you over. But I wasn't worried about Caleb. He'd be okay.

"But he wasn't. Caleb and his crew, good men all, went down with the *Mary Belle*. Sad day. The whole village grieved. I remember it took you a couple of months to recover. Some took longer. Then, you sort of came back. Slowly. And we were happy. Never had children, but we've had a good life."

Lily stood. "And that's your story. Take me back to that horrible day just to prove you love me? I don't get it."

I went to her, wrapped my arms around her stiff body. Whispered, "No, sweetheart, that isn't the end of the story. Remember, after that day, you never made another Happy Voodoo doll charm. You said they were silly, they didn't work, I don't know what all you said. You started making bags of herbs you call enchantments." I dropped my arms, took her hand, and looked into those eyes that seemed to look into my soul.

"That's how I figured it out. You see, maybe your charm did work. That morning I felt bad for Caleb, losing you, so I traded lunch boxes with him. Oh, he didn't know it. I thought it would be a nice surprise. A charm to help him find happiness. A Happy Voodoo from the girl he lost." I watched those eyes darken, and flash with brilliant light. And, I finally said the words that proved my love, proved a love above life itself, proved a love for someone I knew loved another. "Except, it wasn't a happy voodoo, was it?"

Lily's eyes were her soul. The flashing stopped. The color turned to gray, almost a lifeless gray. After a moment the color came back, the sunny blue, and I knew my decision had paid off. She knew I loved her more than life itself.

And her words confirmed it. "Well, I guess this calls for a celebration. I need a shot of sweet tea after that."

Before we headed for the kitchen, I had to tell her again. "I love you, and I'll love you until the day I die."

Lily didn't turn around. She kept walking toward the kitchen. "After we have our snack, I'll tell you exactly what you want to hear. Or, exactly what I want to say, maybe?"

"You are a tease. You make an old man happy."

I was glad to see she got out the tea brewer I'd made for her. It was only an ordinary tea kettle with a strainer added, but tea brewing had become our ritual. She liked to use loose tea leaves and almost always added a few herbs.

As the water began to boil, Lily said, "Oh, there's a tin of spiced pecans up in that cupboard," and nodded toward a cabinet I seldom opened.

"Love your spiced pecans. I didn't know we still had some." I opened the cupboard door, but didn't see anything other than assorted kitchen appliances and cookbooks. "I don't see it."

As she took two glasses out of another cupboard, she said, "Behind that coffee maker."

"Both of us tea drinkers and we have a coffee maker?" I asked as I moved it aside.

"Someone must have given it to us long ago."

As Lily plopped ice cubes into the glasses, I pushed the unnecessary coffeepot aside and reached behind it. "I've never seen this tin before."

"Those nuts are a little different." She flashed a smile and added, "You might call them a tonic. You know, like an apple. One a day keeps the doctor away."

I took a handful and popped one into my mouth. "Taste just the same as usual."

Lily put ice cubes in two glasses and slowly poured the boiling tea into the glasses. She held hers up and said, "Here's to married life."

Usually, she words such a toast as, "Herbs to us." Maybe she'd left the herbs out.

I stirred my tea and waited until she took her first sip before I drank. It was an unnecessary habit I'd begun those many years ago. Still, I looked at the pecans left in my hand and didn't take another.

Lily sat opposite me at our little kitchen table. Together we drank sips of sweet tea. She took one of the pecans, popped it into her mouth, and grinned. One by one, I ate the pecans left in my hand. "You do love me, just a little, don't you Lily?"

"I'll miss you when you're gone," was all she said before she left the room.

That seemed a strange thing to say. Of course, I was sure to die before she did. Was that the love I looked for? The love to last the rest of my life?

Yes, I'd take it.

I stood at the kitchen window and watched my love gather more herbs. She chatted with the neighbor next door.

I'd….

I looked around me as the walls shimmered, the door… I tried to move, but I couldn't. "Lily," I called. "Lily, something's wrong…." Somehow, I must have moved, for I was in my chair.

Lily stood over me, her face sliding back and forth in surges, in pieces.

Her words came in waves. "I've got a story too," she said. Or, was that what she said? Something…. "Those pecans were different. Didn't you hear me? …my tonic… eat one, no more… could be fatal… should have listened closely… won't tell them… hidden… tin of pecans. But your fingerprints are…"

Did I hear… more? Talking to someone not there… the telephone? Something… "Come quickly. I fear it's too late. His heart… My tonic… He must have known." Then… her hand on my forehead… more words. Close… in my ear. The last thing I heard.

"Herbs to you, lover man."

THE BRASS TIARA

LAUREN MOFFETT

Macie was being awfully quiet. I didn't like it. Strike that. I liked the unexpected peacefulness considerably, but I didn't trust why she was being quiet. On most of our morning rides, she talked nearly as fast as she drove her little red speedster, while I gripped the seat edges in terrified silence. My own car couldn't get out of the shop soon enough.

"So, how are you doing?" I asked. Okay, the curiosity was getting the better of me. We'd gone nearly three miles without a word, and worse, we were only going the speed limit. She usually loved taking these mountainous hairpin turns at a racecar speed. Why the sudden caution? Even though it had started snowing, that didn't usually deter Macie.

"Ralphie had to cancel our date last night," Macie replied. I swear a tear caught in the corner of her eye. She opened her mouth to say more but then shut it abruptly. I chewed my lower lip. Macie normally told me more than I ever wanted to know. She was always saying how much she wanted us to be like sisters. I generally nodded and smiled while mentally gagging at the idea of befriending my future stepmother, who was only twenty-four—several years younger than me.

As we pulled into the parking lot of the Autumn Hill Arts and History Museum, I pushed again. Stupid interest. I should have left things alone. "Are you okay?"

"I'm fine, Abby." She wasn't, but if she was going to be stony about it, then who was I to change her mind?

We gripped our coats and walked up the stairs of the historic house which had been recently converted into a museum focusing on local arts and crafts culture. The door was locked. That was odd. We were expected for a staff meeting that was supposed to start in the next few minutes.

"Shouldn't Casper and Olivia be here?" Macie asked, referring to the museum's director and program assistant. Okay, program assistant wasn't the right word. Olivia Turnblatt served as curator, registrar, and education manager for the small place, among a few other odd jobs. "They didn't give me a key."

Macie had recently started as a part-time greeter and gift shop manager. My own fault. When she found out I would be helping the museum with their strategic planning, she begged and begged me to help her get a job there. I guess I'm a doormat.

I shrugged. "We could ask Gadfly, I suppose."

Macie shivered—but not from the cold. "Oh, do we have to? He's so creepy."

The museum was a large, turn-of-the-century Queen Anne style mansion with colorful shingles and a few turrets. Gerald "Gadfly" McGee lived on the grounds in the carriage house and served as caretaker for the house and gardens. In return, he received free rent.

I ignored Macie and walked around the campus to the carriage house, leaving small tracks in the freshly falling snow. Trudging a few steps behind, Macie followed.

I knocked on the door of the carriage house. It reminded me of a hobbit hole from a Tolkien novel. As much as I loved the main building, this cute little bungalow was more my speed. I missed my little rowhouse back in Baltimore, but the museum's contract work and free digs with my dad in his country cabin had pulled me here.

No one answered.

"I guess he's not home." Macie turned to leave.

I caught the flash of a curtain dropping in the front window. "Come on, Gadfly," I said loudly, "we know you're in there!"

"I didn't do anything!" he called out. I turned to Macie, confused by his response. She shook her head.

"What are you talking about?" I asked.

No response. Fine. I didn't feel like dealing with his oddball ways this morning.

"I just need a key to get into the museum. Casper and Olivia aren't here yet," I said.

The door opened a sliver.

"Well, you'll just need to wait for them then."

The door slammed shut. Well, wasn't that just lovely?

Deterred, Macie and I headed back to the front of the museum. We sat on the front brownstone steps. She snuggled up to me, and as much as I detested her doing so, I didn't stop her. It really was cold out. Stupid late February chills.

"Abby, I need to tell you something."

"Yeah?"

Before Macie could say more, a car pulled up. Bronzy, late model sedan. I didn't recognize it as either Casper or Olivia's car. A woman with oversized sunglasses and a Russian style fur hat climbed out. She walked around to open the passenger side door before pulling Casper out by his shoulders. He looked half-dead. His pale skin matched his ghostly namesake. Macie and I raced over to them.

"Is he okay?" I asked.

"He will be. Just drunk."

Casper lay on the asphalt, letting the snow trickle around him. He slowly opened his pale blue eyes, but upon seeing all three of us hovering over him, quickly shut them. He groaned.

"I can't have him at home."

"Are you his wife?" Macie asked.

"Unfortunately." She held out a gloved hand. "Tilly Bergeron."

"Macie Colorado. I'm running the gift shop."

"Abby Tillman, Artifactual Consulting. Helping the museum with—"

"Sure, sure, whatever. Just help me get him inside," Tilly commanded. She pushed a few errant blond curls aside with her left hand.

"We don't have a key," Macie added.

Tilly knelt down and rummaged through Casper's pockets. She pulled out a chain. "House, car… This must be it. Any security code?"

I shook my head. Like with a lot of small museums, Autumn Hill lacked the money and capacity for any sort of security system.

The three of us picked up the trashed Casper and carried him like a casket to the museum. He was surprisingly light, or my workouts were finally paying off. Tilly unlocked the door, and we plopped him inside the foyer.

We started turning on lights. "Where is Olivia?" I asked.

I shouldn't have opened my mouth. Why do I always have to open my mouth?

While Casper lay seemingly dead on the floor of the foyer, Olivia was fully dead in the main gallery. She'd been shot, and the glass vitrine standing beside her had been smashed. The contents were gone.

"I'm going to call 911," Macie said. She raced out of the room.

"Is there anything I can do? Does Casper need help?" I asked.

"He'll be alright," Tilly replied. As we waited for the authorities, she read the remnants of an exhibit label. She whistled, pursing her perfectly red lips. "Looks like someone stole the family jewels. *She* must have been in the way." Tilly gestured towards Olivia.

She was right. The museum's prize possession, the McGee family tiara, was gone. The tiara wasn't necessarily valuable from a lapidarian standpoint. With its twisted brass frame and local semi-precious gemstones plopped in at uneven angles, it was more important to the arts and crafts history of the area. Probably wouldn't be worth more than a few hundred bucks on the black market. Why would someone want to steal *that* then? Was the tiara enough to kill over?

* * * *

The police agreed with Tilly's theory. Or at least they seemed to. I don't know. It didn't seem right to me. There was no sign of a break-in. They must have realized that too, since they questioned Gadfly. The tiara was, after all, from his family. But why steal it? It was only on loan to the museum. He could have taken it back whenever he wanted.

After we were released, Macie and I headed back to my father's cabin. As soon as we returned, however, Macie devolved, staying in her room and rarely saying anything. I appreciated the quiet, but my father appeared so sad, and I knew it wasn't right. After she didn't eat dinner, I put aside my ego and knocked on her door as my dad washed the dishes.

When I didn't get an answer, I slowly opened the door. Macie lay in a lump on the bed, buried under a mountain of blankets. My heart climbed into my throat. I knew what it was like to want to disappear from the world and sleep away pain. As much as I disliked Macie, I hated seeing her depressed even more.

I sat on the edge of the bed. "Macie, what's going on?"

"Go away." It was the most half-hearted order I'd ever heard.

"Something's been bugging you, and this started before we found Olivia, so I don't think it's that—"

She shot up in bed. Even in the darkened room, I could make out tears staining her cheeks. "I killed her."

"What?" That didn't make any sense.

"I really did. I killed her."

"You shot Olivia?"

"No, but it's my fault."

"Macie, why don't you explain what happened?" I asked.

"Well, like I said, Ralphie and I were supposed to have a date night. I wanted to make it really special, so I decided to have him meet me at the museum. I prepared a picnic with a red-checkered cloth and baked my famous baked brie and got his favorite wine—-"

"Okay, so special night at the museum," I said, trying to maintain my composure. I neither wanted to hear about Macie's exploits with my dad nor did I like the sound of her using the museum as her personal playground. Food leads to pest control issues, and wine can stain. Neither are good options in the galleries.

"I stayed late, pretended to leave, and then hid until Casper and Olivia left work for the day. Then, I set everything up. I even..." She paused. I egged her to continue. As much as this was disturbing, I needed to see where she was going with her story. "Well, I even took the tiara out of the case and wore it for Ralphie."

"You didn't," I said, wishing that wasn't true.

"I wore the tiara. And, uhm, maybe all I wore was the tiara…."

"Macie!"

She dove back under the covers. I palmed my forehead. It took another five minutes of coaching to coax her out and get her to continue.

"Then I got a message that Ralphie couldn't come. There was an emergency dentist thing, and he was needed. So I sat all alone, naked in that old house, eating my brie and wearing that damn tiara."

Now I wanted to throw up. Even though I'm in my mid-thirties, everything to do with my dad and Macie tended to make me feel like a grossed-out, insecure teenager. But I couldn't let that consume me. I pressed on.

"So how did that kill Olivia?" I asked.

"She found me. She came back to the museum and discovered me. Oh, Abby, she was so angry. Threatened to fire me. I was going to be kicked out!"

"What did you do?"

"I put back on my clothes and gathered up my stuff. And she was yelling at me the whole time. I felt so humiliated. I got so mad that I threw the tiara at her. It must have hit her hard," Macie said. She broke into another set of sobs.

"And you think that killed her? She was shot, Macie. She didn't die by tiara."

"I know, I know, but I ran out of there before I could find out how badly I had hurt her."

I debated what to do. First there was the issue of comforting Macie, something I really didn't want to do. Would a simple pat on the shoulder work? No, this was Macie. She was a full-on emotional rollercoaster. Biting my lip, I opened my arms and let her tumble into them.

"Please don't tell anyone, Abby."

That was the second issue. Macie shouldn't have been at the museum after hours, let alone eating, naked, and wearing the prize tiara. Combined with Olivia's death, this was going to look bad. She obviously hadn't even told my dad about this. Should I tell him? The police? Her telling me made this my problem. What on earth was I going to do?

Telling the authorities had some pluses. Maybe Macie would go away, and I wouldn't have to deal with her anymore. Then I could just get back to my life. But my conscience nipped at me. Macie was family. Okay, maybe she hadn't married my dad yet, but they had been together for long enough, loved each other, and made each other happy. Even if

I didn't like her, I had to respect that. Besides, there was no way Macie had killed Olivia. I wouldn't believe that for a moment. Just because Macie was annoying didn't make her a killer.

As much as I hated the choice, I decided to keep my mouth shut. I needed to keep fishing for more information. Fortunately, I had some idea as to where to start.

* * * *

The next day I went to the town library and searched through their archives. A few thoughts were bugging me, and I had a feeling that with a little more information, I could piece together the truth. After all, I'm a trained museum professional, so searching records is where I turn to for guidance.

After a couple hours of looking through newspaper articles and local government files, I thought I'd figured out what had actually happened. There were some articles about the tiara's history, a few useful obituaries, and some announcements from the opening of the museum. I even learned how Gerald "Gadfly" McGee got his nickname, which apparently involved a high school prank with some horses.

Unfortunately, everything I found was circumstantial and probably not something that the police would be able to use. I'd need to do a little more investigating—in person.

* * * *

I rounded up everyone at the museum. Casper had recovered from his drinking spree, but Tilly had refused to accompany him. Macie followed me around like a muted puppy. I whispered to her to be ready to call the police and showed her a secret signal to alert her when to do so.

"We need to go to Gadfly's," I told them.

"Really? I don't want to," Macie protested.

"What is this all about, Abby?" Casper asked.

I debated how much to reveal at this point. I felt like Hercule Poirot about to share his theory on the identity of the killer. "Casper, why were you drinking the night that Olivia died?" I asked.

"I don't see how that's any of your business."

"It's important to finding out why Olivia died."

"How is that relevant?"

"Because you were supposed to be here, weren't you?" I asked. Before he could confirm or deny, I started off for Gadfly's. The two of them kept up with me, apparently consumed with curiosity. I didn't blame them. I'd want to know where I was going with this too.

I knocked on the carriage house door. No one responded. I wasn't surprised. Mail had piled up on the doorstep, nearly covering a large package. Gadfly was obviously burrowing in his little hobbit hole. I caught sight of the curtain swishing again and knew he was there. He could likely hear us fine. Good enough.

"Like I said, you were supposed to be at the museum the night that Olivia died, weren't you?" I confronted Casper.

"I didn't come here that night."

"No, you didn't. And it's a good thing you didn't, because you might also have died."

"Abby, what are you going on about?" Macie asked.

"You weren't the only one supposed to have a special date night, Macie. So were Casper and Olivia, and I think that was the night Casper was going to tell Tilly that he was leaving her. Right?"

Casper dropped his head to his chest.

"Thought so. Except that you couldn't go through with it. So instead you drank yourself silly and didn't arrive. You decided to stay with Tilly instead."

The curtain swished again, and I could hear footsteps patter beyond the door. I gave Macie my secret signal. She trotted off toward the museum. Casper didn't pay any attention. He was too engulfed with grief.

"I didn't kill her. You have to believe me," he said.

"I do believe you," I replied.

"I loved both of them. They were both so amazing. But I'm already married to Tilly. I can't just throw that away." He continued rattling on. I didn't really listen. He was just trying to rationalize away his guilt. Instead, I focused on the door.

"Did Tilly know about the affair?"

Casper stopped midstream. "No... I don't know. Maybe."

"Do you know Tilly's parents?"

"What? No. Her mother died, years ago. Her mom's buried in the church cemetery up that road. I think her dad is alive, but she refuses to talk about him."

"She didn't tell you that her dad also cheated on her mom and that her mom killed herself as a result?"

"No, she didn't."

"Abby, please stop," said another voice. It didn't come from behind the door but from behind me. I turned to find Tilly standing there. "I had told Caspy I didn't want to move back to this forgotten little wormhole of a town, but he was adamant. Talked about all the great summers he spent here as a kid. I said it wasn't so great the rest of the year. He didn't listen. I came because I was blinded by what I thought was love."

"What did you do when *Caspy* told you he was hiring Gadfly?" I asked.

"Caspy never told me that's who was going to be the caretaker. Why would he? I generally stayed away from the museum. It was his pet project. He knew I grew up down the street, but why would he have known that Gadfly was my dad?"

"You're Gadfly McGee's daughter?" Casper asked.

"I took my mom's maiden name," Tilly replied, as if that somehow explained everything.

"But when I got the museum—"

"Caspy, you may have fond memories coming out here as a kid. I get that, but I don't. Why do you think I took a job two towns away?"

"We were going to develop new memories here together," Casper pleaded.

"And once upon a time, I believed that could happen too." Tears ran down Tilly's cheeks.

The door beside me opened. Gadfly appeared in the frame, gaunt and lanky. Tears also rolled down his haggard face.

"I just wanted to make things up to you," Gadfly said to Tilly. "I treated your mom plenty bad, but you shouldn't have had to go through the same with this tadpole." He thumbed towards Casper, who slinked backwards.

"What did you do?" Tilly's voice was barely more than a whisper.

Gadfly sighed. He shook his head back and forth, popping the vertebrae in his neck. "When I saw the lights on in the museum, I thought it was them two again—tadpole here and that curator girl. There were two figures silhouetted in the curtains that night. I wasn't going to let him put you through that, so I put a stop to it." His voice wavered between sorrow and pride. Tilly's mouth dropped, and Casper toed the snow on the ground.

"You killed Olivia?"

"I know; I shouldn't have done it. After I shot her I found that she was all alone in there. I thought he was maybe hiding somewhere, but he wasn't. But it didn't matter. I still stopped them."

I heard the first sounds of sirens approaching.

"And the tiara?" I asked, even though I suspected the answer.

"Well, there wasn't any way to tell Tilly that they were over. So I tried sending her the tiara. Thought that'd let her know that she was queen again—that she was always my queen," he said.

I gently kicked the box in the piled up mail.

"She wouldn't accept it, would she?"

"When I saw the handwriting, I knew who it was from. He had been trying to write me for years. I refused to accept any of it," Tilly said. She stopped and knelt down by the box, which was marked "Return to Sender." She rubbed her temples. "Maybe if I had, this could have been avoided. Gadfly… *Dad*, my marriage has been over for a while. I didn't care about Olivia. I just wanted out of here."

The lights of two police cruisers appeared in the parking lot, and the sirens wailed loudly. Macie raced up to us. I guided her away while the three of them cried.

"The cops are here. I'm going to tell them what happened."

"Macie, you didn't kill Olivia," I reassured her. "Let's let them talk first. Then, you can tell the officers about your date night. It's going to be okay."

"You promise?"

"I swear to you." I didn't tell her that she was the other silhouette that Gadfly saw, who he had mistaken for being Casper. Or Olivia. It didn't matter. Instead, I flung an arm around her shoulder, and we walked towards the police together.

THE TRAIN'S ON THE TRACKS

PAULA GAIL BENSON

Patrick O'Reilly, the Senator from Shelton County, stood before my desk in the State Senate chamber holding a tally sheet. He frowned like he did years ago when I used to tutor him in high school math to make my college spending money. Now, God help his clients, he was a CPA.

"So, Senator from Jackson." Paddy addressed me by the county I represented according to Senate custom. He was polling the Senators to see if a majority would vote to end the filibuster on a bill to eliminate the job of a low-level, high profile, irritating public employee. "Do you intend to vote for or against the bastard?"

"Paddy, I know your mama would hate to hear you talk like that." I recently had been elected as the only Independent in the Senate and had no seniority over Paddy, but in our small Southern state, everyone had connections. Old Paddy Cakes would have hell to pay if I told his domineering mama he was using bad language on the Senate floor.

"Damn it, Caro, if Mama had to endure this debate, she'd be talking that way herself. This isn't a college faculty senate meeting where all you do is spend time on meaningless philosophical discussions. It's state government conducting the people's business. We need to make a decision and move on. The train's on the tracks, ready to leave the station. Either get a ticket to ride or wave goodbye."

I paused before replying. As a college theatre professor and playwright, I go by C.L., but I was born Carolyn Louise Mitchell. Usually, people called me Carolyn, but Paddy had reverted to Caro, my nickname from childhood and among close friends.

"You know..." I had to refrain from calling him Paddy Cakes. "...I'm enjoying learning all this legislative lingo. The train is on the tracks. Buy a ticket to ride or get out of the way. Fish or cut bait."

His eyes gleamed. "Exactly."

"Well, except the Senator who told me about cutting bait explained the original meaning wasn't just letting go of the fishing pole."

Paddy rolled his eyes. "Oh, Jeez. I should have known you've been talking with the Senator from Thayer. What did she tell you?"

I glanced beyond Paddy to the short, elegant, gray-bunned woman who had held the Senate podium for the last three hours. Her dulcet tones now underscored my quiet conversation with Paddy.

Emmaline Hartness, representing Thayer County, was a political wife elected to fill her deceased husband's unexpired term and subsequently reelected twice. Senators respected her quiet, forthright demeanor, and her knowledge of where the bodies lay buried and who put them there.

"She said cutting bait used to refer to fishermen slicing up their smaller catches to use as lure for bigger fish. Sort of like me agreeing to vote with you on one issue in hopes that you'll vote with me on another. She called it picking your allies and your battles."

Paddy clenched the tally sheet. "Caro, what she needed to tell you is there's a difference between trading in good faith and trying people's patience. Louis Musgrove's action is an affront to legislative authority."

"Some people call it an innovative approach."

"Well, they're wrong. He should have resigned or been fired by now. If we let him get away with this, any law we pass will be considered a joke. This debate has gone on long enough. The members are ready to go home."

"Then, call the question, Senator from Shelton."

His frown deepened. "Maybe we would if we knew how the votes would fall. Care to enlighten me?"

I rose from my seat, muffling a yawn as I exaggeratedly stretched my arms and legs. "I promise you, Paddy, you'll be the first to know."

Paddy shook his head and glanced at his tally sheet to select his next victim. I pushed my chair under the desk and walked to the center aisle. Gazing back as I neared the door, I saw Emmaline Hartness addressing an almost empty Senate chamber.

"As the people's representatives it's our duty—our sacred obligation—to consider this matter reasonably. To make a determination based on good governmental practices, rather than condemning personalities," she said. Her purple tapestry jacket had a standing collar that framed her face. I knew she wore comfortable tennis shoes hidden behind the podium. She had prepared to argue through the night to defeat the bill eliminating the Family Services Coordinating Council's public affairs office. An office with one employee, Mr. Louis Musgrove.

Last year, the legislature prohibited the state's medical centers from dispensing a non-hallucinogenic oil made from cannabis. That oil provided the only cure for Zara, a child dying from uncontrolled seizures. Zara's grandmother appealed to Louis and he used a significant portion of his public service announcements' budget to film a movie about Zara's plight. Then, he booked it in theatres, charging admission to raise money for Zara and her family to travel to Colorado, where the treatment was legal. Unfortunately, Zara died before making the trip.

I saw the film with a group of legislators. While I grieved that little Zara would never have another tea party in her pink playhouse at her grandmother's rural home, I couldn't let that influence my decision about Louis' position.

Emmaline reached for a disposable cup and took a sip before continuing. "Mr. Louis Musgrove has always been devoted to ensuring that families receive all the help they are due. He has an exemplary public record."

Actually, Louis was a loose cannon. Nobody questioned his devotion to his constituents, but his lack of restraint in criticizing lawmakers' actions made him more enemies than friends.

Emmaline's eyes scanned the balcony seating where visitors watched the debate. She frowned, took another sip of water, then raised her voice. "Mr. Musgrove didn't pass a controversial law that kept a child from getting the medicine she needed. We did that. He found a creative way to deal with that law. Not negligent or reckless, although I know that some of you disagree. He carried out his responsibilities in a manner not prohibited by law."

From the other side of the room, a Senator rose to be recognized. When the Presiding Officer, our chicly sophisticated lady Secretary of State (I know, most states have a lieutenant governor, but we're different), asked if the Senator from Thayer would take a question, Emmaline refused.

"Senator does not yield," the Presiding Officer announced.

Emmaline glanced again toward the balcony, but still seemed disappointed by what she saw or didn't see. She asked, "I wonder, if Zara went to Colorado and lived, might we be congratulating Mr. Musgrove for his initiative instead of trying to end his career in public service?"

Good question, I thought, even though it was subject to an objection under the rules. A speaker couldn't ask a question from the podium. Most members got around the obstacle by prefacing their remarks with "Did you know…."

Sitting alone on a staff bench next to the chamber door was Emmaline's intern, Kent Musgrove, son of the unfortunate Louis. I smiled in his direction, but he wasn't making eye contact.

Continuing to the exit, I glanced at Ted Brennan, the Senate security officer stationed beside the door. He opened it for me, whispering as I passed, "Senator, she needs your support."

He surprised me. Staff didn't comment unless an opinion was requested.

Without reacting, I left the Senate floor and headed to the restroom. Was Ted's concern about Louis' job or Emmaline's stamina?

Usually, Emmaline's granddaughter Juliet stayed nearby during lengthy debates. I hadn't seen Juliet today and wondered where she was.

A second year law student, Juliet spent her free time at the Senate. With her blond braid down her back and her arms loaded with books, she never appeared encumbered. Her always-present, saddle-style, brown leather messenger bag seemed to contain every necessary worldly comfort, particularly her insulin, water, and emergency snacks. If her diabetes had gotten out of control, I would have heard. I couldn't imagine mere class assignments keeping her away from her grandmother's planned filibuster.

From the foyer, through the glass in the chamber doors, I watched Emmaline persevere alone. I admired her a great deal. Her husband died of a heart attack after he had been accused of participating in a vote-buying scandal. Emmaline eventually cleared his name. Even now, she fought valiantly for her cause, despite looking worried. She must have told Kent to face the debate about his father's action and show no shame.

But, where was Juliet?

Emmaline couldn't win this fight. I found myself in the uneasy position of agreeing with Paddy. Louis Musgrove circumvented state law. A child died depending upon an irresponsible use of state funds. Someone must accept blame, and Louis had the target on his chest.

Passing beyond the restroom, I planned to stretch my legs by walking through the lobby until another security officer motioned to get my attention.

"That crazy lady in the Hawaiian get-up is waiting outside, Senator." He nodded toward the doors to the lobby. "I thought you might wanna know before you came face-to-face with her."

So, Zara's adoring grandmother, wearing her signature muumuu and no doubt ready with insults about legislative insensitivity and incompetence, was staking us out. As the officer held a door for a staff member to exit, I saw the grandmother perched at the rope barrier. A brown leather strap appeared to hang heavily across her shoulder, barely visible in the folds of forest green fabric with bright red flowers. Usually, she carried uniquely designed woven clutches (that she pointed in offending legislators' faces) or totes that matched the colors of her flowing garments.

I remembered trying to have a reasonable discussion with her about an intricately decorated tote, featuring an embroidered portrait of Zara. Rather than making small talk, she berated me for mentioning anything but legislative business. To her, I was just another example of an ineffective elected official.

Today, she stood stoically behind the rope barrier, holding a black and white unsmiling head shot of Zara to confront those exiting the chamber. Did she mean to convey that Zara would disapprove of the pending legislation? Where was the colorful embroidered bag with her granddaughter's image?

Thinking of granddaughters reminded me of another one.

"Is Juliet Hartness in the building?" I asked the security officer.

"Haven't seen her, Senator, but I can call around." The officer turned to his shoulder radio.

I waited while he contacted his sources. I might not be able to vote with Emmaline, but maybe I could locate Juliet, who could offer Emmaline comfort and support. Something wasn't right about Juliet's absence. What could possibly keep her away, today of all days?

"Nobody's seen her," the officer told me, but he looked away quickly, as if trying to avoid a follow up request. Not at all usual behavior among our security officers.

"Thanks for checking."

I went to the restroom, where I could sit, think, and have some assurance of privacy while listening to the filibuster, since the sound was piped in. Emmaline and I were the only female Senators. Women staffers used the facility, but the Presiding Officer never did, preferring to retire to her own private one adjoining her office on another floor of the building.

After I was ensconced in a stall, I heard the Senate recess for ten minutes. Moments later, the restroom door opened and someone entered.

"Hello?"

Emmaline's voice. Tense and wavering. I started to call out when I heard her talking on her cell phone.

"I don't want excuses from you, Louis, is that understood? The deposit number has to be correct. I have only a moment before I have to return to the podium. Kent is in the chamber with me. You make certain that money gets transferred into the account. When it's done, send word to Ted Brennan with Senate security. He'll tell me."

After a pause, she said, "Don't mess this up, Louis. I'll make your life hell if you do."

She hung up. Through the crack in the stall door, I saw her looking in the mirror and pinching her cheeks. I pulled back. Did she see me? She walked to the other stall. After using the facility, she came out and washed her hands. She took one more look in the mirror, then left without seeming to notice my presence.

Was Emmaline selling her vote, or using Louis to buy someone else's? Why? And, how was Ted Brennan involved?

I crept from the stall, washed my hands, and patted my cheeks with cold water. A fellow faculty member once told me I was lucky. College politics were all *sub rosa*, while elected officials dealt with matters openly.

Right.

As I entered the chamber, Ted told me to check with the Senator from Thayer. Had she seen me in the restroom and waited to confront me on the floor?

I approached her with my theatre-taught poker face. "You promised me this would be an interesting experience. I'm surprised Juliet's not here to witness it."

Her face was as white as a plaster mask. "I need your help, Caro. I want to pass the podium to you. Will you take it?"

Not the request I was expecting. "We may not be on the same side."

"It doesn't matter. I'll yield if you'll take the floor until I get the matter in order."

Was she asking me to be complicit in a vote-buying situation? "I don't understand."

"I haven't time to explain, but I'd be grateful. Will you do it?"

Her probing eyes bored into mine, seeking those secret places I wanted not to disclose. I had never seen that type of desperation in her before.

"Give me a moment," I said.

"We have no more time."

The Presiding Officer called the Senate to order. I headed toward my desk. On the way, I changed direction and sat by Kent. He didn't notice me until I nudged him.

"Yes, Senator?" he stammered.

"How are you?"

"I'm…." He looked down at his hands and gulped a breath. "It's like watching an accident about to happen and being unable to stop it."

"Why are you here, Kent?"

My question seemed to surprise him. "To assist Senator Hartness."

"Where's Juliet? Why isn't she here?"

He visibly shook. "I don't know."

I glanced at Ted, who watched us from the door. "Are you waiting for a message?"

"A message?" Kent asked.

I paused before answering. "Senator Hartness said you can go. I'll watch out for her now."

He looked uncertain.

"Go on," I told him. "Take the back way. Zara's grandmother's in the lobby."

He stood and I added, "As you go, tell Ted Brennan to check out Zara's grandmother's handbag. It looks exactly like the one Juliet Hartness carries."

A light appeared in Kent's eyes. He nodded, then moved to speak with Ted, who gave me a frown similar to Paddy's before leaving the chamber. Kent looked back toward Emmaline before he exited. She paused in her remarks as she watched the two men leave.

I returned to my desk, remained standing, and reached for my microphone.

"The Senator from Jackson," the Presiding Officer recognized me.

"Will the Senator from Thayer yield for a question?"

Emmaline blinked, turned my way, and replied, "Senator yields."

"Senator, does the legislature have authority to organize state agencies?"

Emmaline nodded. "It does."

"What's the source of that authority?"

"Our state constitution."

"Is that the same constitution we each take an oath to support and defend?"

"The same."

Out of the corner of my eye, I saw Paddy return to the chamber and slip into his seat. I contemplated how to phrase my next question.

"What's the most important part of that oath, Senator?"

She flinched before answering precisely. "The promise you make to serve all the state's citizens."

"And not betray their trust, right?"

Emmaline nodded.

"Have you ever betrayed that trust, Senator?"

Paddy shot up and grabbed his microphone.

The Presiding Officer recognized him.

"Our newest Senator forgets the rules require her questions be both courteous and remain on subject," Paddy said.

"With all due respect, Madame President," I responded. "I believe my questions are appropriate under the rules and ask that you let me continue."

The Presiding Officer had had a long day, too, but after consulting the clerk, told me I could proceed, although she cautioned me that the objection could be renewed at any time.

"Senator from Thayer," I spoke to Emmaline, who gripped the sides of the podium as she listened. I took a breath before asking, "Do you diligently work to maintain the public trust?"

She responded as if taking a wedding vow. "I do."

"And, do you recognize that maintaining the public trust sometimes requires sacrifice?"

Tears welled in her eyes. "Yes."

For a moment, our eyes locked, but I didn't have her talent for probing the conscience. And there were no more questions I could ask. So I faced the challenge. Fish or cut bait?

"Madame President, I request to be heard when the Senator from Thayer yields the floor."

"I yield," Emmaline said.

The Presiding Officer recognized the Senator from Jackson.

Me.

Emmaline gathered her documents into a file folder as I approached the podium empty handed, still formulating in my mind the words I would speak. For a moment, we stood close. I placed my hand over the microphone and whispered, "Even though I don't support eliminating the office, Louis Musgrove has to go. Make that happen and you have my vote. Juliet told me I could always trust your word."

She looked up at me. "Thank you for believing her." Then she moved to take her seat.

I stepped into place behind the podium. A college student serving as a page replaced the cup Emmaline had used with a new one. Glancing down, I saw fresh water lapping against its sides. I looked up to find the chamber filling with members, all watching to see what I would do.

This wasn't the way I would have planned my first speech to the body, but as Shakespeare's Henry V would say… wait, that wasn't a bad way to begin.

"'Once more unto the breech, dear friends.'"

The puzzled looks I received indicated not many Shakespeare fans occupied Senate seats. From years of lecturing to bored students, I knew I needed to get to the point quickly. I hoped Ted was able to check Zara's grandmother's handbag. If I was right, Juliet might be in need of insulin.

"Since I became a member of the Senate, I've been learning about its unique customs and sayings. I've been cautioned to be mindful of the support a bill has. If it has the votes to pass, then the train is on the tracks and I need to decide if I'm getting on board or out of the way. I've been cautioned that being hit by a speeding train of legislation is not a pleasant experience."

From the muffled chuckles, I thought I might have connected with a few listeners. I plunged forward.

"I sense from our discussion and the mood I observe that this particular bill has some traction and is gaining speed. So, now is my moment of choice. And I'm appreciative, as my colleague from Shelton has pointed out to me…" I inclined my head toward Paddy, who nodded back from his desk. "…that decisions made by our State Senate must be both appropriate and timely. We need to accomplish the people's business efficiently and effectively."

That cup of water looked tempting, but I resisted. "I realize that the rules prohibit me from asking questions from the podium, but let me tell you what I've been wondering about this bill. I've heard that the legislature is like the architect, laying out the plan. The executive branch is the builder, and the courts handle any disputes that arise. We have a situation where the legislature has put a prohibition into place and the executive agency has the duty to carry it out, or as the Senator from Thayer speculates, find a way around it. What I'm pondering is why the executive branch agency has not reacted to Mr. Musgrove's creative solution, either affirming or rejecting it, since he is in that agency's employ. It makes me think that maybe there's someone tied to the track that this bill is speeding toward. What I would like to know, if I could ask, is who that might be, whether it's Mr. Musgrove, Zara's family, the Senator from Thayer." I turned to look at her. "Or someone else."

At that moment, Ted Brennan reentered the chamber and walked down the center aisle, which was strictly forbidden to staff during session. I noticed he had a slight limp and that the Sergeant at Arms did not stop him. When he reached Emmaline's seat, he knelt beside her and said, "Juliet's safe. Zara's grandmother locked her up in the playhouse. The EMTs are with her now." Then, Emmaline fainted. And chaos ensued.

* * * *

Later, as we sipped glasses of Crown Royal Reserve in my office, Ted told me the full story. When Kent Musgrove arrived in Emmaline's office that afternoon, he found an anonymous ransom note demanding that his father deposit $25,000 in a bank account to ensure Juliet's release. Emmaline arranged for the cash and dispatched Louis before alerting Senate security. Then they received word the account didn't exist.

Out of desperation, Ted followed up on my suggestion to check out Zara's grandmother's handbag. When he asked if she'd agree to a consensual search, she became belligerent and swung the handbag at him. She missed, but connected with a kick that just missed his groin.

Senate security arrested her for assault and battery. She was in fact carrying Juliet's purse and admitted that she offered Juliet a ride to the State Capitol building.

Juliet had agreed and gotten into the vehicle thinking it was a conciliatory gesture because of Emmaline's support for Louis. Instead of driving to the Capitol, Zara's grandmother clicked the child lock and sped off, taking Juliet to Zara's playhouse, which since the child's death had been outfitted to hold a hostage. Apparently Zara's grandmother sent the bogus ransom note not wanting the money, but hoping to make a legislator suffer, as she had, the loss of a grandchild.

"But how could you be sure about the handbag?" Paddy asked me the next day as I gathered my papers from my Senate desk when the session ended early. After hearing that Louis Musgrove resigned, the Senate adjourned debate on the bill and referred it back to committee.

"I wasn't," I told Paddy. "I just never remembered seeing Zara's grandmother carrying a plain leather tote before. And I guessed."

"Well, that was damned reckless."

I smiled. "Paddy, I'm a theatre professor and the only Independent in the State Senate. Damned reckless is my specialty." I started to leave, then turned back to him. "And you can tell your sweet mama I said so."

BIOGRAPHIES

A legislative attorney and former law librarian, **Paula Gail Benson**'s short stories have been published in the *Bethlehem Writers Roundtable, Kings River Life, Mystery Times Ten 2013* (Buddhapuss Ink), and *A Tall Ship, a Star, and Plunder* (Dark Oak Press and Media, 2014). She regularly blogs with others about writing mysteries at http://writerswhokill. blogspot.com. Her personal blog is http://littlesourcesofjoy.blogspot. com and her website is http://paulagailbenson.com.

Kelly Cochran started college at seventeen where she experienced the downside to using a fake ID, learned nobody believes you when you tell them you saw a UFO, and discovered every decision has a consequence. *Buying Time*, first in the Aspen Moore humorous mystery series, was a finalist in the Next Generation Indie Book Awards. Kelly lives in Missouri with her husband and three dogs, including her short story's inspiration, Skipper the blind beagle. http://kellycochran.com

An IT nerd for twenty-plus years, in her writing **Judith Copek** likes to show technology's humor and quirkiness along with its scary aspects. She is a member of Sisters in Crime, Mystery Writers of America, and Toastmasters International. Judith has published poetry, several short stories and memoir as well as three novels: *The Shadow Warriors*, *World of Mirrors,* and *Festival Madness.* Her website: http://judycopek.com Twitter: @judyinboston Facebook: http://facebook.com/JudithCopek Blog: http://lynx-sis.blogspot.com/

PA De Voe is a cultural anthropologist, which accounts for her being an incorrigible magpie for collecting seemingly irrelevant information. She's published extensively in the social sciences. Her first cozy mystery, *A Tangled Yarn,* was published in 2013. Presently, she's writing a series of short stories set in Ming Dynasty, China. For the past five years, she's regularly posted author interviews on the Greater St Louis Sisters in Crime blog, http://stlsinc.blogspot.com. Her website is http://padevoe. com.

Kate Fellowes is the author of five romantic mysteries, most recently *Thunder in the Night*, for Crimson Romance. Her short stories and essays have appeared in several anthologies, as well as "Woman's World," "Brides," "Romantic Homes," and other periodicals. A graduate of Alverno College, she blogs about work and life at http://katefellowes.wordpress.com. She shares her home with a variety of companion animals, all of them rescues.

Toni Goodyear is a former journalist, winner of the North Carolina Press Association Award for features. Other past careers include ghostbusting (yes, really). Her short stories have appeared in *The Killer Wore Cranberry: Room for Thirds, Kings River Life,* and *Carolina Crimes: 19 Tales of Lust, Love and Longing*. She's completed a cozy mystery, *Trouble Brewing in Tanawha Falls*, and is hard at work on a thriller. She holds a Ph.D. in Psychology, UNC Chapel Hill.

Vinnie Hansen fled the South Dakota prairie for the California coast the day after graduating high school. Author of the Carol Sabala mysteries, Vinnie was a 2013 Claymore Award finalist for *Black Beans & Venom,* her seventh book in the series. Retired after 27 years of teaching high school English, Vinnie lives in Santa Cruz, California. Discover more at http://vinniehansen.com, Goodreads, Facebook, and misterio press.

Norma Huss calls herself The Grandma Moses of Mystery, since her first mystery was published a month before her eightieth birthday. Her years cruising Chesapeake Bay and beyond with her husband in their boat inspired the settings for the story in this anthology and her mystery novels, *Yesterday's Body* and *Death of a Hot Chick*. Her latest book is *Cherish*, a YA ghost mystery (for the grandchildren, of course). Her website: http://normahuss.com

Polly Iyer is the author of six suspense novels: *Hooked, InSight, Murder Déjà Vu, Threads,* and three books in the Diana Racine Psychic Suspense series, *Mind Games, Goddess of the Moon,* and *Backlash*. Her books contain adult language and situations with characters who sometimes tread ethical lines. A former artist, she creates her own book covers. A Massachusetts native, she now lives in the upstate of South Carolina. Learn more at http://pollyiyer.com.

Jim Jackson authors the Seamus McCree mystery series [*Bad Policy* (2013), which won the Evan Marshall Fiction Makeover Contest for freshness and commerciality of the story and quality of the writing, and *Cabin Fever* (2014)]. He splits his time between the woods of Michigan's Upper Peninsula and Georgia's low country. Jim has published an acclaimed book on contract bridge, *One Trick at a Time: How to Start Winning at Bridge*. For more information visit www.jamesmjackson.com

New Jersey writer **Su Kopil** left the 'burbs for a one stoplight town on the Carolina coast where she finds intriguing characters to populate her fiction. Her short stories have been published both stateside and overseas. She also visually brings to life other writers' stories in her book cover designs which can be found at http://EarthlyCharms.com.

Joan Leotta has been playing with words with writing and performing since childhood. Her motto is "encouraging words through pen and performance." Her award-winning poetry, short stories, books, and articles have appeared in many journals, magazines, and newspapers. She performs folklore and one-woman shows on historic figures in schools, libraries, museums and at festivals. Joan lives in Calabash, NC with husband Joe. You can learn more about her work and reach her through http://joanleotta.wordpress.com

Gin Mackey spent years writing for Fortune 500 corporations before finding her passion: writing fiction. She lives and writes on the coast of Maine, and is hard at work on her novel *Disappear Our Dead*, featuring amateur sleuth Abby Tiernan, a grieving widow turned home funeral guide. Gin is past president of the New England chapter of Sisters in Crime. Visit Gin at http://ginmackey.com

Boston-area writer **Cheryl Marceau** spent her childhood moving all over the US, Canada, and the Marshall Islands, amusing herself on the road by making up stories. That didn't stop when she put down roots. She has published three short stories in Level Best Books anthologies, and has a historical mystery in the works. When she isn't plotting miserable things to happen to bad people, she works in a large technology company.

Chelle Martin is a Jersey girl who, when she isn't writing, enjoys coffee shops, art shows, knitting, photography, and the beach. Before writing full-time, she worked for 16 years as a secretary while getting her Bachelor's Degree in Business Management/Marketing. Her two Chihuahuas are the inspiration for her humorous Dog Mom Mystery series, which takes place at the Jersey shore. To learn more about her published work, find her on Facebook at Dog Mom Publishing.

Lauren Moffett (Silberman) is the author of *Wild Women of Maryland* (History Press, expected 2015), *Wicked Baltimore: Charm City Sin and Scandal* (History Press, 2011), and *The Jewish Community of Baltimore* (Arcadia Publishing, 2008). Her museum consultant protagonist, Abby

Tillman, returns in the *Chesapeake Crimes: Storm Warning* anthology. Lauren also runs a webcomic on America's first female detective at http://katewarnedetective.com. Visit her at http://lsilberman.com and http://facebook.com/wickedbaltimore.

Nicole Myers is happy to live in the Pacific Northwest with her husband, two energetic little boys, two cats, and a house bunny. When not writing, she works as a Marketing Project Manager. Nicole devoured Nancy Drew and Trixie Belden books as a child and fancied herself a girl detective at the first sign of any mysterious circumstances. She is currently working on her first cozy mystery series set in the Seattle area.

Melissa Robbins started writing at an early age, inheriting her storytelling ability from her grandfather while listening to his World War Two stories. Melissa is a member of Sisters in Crime and Wichita Area Romance Authors. She lives in Kansas with her husband, kids, and two dogs. Visit her website at http://melissarobbinsmysteries.com.

Georgia Ruth lives in the historic gold mining foothills of North Carolina where she records and shares the stories of neighbors who can trace roots back to Wales and Ireland. Her website is http://georgiaruthwrites.us. Georgia is a member of Short Mystery Fiction Society and has stories published online and in print. Her former careers in family restaurant management and retail sales provide an endless resource for fictional characters and conflicts.

A former journalist and graduate from Humber College's School for Writers, **Tracy L. Ward** has been hard at work developing her favorite protagonist, Peter Ainsley, and chronicling his adventures as a morgue surgeon in Victorian England. She is currently working on the fourth book in the Peter Ainsley mystery series, titled *Sweet Asylum*, due out in 2015. To find out more about Tracy's books follow her on http://facebook.com/TracyWard.Author or visit her website at http://gothicmysterywriter.blogspot.com

Patricia Marie Warren is a romantic suspense writer. As an alumnus of The Writers Police Academy, she can barely resist interrogating police officers on how to get away with the perfect crime. Turquoise Morning Press has published two of her short stories, "Lightning Always Strikes Twice" in *Men in Uniform (Short Story Collection)* and "The Devil is in The Details" in *Currents: A Collection of River Stories*. You can find her blogging at http://TypingOneHanded.com.

Elizabeth Zelvin is a New York City psychotherapist and author of the Bruce Kohler mystery series, which started with *Death Will Get You Sober*. Her most recent work, *Voyage of Strangers*, is a historical novel featuring a young Jewish sailor with Columbus. Liz's short stories have been nominated three times for the Agatha Award and for the Derringer Award. Her story in this anthology is a sequel to the novella *Shifting Is for the Goyim*.

Made in the USA
Charleston, SC
18 May 2016